BIG DEAL

Lane couldn't stand it any longer; she had to be nearer. She climbed into the back of the van and sat on the old tyre. Watching Laurence kissing Carol was both worse and better than she would have expected – the jealousy actually heightened her excitement. Lane was so wet she was pulling at her crotch to get her hot clothes away from her cunt. As she did so, she felt how her cunt had swollen up and how tightly her hard clit pressed against the seam of her jeans. The dildo inside her boxers made the jeans tight anyway, trapped as it was between her belly and the denim. She let her hand rest there.

BIG DEAL

HELEN SANDLER

First published in 1999 by
Sapphire
an imprint of Virgin Publishing Ltd
Thames Wharf Studios,
Rainville Road, London W6 9HT

ISBN 0 352 33365 0

Cover Photograph by The Attard Photolibrary

Typeset by SetSystems Ltd, Saffron Walden, Essex
Printed and bound in Great Britain by Mackays of Chatham PLC

CONTENTS

To Jane,
with love

ONE

The Deal

The deal went something like this: for every time that Lane had sex with men, she would have to bring someone new to their sex life as a couple.

'How are you going to know, sweetheart?' asked Lane, raising one eyebrow. She was leaning against the baby-blue American fridge in Carol's super-clean kitchen, playing the butch shamelessly. Not difficult when you're six inches taller than your girlfriend, and have just had a smart Ross-style crop at the barbers. New combats were helping the look.

But Carol was not easily butched out. 'How am I going to know, *sweetheart*? Let's see now. How did I know this time? Oh, condoms in your bag would have given you away if you hadn't already started acting weird. Like, going for my arsehole. Remember that?'

Lane felt herself blush, which was not good. Something that had been exciting at the time was now being used as evidence against her, or at least as evidence of her dishonesty and inherent selfishness. But Carol was grinning.

'Yeah,' said Lane, trying to regain ground, 'but I won't make that mistake again. What clues will there be next time?'

'There'll always be something, Laney, because you're a crap liar. So, do you agree to my terms?' Carol had now put on her special professor glasses and was glancing between Lane and some

1

paperwork on the kitchen table, as if the interview was nearly over.

Something funny happened to Lane when she looked at Carol in those glasses. When your girlfriend combines being cute and occasionally helpless with being fifteen years older than you and a university lecturer, there are some tangled power dynamics around. At that moment, Lane wanted to tell her to take off her fucking glasses and listen. And then again, she wanted to do whatever Carol told her.

'OK. Agreed,' was all that actually came out of Lane's mouth.

'Good. There, it's not such a big deal, is it?'

'Actually,' Lane replied, 'it's a Very Big Deal.' She spun round and grabbed two beer bottles from the fridge. Cracking them open with her bare hands in a move she'd been practising, she was disappointed to realise that Carol wasn't watching. But it seemed like the worst was over.

'Carrie,' she said to the top of her girlfriend's blonde curls as she handed her a beer. 'What about you?'

The older woman looked up from her work. 'What about me?'

'Well, do you want to sleep with anyone else?'

'Sleep with?' Carol looked at her, clearly amused by the euphemism.

'Do you want anyone else to fuck you?' Lane spelt it out, irritated, her northern accent hard on the consonants.

'No. Not unless you bring them home for me. Or for you. Or whatever.'

'So it's all up to me?' Lane's dark eyes searched Carol's face for clues.

'What we do has always been up to you. It's just that you broadened the parameters by fucking around with fairies. All I'm saying is that, if you're going to do new stuff with other people, you can do new stuff with me too. It's up to you what that is.'

'But you said to bring other people home. So that's your decision.' Even as she spoke, Lane knew that Carol was about to correct her, as usual.

'It's no more my decision than when I say to you, "Fuck me now." If you don't feel like it, you wait. Or you don't do it the way I want it . . . I don't know *who* you'll bring home, do I? Might be nice, might be a bastard.' Carol's blue eyes flickered with flirtation, with her readiness for whatever danger Lane might have in store for her, and Lane grabbed her where she sat and kissed her.

'Love you, babes,' she said.

'Love you too, you slag,' said Carol. 'Now skin up and shut up.'

'Oh no,' Lane replied. 'You're not getting out of this so easily. Suppose you do let someone else fuck your cunt, then there has to be a suitable follow-up for you, too. Here's what I suggest: you must tell me about it, present your arse to me and let me do what you know I want to do.'

Carol stared back at her, apparently caught off guard but trying not to show it. 'Do I have a choice?'

'Why would you need a choice? From what you've just told me, all this is hypothetical. You don't want anyone else, so what's the problem?' Lane watched her.

'Very well.'

'You agree to *my* terms, then?'

'Yes.'

'What do you say?'

'Yes, Lane, I agree. I understand that if I let anyone else fuck me when you're not there, then you will fuck my arse in response.' This was a formal agreement, they both knew that. They weren't playing any more – the edge to their voices came from the seriousness of what was going on.

Until now it had been understood that Carol would not take anything inside her arse. If Lane only touched Carol's arsehole with the tip of a finger, it was enough to spoil the mood, making her nervous and tetchy. Lane had made it clear she would love to plunge a dildo into her femme's behind or push three fingers in there or fuck both her holes at once. But Carol didn't want it.

Lane hardly dared to imagine how mixed her feelings would be if she found out that Carol was sleeping with someone else. Jealousy that anyone else had been in that cunt, that cunt that was meant only for Lane. But the anticipation of finally fucking Carol's behind would be so sweet.

'Good. Then it's agreed.' She sat down opposite Carol and started to roll a joint.

Lane slumped down in the living area of the open-plan flat while Carol finished her work. The room was all bare wood floors and genuine Turkish rugs, simple furniture and big framed prints. Dragging on the end of the joint, she flicked on the TV and watched a chat show. She was far more stoned than Carol, having had most of the spliff, and the result was that she kept trying to think of how she would cope with their deal, but then kept forgetting what she was worrying about.

Her thoughts went round and round. Since meeting Jack, she had realised there were plenty of guys around who would willingly have sex with a woman. Although she hadn't yet been with anyone else, Jack had hinted that he had friends who might be interested. What if she had sex with him and one of his friends at once? Would she have to bring two other people to Carol? Had Carol said, 'Every time you have sex with a man', or 'Every time you have sex with *men*'?

'What's up, pussycat?' asked Carol when she finally left her work and sat down on the sofa. Lane was sitting on the floor and she leant back against her lover's legs and moved her head about while Carol rubbed her short new haircut as if Lane really was a cat.

'Mm-mmm,' purred Lane. 'You still love me, then?'

'Laney, I haven't just this week realised that you're attracted to queerboys, you know. You do flirt with them all the time. And cruise them. And they look at you, as you well know.'

'Cos they think I'm a bloke.'

'Not always. You don't look at them because you think they're women, do you? It's a mutual queer thing.' The hand on Lane's head grew still. 'Well?'

'Yeah, maybe.'

'So, are you brooding on all this?'

'Yeah. I'm not sure about this deal. It's weird. We've been trying so hard not to be "unfaithful" and now we're off into something new.'

'Scared?'

'Maybe. Aren't you?'

'No. Should I be? Because if it's too much for you, then I take it all back. You can stop having sex with boys and just have me,' said Carol. There was silence for a moment. 'Look at me.' Lane shunted on to the sofa next to Carol and took her hand. 'You're a very sexy woman, Laney,' Carol said, looking into her eyes.

'Hey, so are you.' Lane cupped a hand in Carol's crotch and leant over to kiss her.

Their mouths were hungry for each other and Lane shifted round so she was kneeling over Carol, held her face and kissed her with such feeling that Carol started moaning.

Lane's hand moved to Carol's loose white shirt. 'Did you go to work like this?' she asked. 'With your blouse undone and your underwear showing? Like a slut?' Carol gave a moan. Lane ran her hand down inside the shirt and over her lover's shiny red body-stocking. 'Answer me!'

'Yes.'

'Yes, you went to work like this? What will people think? They'll think you want them to look at you, to imagine you in just your underwear, won't they?'

'Yes.' Carol looked at her, pleading. Lane could see she wanted to be fucked, already needed it. She didn't want to be interrogated. But certain things had to be said. Even as she spoke to her lover in this way, Lane grew wet with desire, with the power she had over this woman and the need between them.

'Carrie, I have to take some of your clothes off now, but I won't be fucking you yet. I just need to look at you.' She undid the white shirt and pushed it down over Carol's tanned shoulders, kissing each one as she bared it. She stroked Carol's arms, enjoying both the muscle that came from daily exercise and the warmth of her flesh. Carol worried about her weight but, to Lane, this extra weight was a pleasure, flesh to enjoy.

Slipping Carol's shirt down to her elbows, Lane decided to leave it there so she could enjoy her lover's half-dressed state. Her hands moved to the older woman's waistband, finding the zip at the side of the black trousers and sliding it undone.

'What are you going to do to me?' asked Carol, her voice quivering with excitement.

'Whatever I want.' She pulled the trousers off, revealing the rest of Carol's red silk underwear and the press-studs that held it together near to her clit.

'Whatever you want? What if I don't want it?'

'Let me see now, do I care?' Lane looked at her, knowing that the intensity in her own eyes would be reflected as fear and excitement in Carol's – and it was. 'No, I don't care. When I say I'll do what I want, I mean it. I think you know that.'

Carol shook her head against the back of the sofa and raised her shoulders as Lane moved in to kiss her. 'No, get off me.'

But Lane nuzzled her neck, at the same time running her hands down over Carol's full breasts and the slight swell of her stomach. Carol was struggling, moaning, 'No, no,' while her breathing grew heavier.

'Now I've got you, babes. Now I've really got you.' Lane grabbed both Carol's hands and pulled them to her mouth to kiss them, gently and carefully; both sides, every finger. Then she suddenly pushed away, pinning Carol's hands to the back of the sofa while pushing a knee between her thighs. Her lover gasped and again shook her head from side to side, struggling under Lane's light grasp.

They had a kind of code between them, but it never had to be discussed. Perhaps twice or three times since they had been together, Carol had said, 'No, Lane, get off, don't do that,' but in her normal voice – something close to her professor voice actually – and it was dead clear that she meant it. The last time it had happened was just last week, when Lane had gone for her arsehole with the strap-on. Then Lane would stop (although they both knew that Carol would be punished in some way for failing to comply). But anything else, like thrashing about or begging or even crying, was to be expected.

Lane was now kneeling on the sofa in front of Carol, one knee moving slowly, lightly and determinedly on the thin crotch of that red silk. Her own crotch, still encased in her khakis, rubbed against Carol's naked thigh. She prolonged this for as long as she could bear it, knowing that it was too long for Carol, whose eyes searched her face, pleading wordlessly for release.

Then Lane let go of her lover's hands to push the delicate straps of her bodystocking down over her shoulders and unwrap those full breasts. One at a time, Lane sucked Carol's whole breast into her mouth and, holding it there, sucked and chewed on the nipple. 'I love your tits,' she said as the first slid from her mouth and she moved to suck on the second. Carol moaned. As Lane sucked the other breast into her mouth, Carol pushed her chest out to show her keenness.

Lane slid a hand down between Carol's legs, gasping herself as she felt the outline of Carol's hair and of the wet lips of her cunt. The fabric was soaked and Lane needed to take a proper look. Leaving her lover's breasts hanging out of her underwear, Lane bent to view the dark patch of the bodystocking. It was an oval a little larger than Carol's labia. She fingered it. Carol was moaning loudly. 'Fuck me,' she mumbled.

'What did you say?' Lane's voice was firm and Carol seemed to tremble under her.

'Fuck me. Please.' She searched Lane's face to see if she would get her desire. But her voice betrayed the shame she felt in asking, and her fear that she had broken the rules.

'Who decides when and how I fuck you? Who decides if I even want to fuck you?' asked Lane, her fingers grabbing at the silk and pinching together Carol's cuntlips.

'You do.' Again that mumble, Carol's eyes downcast.

'I can't hear you.'

'You do. You do whatever you want.'

'That's right. As long as you understand.' Lane unzipped the fly of her combats, then paused to take off her shirt, revealing the ribbed khaki vest she wore underneath. She was still wearing her boots, in contrast to Carol, who was nearly naked: the one-piece covering her belly and cunt, one breast loose and the other partly trapped under the thin fabric, the shirt hanging from her arms.

Then Carol watched, unblinking, as Lane reached through her flies and through the opening in her cotton boxer shorts to pull out her black rubber cock. Carol's hips were moving back and forth already. She had known it would be the cock today, had felt it hard against her when they first greeted each other that evening (or so Lane hoped). Throughout their negotiations about the Big

Deal, Carol had known that whatever power she had at that moment would last only as long as Lane's trousers were zipped.

Now that the time was here, Lane had to exercise careful control over herself. 'If I really do whatever I want,' she said to Carol, 'then you might get hurt. So for your sake, I will try to be careful. But you have to understand that I can't always stop myself and it is possible, for instance, that I won't be able to enter you without hurting. Do you understand?'

'Please don't hurt me,' gasped Carol. But Lane was already unsnapping the studs of the red silk, which fell apart to reveal wet hair, a cunt that seemed to spread wider before her eyes and a clit that was already hard. Lane rubbed her palm over all of this and enjoyed the smell that rose from Carol's cunt. She pushed the wet hand into Carol's face and watched her lick it.

Then the hand went back to that wetness, lightly touching and probing as Lane felt herself going hot and red in the face with the effort of not just plunging into her lover.

'I'm going to fuck you now, Carol,' she said quietly and determinedly.

She motioned for Carol to kneel up so she could get inside her. Lane gripped her cock and rubbed the head between Carol's thighs, gathering the dripping juices until the warm silicone was wet and sticky. Then she started to guide her cockhead to Carol's hole, while using her other hand to steady Carol's head.

She kissed Carol's cheek and slid in the first inch of the dildo, but as Carol gasped with gratitude, Lane couldn't stop herself from thrusting. She flinched as she heard Carol cry out. 'I'm sorry,' she whispered, kissing Carol's face softly and then waiting for her to slide down, taking the rest of Lane's cock inside her, gasping and groaning.

At that moment Lane felt all her strength and love pumping through her. Her job now was to fuck Carol without getting so excited herself that they became distracted from what was important: that Carol should come while Lane filled her.

Carol was already so aroused that Lane knew she needed her clit to be touched. 'You can touch yourself soon, but not yet,' she told her.

'You!' Carol demanded in a low moan.

'What?'

'You touch me!'

'Are you making demands?' As Lane asked this, she thrust hard inside Carol, wrapping her arms tight around her and pulling her down, so that the movement rammed the cock against Carol's insides.

'Ow! No! You decide. But if you want to touch me, then please do!' Carol's voice was submissive but desperate.

'Touch yourself,' said Lane as if it were a punishment, and her lover obeyed, her fingers moving on her long clit. Lane's head dipped and she started to suck on Carol's breasts, rubbing her head between them and feeling it enclosed by the soft flesh. Then she moved to suck the other breast, now moaning herself. She could never believe her luck at moments like this, to have a lover who needed to be fucked and sucked and overcome like this.

Now Carol was building to her climax and Lane held her tight, her own face pressed so hard into the older woman's breasts that she could barely breathe, her hips moving fast to push the dildo up and down inside that warm cunt. Carol was saying, 'Oh, Lane, what are you doing to me? Oh, God, I can't . . .' and then she came, moaning and moving on Lane and grabbing Lane's hair to pull her towards her, to kiss her.

The kiss lasted only a few seconds but sealed their love, the deal they'd made today, and their understanding of the sex between them.

They stayed like that, Lane's cock deep in Carol, until Lane knew she too had to come. She pulled out of Carol, who groaned in protest and in pleasure; then she held her dildo in one hand and touched her own clit with the other, her eyes on her lover's gaping cunt which was still pulsing with the aftermath of orgasm.

It only took a minute for Lane to bring herself off. Carol didn't attempt to touch her, and Lane knew it was partly her lover's exhaustion and laziness, and partly because they both knew that Lane loved to touch herself like this, rubbing her clit faster and faster while her breathing all but stopped, until her open mouth let out a deep groan. She kept her eyes on Carol's sex as she shuddered to a climax, then reached out her musky hand to wipe it across her lover's breasts.

Carol smiled as the younger woman fell down between her legs, kissing her pubes and giving a little lick to that gorgeous clit.

They slumped there, Lane rubbing her face in Carol's wetness as Carol stroked the cropped hair at the nape of her toygirl's neck.

By the time they had pulled off their musky clothes and were naked in Carol's mezzanine bed, just under the ceiling, it was late. Lane felt uneasy and sensed that Carol did too. 'Are you all right?' she asked.

'Yes. Are you?'

'Yeah. But I keep thinking about this deal we've made, the Big Deal.' Lane rolled her eyes.

'What's that mean? That you don't want to go along with it?' As Carol asked this, she tugged on both the silver rings that looped through Lane's nipples.

Lane shrieked and fought back. 'Stop that! I need to talk to you!'

'So what's the problem?'

'Suppose I had sex with more than one man at a time? How many new people would I have to bring to you?'

'As many as you had sex with, of course. Is the concept too difficult for you?' Carol was enjoying regaining the upper hand, slipping into academic mode.

'So I could just bring everyone I'd just shagged and have them shag you, couldn't I?'

'Well, in theory you could. But in practice, I don't think I'm going to stick around very long if you make me have sex with several gay men at a time. That's not why I became a lesbian.'

Lane laughed. 'Don't give me that shit. You "became" a lesbian because a sexy androgynous dyke wanted to fuck you,' she said, describing Carol's old friend and ex-lover, Al.

Carol wouldn't admit defeat. 'You know what I mean. I'm not a gay boy, Laney, so don't try to make me into one.'

'I don't want to. I love you just the way you are.'

'Yeah, me and an army of gay men. Very flattering.'

'Are you jealous?' asked Lane, tentatively.

'Of course. And I'm wondering why you'd need more than one of them at a time. But it's kind of a turn-on, thinking of you going out for what you can get – and then finding someone special to bring home for me as well . . . But it's got to be girls, for me, Laney. No blokes in this bed.'

'But you used to be straight,' the younger woman pointed out.

'That's not the same thing and you know it.' Carol started to make herself comfortable, wrapping an arm around Lane and yawning.

It never took long for her to fall asleep, but Lane wasn't prepared to let her. 'Hey,' she urged, 'you need to practise. It won't be long before I bring someone home to fuck you and I need to be sure you'll get it right.'

'Not now,' said Carol.

'Yes, now.' Lane rolled her naked lover on to her front, oblivious to her protestations.

'I can't do it any more. I'm exhausted,' moaned Carol. But she was already grinding her hips sleepily into the mattress and she spread out her arms as if expecting a body search.

Lane looked lovingly at Carol's body. It wasn't often that they were completely naked together, and now Lane lay down on top of Carol and they both murmured their appreciation of the soft warmth between them. Carol liked to be trapped – Lane knew that – but this time she was going to be tender with her.

Filled with love for the woman she had already fucked so thoroughly that evening, Lane spread her own arms out on top of Carol's. Their hips moved in unison. Lane was kissing the back of her lover's neck and listening to her moans. Then she slipped a hand under Carol to feel her breasts and pinch her nipples. Enjoying the sleepy passivity of the woman under her, Lane moved her hand to touch Carol's clit, so that each time the trapped woman ground her hips into the mattress, she was rubbing against Lane's fingers.

Their quiet groans gathered pace together. In the seconds before Carol came, Lane was taut with expectation, barely moving. Then Carol bucked and screamed and her spasms went on and on while Lane kissed and bit her neck and shoulders, whispering, 'That's it, good girl, my good girl.'

★

'How do you say thank you?' asked Lane when Carol was calm and still.

'I don't know,' replied her femme. Lane was still half on top of Carol, twisted round her and holding her tight.

'I think you do.'

'Fuck you with my fist?'

'That's right. That's what I want.' She almost took pity on Carol, who was clearly drained and sleepy. But Lane wasn't finished yet.

Lane was so wet that the very wetness seemed to be driving her to be filled and fucked. She took the lube from the little set of drawers on the table next to the bed and handed it to her lover.

'I want you to fuck me with your whole fist. If I say stop, then stop. OK?' she asked, as usual.

Carol nodded, but that wasn't good enough for Lane, who liked proper obedience. 'Do you understand?' she asked.

'Yes.'

The blonde woman touched Lane's cunt, brushing her fingers gently around the opening. Lane was lying on her back with her knees raised and her legs wide open. There were pillows behind her head and she pushed them down behind her back in preparation for what was to come.

As Carol knelt between Lane's knees, Lane hoped she wouldn't go too fast. Really, Lane hadn't trained her properly at the start and she seemed to take some pleasure in getting it wrong.

Already – too soon – Carol's knuckles were grinding against Lane's pubic bone. But the young butch decided to relax and take it. She put her hands under her head to keep herself still, and concentrated on keeping her cunt relaxed. And, like magic, the fist slipped inside her in a quick and agonising slide that made Lane bellow like an animal. Her eyes were wide with shock and gratification.

'Oh, good girl, my good little femme,' she said.

She was rewarded for this belittling phrase with an internal bashing that made her twist in panic on the bed. A wicked grin was playing over Carol's face as she bent forward to kiss her victim. Lane wrapped both arms round her and was able to haul herself up so she was sitting on Carol's fist while plunging her tongue equally deep into Carol's mouth.

Locked to her lover, her back against the wall, Lane felt herself drowning in the pain and the satisfaction of being so very full. It wasn't long before she pulled her mouth from Carol's to bellow louder than ever and push her fister down on the bed with her where they writhed and thrashed against each other.

'So fucking good,' Lane said quietly as they settled. Carol slowly pulled out her arm and emptied Lane out, making her sob. They fell asleep, Lane's tears forming tiny streams across Carol's breasts.

TWO

Like a Man

Lane wondered why Carol hadn't asked more about what she and Jack had done. In fact, Carol hadn't even asked if it *was* Jack. She didn't want to know, apparently. Was it jealousy, or just that the thought of Lane with men was a turn-off for her? Lane hadn't even been able to tell her that she and Jack had only had sex once – so far.

On a rare evening alone in her own flat, Lane lay down on the bed, stuck her hand through the fly of her boxers, and thought back on that first time with Jack.

Soho was alive with the first frisky days of spring as Lane walked through from Covent Garden, where she worked as 'webmeister' for a design company. There was quite a crowd of queers outside The Corner, enjoying the lukewarm night. She pushed past them to get inside the trendy drinking hole, then wound her way up the stairs from one bar to the next. As he'd promised, Jack was waiting for her in the top bar. He looked gorgeous in a tight white T-shirt and baggy combats.

Lane had a pang of guilt, knowing that Carol was round the corner in Chocolate Bar with her friends tonight. Lane could pop in to say hi, but she wasn't going to. She wasn't even going to tell Carol where she'd been.

She smiled at the handsome skinhead she'd known for so long.

'Hey, bro!' she called. Jack was sitting at the bar and gave her a sly smile.

'Get over here, girl!' He grabbed her and wrapped his arms around her without getting up from his barstool. His bear hugs were usually suffocating and this was no exception.

'Oi, let me go, Jack!'

As he complied, he took a good look at her, then took hold of her chin and kissed her on the lips. Their mouths opened and Lane felt a surge of lust as Jack's pierced tongue played with hers.

But she pulled away. 'People will talk, Jackie-boy!'

'Yeah, tongues will wag,' he replied, sticking out his tongue and waggling it lewdly at her, the stud glinting like an added obscenity. He bought her a vodka and cranberry.

She thanked him and then confessed. 'Guess what, I'm dead nervous, Jackie-boy.' It wasn't the first time they had kissed, but it was the first time they had met up with this particular mission: to fuck.

'Get that down you and I'll take you home and sort you out, darlin'.'

'Hey, give me a chance.'

She insisted they stay for a couple more drinks, so they sat and chatted about people they knew from college. Then Jack said the time had come, and he led her from the bar and through the cool evening air to his flat off Tottenham Court Road. As they went up in the lift of the modern block, Lane took his hand.

'Thanks, Jack,' she said.

He smiled at her and shook his head. 'Hey, don't put yourself down. Thank you for the idea, sis.' They had been *brother* and *sister* since their college days. There had often been moments when it seemed like they would have sex. But Jack would break the frisson every time with some remark like, 'Hey, if you were a guy I'd have your pants off by now, sis,' and they would both back off.

It was only in the last few weeks that they'd started having goodnight snogs, and eventually Lane had told Jack her fantasy: that he would be the first person to fuck her up the arse and would teach her how to 'take it like a man'. She had also told him how she hoped to go with other men. He promised that, if she could take his cock, he would help her to find other guys who wanted to fuck her.

Now he was leading her into the small bedroom where her fantasy was going to come true. Brightly painted in blue and lime, the room had three giant abstract pictures, all created by Jack who was a graphic designer.

Tall and muscled, he took over the small room with his presence. He stood in front of Lane and wrapped his arms round her to stroke her arse. Bending down, he kissed her gently on the lips and let her be the one who pushed her tongue into his mouth. Then his piercing was rubbing on her tongue and knocking against her teeth as his breathing grew heavier and she felt his cock harden against her. Enthralled, she cupped his thick erection. She rubbed a hand up the length of it and raised her eyebrows at him.

'Well, hel-lo, big boy!'

He moved her hand away. 'You don't really want to handle the goods, do you? You're a dyke, remember?'

'A dyke who wants to be your boy for the night,' she said, blushing with the truth of it. But he was almost right about her feelings for his cock. Her teenage experiences with boys had involved one too many dicks in her mouth. What she liked was the implied power of his cock inside his trousers, the mystery of that bulge. She liked the size of it and what it could do to her.

And what she wanted was the power of that cock up her arse, the possibility that it could transform her for the night – from butch top to gay bottom.

They pulled off each other's T-shirts. They were dressed almost identically and the vests fell at their trainered feet. Jack touched her breasts with what seemed like reverence. 'I've never done this, sis,' he said.

'I know, bro. Do you like them?'

'Yeah, they're cute.'

'Cute?'

'Er, sexy?' He cupped one breast in each hand and let his thumbs play over her nipple rings. Lane gasped.

She felt strange being the small one instead of towering over Carol. She gave in to it and let him take over her, stroking and then kissing. His mouth moved to her breasts and she gasped as he chewed on a nipple and his tongue piercing played with her nipple ring. The metal made her nipple stand proud and it felt like he was starting to scratch an itch that was getting bigger all the time.

Lane felt her cunt swelling as Jack put a hand in her crotch. She had decided not to pack her dildo in her pants tonight, but wondered if she'd done the right thing as something like disappointment seemed to cross her friend's face.

'Turn around,' he said.

She did so and he told her to take off her trainers and trousers. She realised that, just as she so often did with Carol, he was going to keep most of his clothes on to fuck her.

Jack stroked her back and bum, pushing his hands down inside her boxers and gripping her cheeks. 'That's a good arse you've got there, Lane,' he said. He moved in closer and kissed her neck, then bit into it, making her cry out. 'Do you like that? Do you want me to bite you?'

'Yes. Hurt me,' she said firmly, as if she was in charge.

'OK.' He pushed her down on the bed on to her side. Lying down behind her and pressing his firm body into her back, Jack grabbed her nipple rings and gave a sharp tug as he bit deep into her neck.

Lane put her fist in her mouth, determined not to cave in. Wasn't this what she'd wanted? 'Kiss me, Jack,' she said when her hand was out of her mouth – suddenly doubting whether he really desired her. His strong arms turned her towards him and his mouth dispelled her doubts as he hungrily kissed her.

It was new, the firm, demanding way his tongue took her lust out of her mouth and into his, as if they were feeding on each other, and she gave him back just as much. She pulled his T-shirt out of his combats and ran her hands over his smooth, firm chest. She pulled the T-shirt over his head and felt empowered by the fact that he let her do it. They wrapped their arms around each other and the feel of his flat chest against her tits felt so alien that she was reminded of the big departure she was taking by being on this bed with this man.

As they kissed, their hands roamed over each other. He lingered again over her bum, gently pulling apart the cheeks in a hint of what was to come.

'Have you practised?' he asked her.

She knew what he meant. 'Yeah, with a dildo. But it wasn't that big.'

'You'll be OK, sis.'

'Could you stop calling me that, just for tonight? Lane would do fine.' She knew she sounded nervous.

He smiled. 'You got it. Take off your boxers.'

She did as he said, throwing the striped shorts to the floor. 'Jack, you haven't forgotten what we said about staying safe?'

'I'm always safe. That's not what's scaring you, is it?'

'No. I'm not sure whether I can really go through with this. But I want to.'

'You will, sis.' He shook his head to correct himself. 'Sorry, Lane.'

She kissed him and he reciprocated keenly, but his breathing was heavy and she wasn't surprised when his lips left hers and he spoke again.

'I think we're ready to start,' he said, struggling to speak calmly. He was clearly excited. 'Lie back.' He unzipped his khakis and she stared as he released his long, thick cock, which was the size of the dildo she often used in Carol. It was standing proud. He knelt between her legs and kissed her breasts. She was breathing as deeply as him now, fired up and ready, and she raised her knees and realised her arse was involuntarily grinding into the bed.

With a lubed finger, Jack went straight for her arsehole, pressing against it. 'Can you take that, Lane?' he asked.

'Yes.' She breathed deep and let him in. His finger pushed into her, delving as far as he could reach. 'That's good,' she said, gasping. Then she felt the pressure on her hole again as another finger slipped into her. Soon he had three fingers in her.

'Jack, that's enough, I can't take any more,' she moaned, her hips moving up and down as his fingers worked her tunnel.

'I think you can,' he said. His voice had deepened and his dark eyes had narrowed. She looked at his determined face and knew that she had chosen a man who would not be distracted from the task they had set themselves.

'Get on all fours now, Lane,' he said, and she did so while he unwrapped a condom.

Naked and frightened, Lane tried to prepare herself for what was to come. Jack was already rubbing more lube around her tight hole. Then she felt his hand on her arse cheek and something big pressing into her behind. It felt almost too big to fit between her cheeks. But even as the panic rose in her chest, Jack murmured, 'It's OK, you can take it.'

She believed him and, as she relaxed, the head of his cock slid past her sphincter and she screamed in thrilled pain, knowing that there was more of this to come, the pleasure as intense as the pain. 'Jesus, Jack, that fucking hurts!' she said.

'Hey, hey, it's OK, Lane. It's OK.' He was stroking her arse and then his firm hand reached to her breast and he stroked it, took hold of the nipple ring and teased her with it. She was moaning now and, holding her by both nipple rings, he pushed into her so that her tunnel gave way around his cock as it delved inches inside her. Then he waited, while she moved her hips in circles, welcoming his dick into her arse.

'Take a bit more now, Lane.' His voice was more urgent and she realised he was desperate to get deep inside her. She felt the wetness from her cunt seeping down her thigh at the thought of Jack's need and she gave in to him. He knew it and thrust deeper inside her. This time her scream was louder than ever, the pain searing through her insides.

'Nearly there,' he said. With one hand on her rump, he pressed into her again. Lane let her hole relax. Slowly, but not slowly enough, he slid in further, groaning all the time. She was opening to him and her tunnel was filling up with his meat. And all the time she was screaming. It was like letting Carol's fist into her cunt except that she had less control.

'Oh God, it hurts,' she screamed. 'Fuck me!'

He pushed his full length into her until she could feel his balls pressing against her arse, and her whole body buckled with the pain and fulfilment. Then his hand reached round to her clit and, to her amazement, started to move amateurishly on the swollen bud.

He began to thrust inside her in long, slow movements. Lane had no choice but to move in rhythm with him as this strong man fucked her arse as if she was a man. She felt his whole body leaning into hers and then a shock as he bit into her shoulder.

'How's that? Do you like me fucking you?' he asked.

'Yes, yes, I need it, fuck me,' she replied.

As she felt him building to climax, his thrusts coming faster and his shouts no longer in words, so she let herself give in to the experience of being overpowered by Jack. The feeling in her clit was secondary to the pummelling in her gut, but it was the knowledge that this man was about to empty himself inside her that made Lane come, screaming obscenities as they climaxed together.

He was slamming against her arse, his dick stirring up her guts, but Lane collapsed as she came, bringing Jack down on the bed with her. He clutched her to him, his arms wrapped around her chest as his whole body pressed into her back. He was biting her neck again and she kept coming, amazed at how he had fulfilled her dreams.

'Coming out now,' he said finally. Inch by inch, she felt his cock slipping from her arse and her tunnel closing up behind it.

'So good,' she mumbled, 'so good.' As his cockhead left her, her hole clenched. 'Jack,' she gasped, turning over and reaching out to him.

She wrapped her arms round him and they kissed. 'You are one good fuck, Lane,' he said.

'Takes one to know one,' she replied, disengaging from him. 'But will you be telling all the boys how good I am?'

'Not just yet. I'll keep you to myself while I train you up. You're not quite obliging enough, but it shouldn't take long to correct that.'

She kissed his chest. 'Can I stay?'

'Can you stay? Well, let me see now.' He clapped his hands and a projection of a clock appeared on the ceiling for just long enough to see that it was midnight. It was a trick she had seen quite a few times since he'd bought this treasured gimmick. 'My next client is in half an hour . . .' He broke off the act and grinned at her. 'You'd better fucking stay. You owe me breakfast.'

'Did we have a deal?'

'Don't you remember?'

'No. But if that's the price of an expert fuck, it's cheap.' She looked at him. 'Are you going to sleep in those trousers, or can I take them off you?'

Jack stretched out on his back and gave her a cat-got-cream look. 'Mmm, strip me, sister,' he said.

Remembering that first fuck, Lane moved her finger fast on her clit and quickly brought herself off. She needed to have him inside her again, and soon. But that meant that she needed to start recruiting the women who would fuck Carol in return. Because breakfast wasn't going to be enough to satisfy that particular deal.

THREE

At Her Feet

The week after the Big Deal was struck, Carol took a night out from the intensity of her relationship with Lane, to go to dinner at a student's house. Marg was taking Carol's Lesbian Writers module on the Twentieth Century Literature course – and referred to it as Twenty Clits. In fact, everything about the nineteen-year-old was cheeky and immature, except that she had a keen intellect. She lived in the same north London terraced street as Lane, but Carol had never been to the flat before.

Carol had assumed that Marg was giving a dinner party for a few like-minded students and had asked her lecturer along as an added frisson. Many of the students saw socialising with the staff as a grown-up, exciting thing to do; although others, of course, thought it was geeky.

But when Carol got to the flat, Marg led her into a small living room, empty except for a girl who was introduced as Amy and seemed to be the flatmate. Carol thought she'd seen her around campus. The room seemed to have been furnished by a taste-free landlord in the seventies but the girls had made the best of the flowery decor by lighting it subtly with candles, and chucking Indian throws over the battered suite. There were cheap rugs on the floor, only partially covering the maroon flowered carpet.

The result was a cosy mess, even though it wasn't actually untidy: books and records were on shelves and magazines were piled high on a coffee table. The wallpaper was mostly hidden by posters that ranged from a photo of Toni Morrison to a giant dayglo marijuana leaf.

'I'm real glad you could come,' Marg said in her American accent.

'Isn't anyone else coming?'

'No.' That was all she said. Then she just smiled at Carol and looked around the room, apparently waiting for her tutor to initiate a conversation. Carol felt no such obligation. Instead she took the opportunity to have a good look at her student.

Marg ('Think margaritas,' she told anyone who mispronounced her name, 'not non-dairy spread') was a redhead. She had one of those hairstyles that the students did to each other when they were drunk but always seemed so delighted with. It made her look like a crusty, with a little tail at the back, Tin-Tin tuft at the front, and the rest unevenly shaved close to the scalp.

But she was a good-looking girl, with a perky face and lively green eyes, a little bud of a mouth and a lithe body. Tonight she was dressed in ex-army combats dyed purple and a T-shirt with a big orange sun design. The dramatic Celtic tattoo that ran round her upper arm was revealed as Marg rolled up the sleeves of her T-shirt.

Amy, who had by far the better hair – longish braids with the odd bead in them – returned from the kitchen with a bottle of wine. Carol realised with a jolt that they'd been sitting in silence.

'D'you both want some wine?' asked Amy, with a slight south London drawl.

Carol nodded and thanked her. Amy made quite a contrast with her pale, scruffy flatmate. She was an elegant girl with a long, pretty face and light brown skin, and was wearing a tailored blouse and trousers.

'The thing is –' Marg suddenly began, as if about to make an important declaration.

Amy shot her a look. 'The food's ready, Marg, d'you want to come in the kitchen with me?'

They went through a curtain of bright plastic beads and Carol could hear low arguing. Presumably something was wrong with the dinner and Amy thought she could sort it out without any grand announcements from Marg.

In fact the dinner was fine, if predictable: a risotto with salad and then ice cream. They chatted about literature; Amy was studying French but she was well read in both languages. Carol felt that the girls were keeping her on her toes, especially as they kept filling up her glass and she was now quite drunk.

It was when Amy went to make coffee that Marg made a move. She asked Carol to sit on the floor with her. 'I want to show you something.' Drunk and happy, Carol sat next to Marg and watched the girl take off her T-shirt to reveal another tattoo, this one running all round her belly button and in a similar Celtic design to the one on her arm.

She was not wearing a bra and her smallish breasts were as perky as her face. Carol stared. 'That's, er, very nice. Great.' She felt like the grown-up prude.

'Have a good look. That's why I said to sit next to me. Touch it if you like.' Marg took Carol's hand and placed it on the tattoo.

The older woman dutifully stroked the black design, which did look dramatic against Marg's pale skin. Her awkwardness melted away as she looked into Marg's eyes and saw the girl was playing with her and that the whole thing had been pre-planned. There was a satisfied look and the beginning of a grin on Marg's face as she leant in and touched Carol's cheek.

'Do you want to see the third one?' she asked.

'You've got three breasts?'

Marg laughed. 'You don't see my third breast on a first date!'

'Oh, we're on a date now?' Carol asked, all innocence.

'Just a figure of speech.'

'So, why *three* tattoos?'

'I figured while I'm in the UK I should take advantage, like, get in touch with my Celtic roots the hard way.'

'Does it hurt a lot?'

'While it's being done, yeah. But I kind of like that.' Marg kissed her lightly on the lips, then, when Carol didn't back off, lunged in and stuck her tongue fiercely in her tutor's mouth. Carol was fired up with the thrill of this sudden encounter and her own tongue explored Marg's mouth, their teeth grinding against each other as the girl daringly pulled up Carol's tight top and stroked her naked breasts.

'Marg,' Carol said tentatively, 'this isn't exactly approved behaviour between tutor and student, you know.'

'I'm not complaining, am I? I won't tell anyone, Dr Maitland.'

Carol weighed it up. She wasn't marking Marg's term paper on Twenty Clits because a colleague who was an expert in the girl's chosen author had offered to do it. So did it matter? There was only half a term to go and then Marg's exchange ended and she was going back to the States to finish her degree. If Carol was going to feel guilt, it should be over Lane.

Perhaps it had something to do with the fact that Lane had been 'playing away from home', but Carol didn't feel guilty about what was about to happen. Instead she felt excited and desired. All the worries she'd been having recently about turning forty, about ageing and gathering cellulite, were evaporating as this teenager probed her mouth once more.

Then Marg pulled away. 'The thing is –' she began, and Carol couldn't help but laugh at the serious way this topless youngster was once again trying to make an announcement.

'Yes?' she asked in what Lane would call her professor voice.

'Well, y'know, Amy and me don't go for each other, we're just friends. But we've both got kind of a crush on you. So we were wondering –'

'You've brought me round here on the pretence of having a dinner party so you can both have sex with your lecturer?' Carol feigned annoyance. Apparently she was a good actor, because Marg looked as if she'd been slapped.

'Yeah, I guess it looks that way. But we didn't mean any disrespect.'

'Come a little closer and say that,' Carol demanded.

Amy came back in to find them pulling at each other's clothes. She coolly discarded her own blouse and the flimsy white trousers and sat down next to the others with a glass of wine, watching.

Knowing what she did – that she was desired by both girls – Carol soon pulled away from Marg to reach out to Amy, who willingly came to her. Carol saw that the girl's face was gleaming with a light sweat and, as she watched, Amy's mouth opened slightly and her face moved closer. Their lips met and Carol was able to enjoy the contrast between Marg's aggressive style and

Amy's more subtle, getting-to-know-you kiss. They luxuriated in each other, running their hands over each other's backs and breasts. Amy was wearing a black cotton sports bra and pants, and Carol played with this underwear, tugging at the elastic and slipping her fingers inside.

Marg was walking around, watching them from different angles, probably feeling left out.

'I should tell you that I'm not into pain,' Carol said as she watched the redhead unhooking a whip from the wall.

'But I am,' said Marg, handing the whip to her tutor.

Carol had never used one and wasn't sure she wanted to start now. The whip was made entirely from leather, with a thick, plaited handle and a long thin strap. She glanced at Amy for help but the girl smiled and shook her head.

'Marg and I have this deal that we won't do anything directly to each other. It would be too embarrassing afterwards,' she said straightforwardly.

'A deal, huh?' asked Carol, thinking of Lane's adventures. 'Never mind my embarrassment when I see you on campus and know you're thinking, "Oh, there's Dr Maitland, who whipped my flatmate so incompetently the other night."'

'If you don't know what to do, I can show you,' said Marg, who was trying to look calm but seemed to be hyperventilating.

'You're rather missing the main thrust of my concern, Marg, but OK.'

Marg took the whip and started to demonstrate. On the wall was the publicity poster for Pulp's album *This Is Hardcore*, with a picture of a naked, prostrate woman, looking helpless.

As Marg showed her how to hold the whip and how to lash someone correctly, slicing the whip down on one arm of the settee, Carol felt disturbed by the image on the poster. She said so.

'It's not a woman, it's a mannequin,' claimed Marg. 'Do you know their music? It's kind of ironic. It's like, the poster's a comment, you know?'

Carol shook her head. She didn't know, she suspected it was bullshit, but she was endeared by the way Marg could always justify herself, even in the middle of showing her tutor how to give her a sound whipping.

'Now you hold it,' Marg told her. 'You really never done this before? You'll soon get it. Go on, have a try.'

As Carol gripped the whip, Marg encouraged her by miming the action herself, bringing down her arm and flicking her wrist at once. Carol copied. The whip thudded against the sofa.

'Good, nearly there,' said Marg. She took hold of Carol's elbow, dissatisfied with her angle. She gently guided her as Carol took another swipe at the sofa. There was a satisfying swoosh and crack from the whip.

'Yes!' Marg approved.

Her lecturer raised an eyebrow at her. 'I have the idea now, Marg,' she told her formally.

'You sure do, Doctor M. Cool!'

To stifle her exuberance, Carol reached out and pinched one of Marg's small rosy nipples, then twisted, hard.

'Ow!' Marg screamed and spread her hands out in supplication. Now she was Carol's. 'Do what you have to do,' she said submissively, 'but if I holler "Emergency!" then you got to stop, OK?'

'OK.' Endeared still further by this plain speaking, Carol let go and Marg fell to the floor, where she pulled off her white Y-fronts and crouched before Carol, her arse in the air. It was a beautifully decorated arse, with the third tattoo, a Celtic cross on one white cheek. Carol felt a shock of delight and power run through her.

As Amy stood aside, the lecturer took aim and flicked the whip at her student's backside. It barely touched her. The second lash was right on target, eliciting a moan from the teenager which made Carol flush with excitement.

So this was what it was all about. Even when she fisted Lane, Carol had never felt this, because Lane had the power. But here with these girls who saw her as some kind of goddess, with Marg at her feet like a supplicant, Carol felt a burning stillness which kept her nailed to the spot, wielding the whip. She lashed and lashed at the girl's beautiful behind, watching as red weals came up across the tattoo, hardly hearing the mounting screams that came from Marg's mouth.

She stopped, to take Amy in her arms and kiss her. As she hoped, Marg twisted her head round to watch, without changing her abject position on the floor. Amy keenly slipped her hands in Carol's pants and stroked her bum. Carol mirrored the movement, pulling Amy's groin into her own, so their fannies ground together. Then she gently pushed Amy away.

'I have to finish with Marg,' she said. 'She's waiting patiently like a good girl.'

Marg whimpered. 'Ten more,' said Carol heartlessly. She lashed at the girl with all the strength she had, slicing across her bare flesh mercilessly, like a practised dominatrix. Carol felt herself growing taller and stronger with each lash of the whip, even as Marg curled into a smaller ball and started to weep and shudder beneath the blows.

Amy was counting aloud. When they reached ten, Carol knelt behind Marg and put a hand on the smarting tattoo, making the girl wince and cry.

'Stay there,' she ordered. She gestured to Amy to kneel with her. 'What do you want, Amy? What did you imagine yourself doing with me?'

The brown eyes looked steadily back at her. 'I imagined sitting on your face,' said Amy.

Carol nodded. She was not used to the active life when it came to sex, however active she might be in the rest of her life. With Lane, she barely lifted a finger, except under orders. And those orders were quite infrequent, as Lane often preferred to fuck Carol exhaustively and then just rub her own clit for a couple of minutes to make herself come.

But now there were two young girls who wanted to be used by Carol, and she was revelling in it, full of energy, not even thinking about her own release. Was this how it was for Lane?

Amy said, 'I know what else Marg wants, too.' Carol nodded encouragement, and Amy crawled over to a sports bag sitting on a trunk, and took out a fat dildo in two-tone purple and white. 'She wants to beg you to fuck her with this,' she explained.

Again, Carol nodded as if all this was normal, as if fucking with purple dildos, whipping and licking were requests she got every day from her students. 'Is that what you want, Marg?' she asked.

The girl whimpered, apparently reduced to a wreck who couldn't speak. She was soaked in sweat and breathing very heavily. Then she pleaded in a broken voice, 'Please fuck me with the dildo, Dr Maitland.' She said it without moving, her arse pointing at Carol, as if she did not deserve to face her abuser – nor to use her first name.

Carol turned to Amy, who was pulling off her own pants in readiness for what was to come, revealing a narrow triangle of dark hair, as if she had shaved it to make a neat pointer to her cunt. With the two naked girls before her, Carol had to steady her nerves for a second. It was the kind of fantasy she had never even let herself entertain in the shadier reaches of her psyche. You don't fuck your students, so it's best not to even think about it. But now they were begging her to do just that and she felt liberated.

She saw what to do and gave instructions. 'Marg, crawl under the table,' she said, sweeping the magazines to the floor. 'Amy, sit on the table.'

Arranged this way, Carol had them presented to her beautifully. As she watched the naked girls take their positions, she felt her own juices start to soak through her pants and dampen her thighs. There was a fire in her belly but she felt as still as a rock. She surveyed the scene. Marg was under the table, her whipped arse sticking out in readiness.

'Please fuck me with the dildo, Dr Maitland,' she said again, louder this time but in a shaky voice.

Amy was sitting on the table, her brown legs wide open to reveal her cunt, her feet swinging wide of Marg's tattooed arse. Perfect.

Carol approached them without words. She knelt and spread Marg's legs wider, waiting until the girl repeated the plea once more: 'Please fuck me with the dildo, Dr Maitland.' Then slowly but without foreplay she started to push the fat dildo into Marg's gaping wet cunt. At the same time she pushed her face into Amy's hot fanny and licked it out, slurping and nibbling as Amy grabbed her head and pulled it in tighter.

Carol was able to touch Marg's clit while she worked the big toy in her, and while she licked hard on Amy's clit. She was very aware that she was the only woman still wearing her pants; the skimpy pink nylon was soaked, but they were a badge of her power.

She listened to the girls' moans, trying to get the timing right in the way that Lane might do with her.

Amy whispered, 'Dr Maitland, I can't believe you're doing me,' and Carol herself came at the sound of this perverse formality and respect, her backside quivering as she forced herself to continue bringing the girls to climax.

It took only seconds before they were all coming together. Carol left the dildo in Marg and started spanking her, without thinking or knowing what she was doing, while they were all still in the throes of orgasm. Amy's legs were still wide and she pulled Carol's head back into her lap as soon as she could grab it. The frenzy was full of groans and shouts and Carol felt stripped of herself and renewed.

It was when she woke at dawn on the floor of the living room, covered in a throw, the two girls curled on either side of her, that the pounding thought came to her: the Big Deal. If Lane found out what had happened – and Carol certainly had no intention of telling her – then she would insist on taking Carol up the arse. In her drunkenness last night, Carol had forgotten her own side of the bargain.

Trembling, Carol woke the girls and made each of them promise not to tell a soul what had happened. Sleepy and bemused, they each swore to keep the secret, kneeling before her like disciples. They were wrapped in bedspreads but these were falling away, revealing both girls' smooth breasts.

'Hey, Dr Maitland,' said Marg, 'we could just tell any girls that might be into it, you know? Anyone who might come along next time?'

'What makes you think there will be a next time?' asked Carol. 'What makes you think I want other people involved?'

Marg apologised. 'I guess it wouldn't look too good if anyone told the Prof, huh?'

Carol just nodded. It certainly wouldn't look too good, but at least Professor Jones was unlikely to punish her for this abuse of power by fucking her up the arse.

FOUR

All Boys Together

'Carol knows about us,' Lane said suddenly after a shot of Aero Mint vodka.

Jack raised a pierced eyebrow and placed a finger dramatically against his temple. 'And what does she have to say?'

'Well, actually, I don't think she knows it was you; she just knows I've had sex with a bloke. In fact, she probably thinks I've done it loads of times already. We didn't talk details, we just made a deal.'

'Huh?'

'I can't really tell you about it, Jack, it's private. But it's cool. We're OK.'

'So you won't mind if the whole of Soho sees us together this time. Our secret is out.' His dark eyes twinkled mischievously as he kissed her neck.

'Oh, right! Cos my friends wouldn't bat an eyelid if they knew, of course. I'd rather not make any announcements in the *Pink* if it's all the same to you, bro.'

'But you must have told Annie?'

'God, no! No, no, no! Absolutely not. I'd like to keep her friendship.'

He could not respond because someone forced his way between the two of them to get to the bar.

Jack got up. 'Let me take you away from all this.' He grabbed her hand and hauled her from the stool, and suddenly they were winding down the stairs of The Corner, Lane's head spinning from the vodka. 'I've got plans for you, darlin',' whispered Jack, just before he bit her neck and made her scream in front of the crowds of people who were drinking outside the bar.

'Lane Wolfson! What are you up to?' The voice was familiar, as was the bitchy tone. It was Carol's colleague, Petra, giving Lane a knowing look as if she was planning on blackmailing her. 'Who's this you're with?'

'This is my old friend, Jack. We were at art school together.'

'Oh really?' Petra arched an eyebrow. What an infuriating woman she was. Tall, dark and slim, she had the good looks of a model, rather than the good looks of a dyke, which Lane preferred. In fact, Petra was bisexual. If Lane hadn't known any other bisexuals, any nice or amusing ones, then Petra would have confirmed all those stereotypes about the flirt who goes for anyone, any time. Luckily, their paths rarely crossed.

'Does Carol know what you're up to?' Petra asked, again in that bitchy, almost threatening tone. Had she seen Jack biting Lane, or only heard the scream that Lane let out?

Playing it cool, reminding herself that she was worth more than Petra any day, Lane replied, 'Carol and I don't have to check in with each other twice a day, Petra. Does your husband know you're here?'

'We're not married.'

Lane knew perfectly well that Petra and Anil weren't married. But it wasn't for any bohemian or queer reason, only that this irreligious white woman didn't go down well with his family. And what was she wearing, anyway? Some kind of power suit and a nasty, whirly shirt.

Lane felt Jack's reassuring hand on her shoulder. 'This is Petra,' she said.

'Pleased to meet you, Petra,' he said, shaking the woman's hand. Lane caught a strange look between them which she couldn't identify.

'We've got to go,' she said, taking Jack's arm and guiding him away from the crowded pavement and into the road, without a backward glance.

'Who's that?' asked Jack.

'Just some conniving bitch that Carol works with. They seem to get on, but I don't trust her as far as I could throw her bitchy arse.'

Jack laughed and they strolled through Soho Square in the dimming half-light. Lane noticed how he glanced at a gay man who passed them, sizing him up.

'Do you cruise here?' she asked, as they rounded the corner of the little half-timbered house in the centre of the square.

'No. My activities centre on Russell Square,' he replied. 'I'll have to take you there some night, sis, when I've broken you in properly.'

'I might go by myself.'

'You will not.' Stopping, he drew away, so that her arm fell from his, and looked solemnly at her. 'If you want to be trained, then that's what I'll do. But we have to trust each other. And when you start talking like that, I can't trust you. You do not go cruising until I say so, and then you go with me, understood?'

'OK.' She admired this in him, the way he took control so determinedly. It reminded her of the way she was with Carol sometimes, in command.

The pact made, they cut through to Centrepoint, then up Tottenham Court Road to his flat. Lane felt their old familiarity, but also the sexual tension between them which had hardened, since that first night together, into a threat or a promise. His hand was on her bum as they entered his block of flats and her heart quickened in expectation of what he would do to that bum. The memory of his cock up her arse was already real in her body, like a presence.

'There's someone I want you to meet,' Jack said, his voice deep and serious in the empty, marbled lobby. He pressed the lift button. 'He's upstairs now and he's very interested in what I've told him about you.'

'Who?' Lane could barely get the word out for nerves. She hadn't realised Jack's plans involved another person.

'He's called Matthias. He's Greek but he's lived here for a few months. Back home, he trained younger men. He's got a thing

35

about it. Getting them ready for his cock and for other men's cocks.'

Lane felt excited and scared as they got into the lift – feelings which were becoming familiar when she was around Jack. 'What will he want to do?'

'He will help me to train you, that's all. That's what you want, isn't it?'

Lane couldn't bring herself to nod. She wanted to say, 'Yes, in my fantasies – not in real life!' But she couldn't speak. It was as if Jack's certainty and control had silenced and oppressed her. Her stomach lurched as the lift stopped suddenly at Jack's floor. What was waiting for her behind that door?

He opened the door in question with his key, then took her by the shoulders from behind and half guided, half pushed her into the hall. Straight ahead was the bedroom where he had fucked her last week. To the right of that was the living room, where the light was on. A smell of foreign cigarettes filled the air, which made Lane think of some holiday, but she couldn't grasp the memory.

Jack pushed her into the living room and she almost fell. Recovering herself, she looked around the small room to see a dark-skinned white man in a smart green shirt and pale chinos, wearing good leather shoes. He was sitting on the sofa smoking. He looked at her with a faint and threatening smile on his face.

'This is Matthias,' Jack told her, as if introducing the boss. 'Matthias, this is Lane.'

'How do you do, Lane,' the visitor said. His voice was low and teasing, but in command. The Greek accent was quite strong and seemed to add weight to his words. She looked him in the eye and noticed he was handsome in a brooding way, dark and dangerous.

Jack sat next to Matthias and they kissed. Lane was surprised to watch as their mouths opened and Matthias gripped Jack's stubbled head with both hands to draw him in. She stood, faintly foolish, but knowing instinctively that she shouldn't sit down unless they told her to.

Finally the two strong men drew apart and both turned to appraise her. 'I'll tell you what I've done with her so far,' said Jack.

But Matthias stopped him. 'I think we will say "him" tonight,' he said firmly. 'All boys together, yes?'

Jack raised his pierced eyebrow, but not in astonishment. Rather, he looked titillated by the suggestion. Lane, though shocked, felt herself grow wet with anticipation. So he wanted her to be a boy with them? Wasn't that what she wanted?

Continuing his explanation, Jack told Matthias, 'She . . . *he* was nervous last time. He had never been with a man before or felt a man's cock up his tight arse.' Now Lane was dripping, she could feel the cotton of her boxer shorts dampening and sticking to her thighs as Jack went on describing her in this strange way. 'He is keen to learn and it didn't take me too long to get in there, given that it was his first time.'

As Jack spoke, Matthias's hand moved to his own cock, which he stroked while he listened. 'I put Lane on all fours on the bed and fucked his arse,' said Jack. 'He took my full length and I came inside him. I was quite satisfied with him, especially that he could take all of me.'

'Yes, you are big, Jack,' Matthias said thoughtfully. His cock had hardened and Lane looked at the way it pushed his trousers away from his body. He was older than either of them, in his late thirties, perhaps. He didn't look particularly gay, but he reminded her of a straight-looking Mediterranean guy who had once followed her around a park, chatting and trying to get a date. He had been sexy but there was no way that Lane was going off with someone she met in the park. Not back then, anyway.

'I think,' Matthias continued, 'that I will take your friend myself tonight. Perhaps you may join us by taking the other end, Jack?'

Jack nodded and glanced at Lane, who stood shaking on the rug in the centre of the room.

'Give him something to calm him down, Jack, for God's sake,' said the older man. Jack nodded once more and went into the kitchen. While he was gone, Matthias just stared at Lane as if she were some item that he wanted to buy. Jack came back with a bottle of red wine, which seemed fairly foolish after the vodka. But Lane was in no position to argue when he handed her a chunky pewter goblet filled to the brim with the heady liquid.

She took a swig as Jack opened a small wooden box and took

out a ready-rolled joint. He lit it and sat next to Matthias. Simultaneously, each man felt for the other's cock through the cotton of their trousers, without looking away from Lane.

'Please can I sit down?' she asked tentatively, her legs like jelly. Matthias gave a roar of laughter.

'On the floor, Lane,' he ordered. She collapsed on the rug. 'Good boy,' he responded, as if speaking to a dog. Then, 'I think we will have him in here, Jack. Yes, I like that. Let him have the joint.'

Jack leant over to hand the thin spliff to Lane, who greedily took several hits, eager to lose her inhibitions. She felt so nervous that she doubted whether she would be able to go through with what they had in store for her. But was there any way out? She could stand up right now and leave the room, leave the flat, go home or even go to Carol's and climb into her safe, cosy bed, whether Carol was there or not. But instead she sat cross-legged on the floor, waiting for her ordeal to begin at the hands of these unsympathetic men.

Even as she had these thoughts, she noticed Matthias growing impatient. He was shuffling in his seat and watching her. 'I need the boy to be ready very shortly,' he said in his formal English. 'Undress him now.'

Jack got up and took the joint from Lane. 'Stand up,' he said. Lane gasped with shock, because all the gentleness that he had mustered in their last encounter was gone now. He seemed as hard and harsh as Matthias, not like her old friend at all. Still, she stood and allowed him to take off her top and expose her small naked breasts to the stare of his Greek friend.

'That's enough. It's not the breasts that interest me,' Matthias said grimly. 'It's the arse, always the arse.' Jack turned Lane so she had her back to the other man, then pulled down her jeans and boxer shorts with one swift movement. She heard Matthias's groan as he saw her bottom exposed to his gaze, and she felt violated already.

'That is what I want to see. He may sit on the table,' said Matthias. Lane sat with her back to him, her trousers and pants around her ankles, while Jack returned to his wooden box and produced a small bottle. He opened it and the stench of poppers filled the room. Lane almost retched as he shoved the bottle under her nose and held her head to it roughly.

She inhaled and felt the chemicals searing through her head and pumping in her heart. Remembering the last time she had taken poppers, when she had been terrified that her heart would burst, Lane quickly jerked her head away and was relieved that Jack let go of her.

But now Matthias was getting up and he took hold of her from behind, wrapping his arms securely around her. 'Take off the trousers, Jack,' he ordered, and he was obeyed as Jack undid her trainers and pulled them off, followed by the jeans and shorts, till she was naked. 'Remember,' Matthias said quietly and threateningly next to her ear. 'You are our boy tonight. Do you feel it?' Lane nodded, and felt the borderline between the sexes melt away so that Lane was neither man nor woman, but their androgynous boy, to be used by them.

Lane's breasts yearned to be touched, but it would not happen tonight. Tonight there were other priorities and no female desires. Knowing what the men wanted from that body, Lane was not surprised when Matthias let go and shoved Lane face down across the low table. Lane's knees were on the floor, arse sticking in the air at the edge of the table, face pressed against the table. Jack was padding out of the room and it was Matthias who was feeling the naked arse that was presented to him. Lane gasped as those hands moved expertly, stroking and then parting the cheeks.

Now Jack was back in the room and one of the men was ripping open a condom packet. Lane caught a glimpse of Jack's mammoth erect prick but looked away, afraid to see too much. The drink, the blow and the poppers were working their varying effects in the wired body that now waited to be fucked. Lane felt high, tired, wired. Then the cool wet feel of lube being rubbed into the anus. Then a hard cock straining around the hole.

'No! Not yet!'

'Ah, yes,' moaned Matthias, uncaring, pushing his cock against Lane's hole until it started to open to him. Jack took hold of Lane's hair and gave a rough tug towards the poppers which he had once again in his hand. Lane inhaled, remembering that this was supposed to relax the sphincter.

Sure enough, the next sensation was of Matthias's prick sliding painfully inside, of the arsehole opening and giving in and of pure lust as the lining of the rectum received the slide of this cock. It wasn't as big as Jack's but Matthias had none of his friend's patience and was moving inch by inch into Lane's arse within seconds.

'Good,' said Matthias through heavy breathing. 'Good boy.' Lane thought of the phrase, 'good girl,' that she'd used on Carol. Now the power was not Lane's but someone else's, someone who cared only for himself.

'Please be careful,' begged Lane, whose hands were gripping the sides of the table. But the man plunged in deeper.

With deliberate breaths, in between moans, Lane was able to control any feelings of panic or pain. Certainly the pain was there, but it was less than the lust or the submission.

Now Jack was straddling the table and grabbing Lane's head. 'I'm going to fuck your mouth now with my cock, Lane,' he said insistently, single-minded in his need.

Sure enough, he pushed that big cock into Lane's mouth. Any disinclination for fellatio which might have been in Lane's mind last week was irrelevant as Jack's dick forced its fat way in. Once again he was fully dressed, as Matthias seemed to be. Lane was barely moving, except for the grinding of pelvis against wood, as both cocks pushed into those holes up to the hilt.

'Take it, take it,' chanted Jack through gritted teeth. There was no love there, only a demand that he should be fulfilled. Lane clung to the table, face uncomfortably held by Jack while he pumped that mouth, packing it with his meat.

At the other end, Matthias was muttering: 'This is the way to be fucked, you see? Fucked and fucked by me, filled with my cock. You see? Now you are truly our boy, for us to take.'

Unable to scream but filled with the feeling of a scream, Lane realised that it was nearly over. Although it had just begun, they were all so hyped up that there might only be seconds to go. Suddenly the two men were leaning in towards each other over the prostrate Lane, kissing noisily as they continued their ever-faster thrusts. Lane's guts were pounding with the back and forth probing of Matthias's cock as louder groans escaped from the men.

Suddenly, both of them were shouting, 'Take it!' and 'You see, you are our boy!' and Lane felt a climax building in all of them at once. Lane's whole tunnel tightened around the stranger's cock as he shouted out and came, while Jack plunged down Lane's throat and came in choking fountains of liquid.

Lane's own body was out of control, banging against the table, breasts squashed, cunt soaked, arms wrapped under the table to gain some stability. No one had kissed Lane throughout this 'training'. Now, once again, the two men were kissing each other. But why should Lane expect anything else? They were doing this for themselves, for the power to be gained by fucking someone they controlled – someone who could barely breathe now, mouth full of spunk and cock, arse packed full and still in spasm.

Finally, they both withdrew at once. It was as if Lane's whole body exhaled violently. She lay, shattered, across the table. Matthias peeled off his condom, then the two men sat back down on the sofa and tucked away their cocks, zipping their flies. Jack picked up the wine bottle from the floor and poured them both a glass of wine. No one spoke.

Lane woke, not from sleep, but from something deeper, almost as if she had passed out. She did not know whether minutes or hours had gone by. Her body ached. She dragged herself from the table and fell across the sofa, registering the fact that she was alone, before she once again fell asleep.

But not for long. Jack woke her with a kiss on her lips, then lay down with her in his white vest and Calvin briefs. Gently he kissed her on each breast. She felt that her womanhood was being restored as he carefully sucked at each nipple, stroking her sides as he did so.

'Are you OK?'

'Yes,' she said sleepily.

'Matthias needs to speak to you.'

'OK.'

Jack called the other man, who came in from the bedroom, wearing Jack's striped cotton robe. 'You did well,' Matthias said, standing in the doorway. 'Jack and I believe you are ready for other men.'

Lane nodded as Jack stroked her shoulder. 'Yes,' she said.

'Good. Jack will take care of you. I try not to fuck the same boy more than once. You may not see me again.' Matthias left them and they slept on the sofa in each other's arms.

FIVE

Fuck My Femme

It was late by the time that Lane let herself in to Carol's flat. It had taken some time to find the right women but now she had them. What had gone before was bizarre, but that's what you get if you go looking for a certain kind of person in a certain kind of place.

Carol was standing at the chrome railing of the mezzanine bedroom area in her knickers, looking down on Lane. 'You startled me,' she said accusingly.

Lane looked at Carol. She wore dark-pink satin knickers with lace panels, and nothing else. Her full breasts were tanned and soft. Lane climbed the metal staircase, reached out and held one breast in her hand, and watched Carol melt a little. 'It's time. I've got people outside who need to fuck you. Put that coat on, the long leather one.'

Carol looked startled.

'Now?'

'Yeah, now. Put the coat on.'

'Fetch it for me,' she said, her urgent tone almost hiding her fear.

'Come with me,' Lane demanded. She saw that Carol was looking around the room to see what to bring. 'Don't bring anything, just come with me.'

Lane went back downstairs and took down the black coat she

had chosen for Carol from the retro coat-stand near the door. She turned back into the main room to see that Carol had followed her and was gripping the back of a sofa as if she needed support to stand.

'Put this on, hon,' said Lane, her voice softening. Standing behind her, she helped her lover into the coat, then took a red bandanna from her pocket. 'And then this.' She realised that Carol was confused and unsure as the blindfold was suddenly wrapped around her eyes. Lane had never blindfolded her before but, because she had tonight all planned out, she felt nothing but a mounting thrill.

'Why?' asked Carol.

'Because you don't need to know who they are, do you?'

Immediately, Carol's breathing quickened and she murmured, 'No, you're right. I don't need to know who's going to fuck me, if you've chosen them for me.'

'Good.' Lane bent Carol forward over the back of the sofa and hitched up the back of the coat to stroke her arse through the satin of her pants. Then she slipped a hand lower to slide lightly over her cunt. At the same time, she pressed forward with her hips so that Carol would feel the hard ridge of the silicone dick that strained in Lane's jeans. The trapped woman let out a moan.

'Can't you fuck me, now?'

'I'm sorry?'

'Please,' said Carol, remembering her etiquette. 'Please, I need you in me. I don't want to wait for them.'

'But I want you to,' Lane replied, jerking Carol back to a standing position. 'I've brought them here because I need to see them fuck you, and that's what's going to happen.'

'Aren't they coming in?'

'It's time that you shut up, Carol. It's time that you just came with me and you'll find out what's going to happen soon enough. OK?'

'Yes.'

'Say it like you mean it, like you really understand what's going on here. Because this is important.' As she spoke, Lane took a leather handcuff from her small backpack, slipped it round one of Carol's wrists and pulled the strap tight through the buckle.

'Yes, I know you need to see them fuck me, to watch it,' Carol said. 'I'll do what you say, Lane.'

Satisfied with this response, Lane wrapped the second cuff round the other wrist and then linked them together with the metal catch, so Carol's hands were caught behind her back.

'Good. Let's go.' Taking hold of Carol's arm above the elbow, Lane started to steer the blindfolded woman to the door, noticing that she wore no shoes on her small feet. She pushed her outside and shut the door. Already the van was revving up.

'Who are they?' Carol suddenly asked in a frightened voice.

'Don't fucking start that again,' Lane said aggressively. 'Do you trust me?'

'Yes.'

'Go along with whatever I say. Absolutely, whatever I say. OK?'

'Yes.'

Lane walked Carol to the van and opened the double back doors. She picked up her lover and threw her into the back. Two of the women were sitting there, one on a spare tyre, the other on an old suitcase. Standing in the street, Lane bent into the van to kiss Carol on the lips and enjoyed the surprise she felt coming off Carol. The blindfold had prevented her from anticipating the kiss. Lane pulled away before her lover could get enough, and slammed the van doors, then took her place in the passenger seat.

Next to her, the driver nodded in approval and drove off. Lane gave directions curtly, sometimes just indicating right or left with her hand. They drove through the empty night streets towards the bleak industrial estate a few miles away. Lane took a ready-rolled spliff from behind her ear and lit up, toking away to release the tension.

Eventually she asked, 'Who wants this?'

'Yeah, ta.' As she turned to hand the joint into the back of the van, she heard the familiar gasp of her femme. The smallest of the gang, a woman in her thirties, Asian British, Carol's height but as slim and flat-chested as a lean youth, was on the floor, leaning her cropped head towards Carol's curls as she pushed her hand roughly inside the leather coat. It fell open to reveal Carol's vulnerable breasts, which the woman handled as if they belonged to her, pinching a nipple as she breathed into Carol's hair. She broke off for a second to grab the joint from Lane but even as she held it to her mouth, she was pinching Carol's nipple again with the other hand.

Turning to face the road, Lane tried to concentrate on giving directions. She had never before seen anyone touching Carol like that and it filled her with lust and with an anger she had not anticipated. How dare that stranger touch Lane's lover's breasts? If she had found them together like that, Lane would have wrenched the woman away, throwing her to the floor of the van and telling her to watch how it should be done.

Instead, Lane knew that she had told these women to have their way with Carol, that she had instructed them to fuck her femme and that they were preparing to do just that, in whatever way suited them. Lane was not as much in control as she had pretended to herself in her fantasy version of how this night would go.

As they pulled into a dark car park behind a concrete warehouse, Lane heard Carol call her name and turned to see that the butch, Ash, who had rich brown skin and intense, deep brown eyes, had pushed Carol down to lie full-length on the dirty metal floor and was rubbing a hand between her legs.

'I'm here, babe,' Lane reassured her lover. 'Let her do it.'

'OK.' Carol's voice seemed sad and resigned, but then Ash started to kiss her breasts and Carol moaned the way she had when Lane touched her cunt in the house.

Mesmerised, Lane stayed in the front seat, but swivelled round to watch the action. The woman in the driving seat was also watching. Ash was wearing a tight white T-shirt, jeans and DM boots. She stroked Carol and looked across at her friend in the back of the van. This was Laurence, a broad and muscled French-woman with dark eyes and a rugged and commanding face.

No one spoke as Laurence pushed up the sleeves of her plain black leather jacket to reveal her thick white forearms. She got up from the tyre where she was sitting and crawled over to her friend. Instead of touching Carol, she crouched by Ash to watch her hand moving outside Carol's satin knickers.

'Tease her with one finger,' said Laurence in her thick French accent. 'But not her clit. Just tease around her cunt.'

Ash smiled in complicity. 'Keep her waiting,' she agreed.

'Lane!' They all stared at Carol as she continued in a shaky voice. 'You said you would be in charge.'

'No, I didn't.'

'You told me to do whatever you said.'

'Yeah. And now I'm saying, let them do whatever they want. Be quiet now.'

'What will they do?' Carol asked from her prone position.

'Whatever they want. Aren't you up to this?'

'Yes,' gasped Carol. 'Yes, I am. I need it.'

Turning to the other women, Lane told them: 'Keep her quiet.'

Laurence shifted over to Carol's head and then Carol's face was hidden from view. All Lane could see was Laurence's thick dark hair as the woman kissed Carol while Ash teased their captive's cunt.

Lane couldn't stand it any longer, she had to be nearer. She climbed into the back of the van and sat on the old tyre. As it was on a ledge, she was raised up above the women. Watching Laurence kissing Carol was both worse and better than she would have expected. The jealousy actually heightened her excitement. Lane was so wet she was pulling at her crotch to get her hot clothes away from her cunt. As she did so, she felt how her cunt had swollen up and how tightly her hard clit pressed against the seam of her jeans. The dildo inside her boxers made the jeans tight anyway, trapped as it was between her belly and the denim. She let her hand rest there.

No one spoke as Ash pulled downward on the gusset of Carol's dark-pink pants, which were now so much darker from her juices. How Lane longed to grab at those pants, to suck that juice from them and then suck on Carol. But although her legs were tingling with the need to move, to jump down and push the others away from her lover, Lane still restrained herself, sitting perfectly still except for the imperceptible movement of her middle finger against her clit as her hand rested in her crotch, the thumb in line with the bulge of her dildo. She would look like a man holding his balls to anyone who didn't recognise her as a dyke.

Laurence was still kissing Carol and they were both letting out moans, but Laurence was in charge, her hand wrapped in her captive's blonde curls to keep her head trapped against the floor.

The woman in the driving seat, who had an impressive tattoo of a bird of prey in flight on one forearm, shoved a tape into the slot on the dashboard.

'Bit of music, girls?' she asked even as the unmistakable tones of Freddie Mercury in full throttle and mid-song broke the silence: 'Big-bottomed girls, you make the rocking world go round!'

'Sorry!' she said in her north-London accent. 'Didn't know it was on that track. No offence. I mean, if anyone's got a big fat arse, it's me – and I'm proud of it!' It was true that she was a big woman and she certainly showed it off. She was wearing a T-shirt with the arms ripped off and tight leather trousers.

'Shut up about your arse and get over here, Hawk,' said Ash. 'Look what I'm getting my mouth round.'

As the beat of the loud music made the whole van vibrate, Lane stopped trying to control her hand in her crotch and let it move in rhythm with the song. She watched as Laurence continued to kiss Carol as if neither of them would ever need to come up for air. Meanwhile, Ash pulled those pink knickers down over Carol's thighs and down further to stretch between her knees. She left them like that so there was only just room to get her tongue in between Carol's legs and move on her clit and cunt.

Then Ash stopped long enough to say to Carol, 'I'm going to lick you till you can't stand it and then I'm going to fuck you. We take turns in this van. The others will want to play with you, I expect, but they'll want to fuck you too, lick you, whatever, when I'm done. D'you get it? It's going to go on a long time, sweetheart.'

Laurence pulled her face from Carol's to let her reply. Lane said, 'It's OK, Carol. Let them do it. I'll be watching. I'm already rubbing my hard cock and my hard clit while I watch.'

In response, Carol did nothing but moan. She had often told Lane that her biggest fantasy was to have people fuck her while she was powerless, so that she would have no responsibility for their pleasure, might not even know who they were. Now that fantasy was coming true and Lane knew that, whatever fears her femme would have right now, she longed for it all, deep in her cunt and deep in her spirit.

No wonder Carol felt no need to speak but only groaned once

again as Ash moved back to that clit. Finally, Hawk had dragged herself away from the sound controls on her tape deck and was climbing into the back of the van where she pushed her way into a vacant space: the space where Carol's breasts were exposed between the gaping lapels of her leather coat. Hawk, whose hair was shaved tight to her scalp all over, immediately dropped her head to Carol's tits and rubbed it between them.

Lane watched as all three worked their hands and faces over her lover's vulnerable body. What would they have to do before Lane stopped them? She couldn't imagine what they would choose which wouldn't turn her on so much that she would let them do it, even if she knew that Carol would hate it. Except one thing.

Now Ash was kneeling up further, unzipping her jeans and pulling them off. 'I like to feel the flesh of a woman against my flesh while I fuck her,' she said, maybe to Carol or maybe to all of them. She took off all her clothes except her T-shirt. She had a thick bush of shiny black hair that looked lush against her brown skin and Lane longed to touch it. Realising with amazement that she could do just that, she finally got down from her perch and kneeled next to Ash, stopping her from going back to Carol for just long enough to rub a hand through that bush. Ash grabbed her head and kissed her deep on the lips, then pulled Lane's hand away and licked it to savour her own taste. Then Lane kissed her again to share that rich flavour.

They both grinned, glancing at Carol where she lay spread out and exposed on the floor, and noting the thick juice that dripped between her thighs.

'Let me help you with that,' Lane said to her new friend. She rolled Carol's wet pants right down her legs. 'Who's touching you now, babe?' she teased her lover.

But Carol was unable to speak because Laurence was kissing her again. Hawk was still rubbing her face around and between the femme's full tits. It was hard to tell if she was licking or kissing or just rubbing her head around.

Lane knelt back on her heels and watched the others. She slipped her cock out of her jeans and played with it. By adjusting the harness, she pushed the base of the cock down to rub against her clit more. Now she could just ride on her own heels and get enough sensation. Queen were singing, 'Don't stop me now,' as Ash plunged her fingers into Carol's wet cunt and Lane groaned as loudly as her captured lover. It was like Ash was fucking Lane, like Lane was fucking Carol, like they were all acting on each other, with that angry undercurrent that kept telling Lane that it wasn't all right to do this, that this was dangerous shit.

Hawk shifted round to Carol's head and grabbed at Laurence's head so she could kiss her friend roughly and then kiss Carol. The three of them were all kissing at once although Carol didn't have to do anything except let them do it to her.

Lane looked at her lover, trapped against the floor in a position in which, the butch knew, it would not be easy to climax. Carol liked to be able to move. Lane looked at these strangers fucking her girlfriend and she slipped her own hand inside her own shorts and thought how this was the most sexy thing of all: to watch your ultimate fantasy and bring yourself off, not rely on someone else who might not be up to the task in hand, so to speak. Just do it yourself.

She couldn't wait. So she told her blindfolded lover, 'I'm touching my clit and my cock right now, Carol. I'm watching them fuck you and kiss you and hold you down. Know what you look like?' As she spoke she realised that all the women's breathing was deep and heavy and they seemed to be mesmerised by Lane's voice. 'You look like a whore, on the floor there being fucked by strangers. And you are a whore, because they've paid me.'

She took three £20 notes out of her jeans pocket with her free hand and rustled them. 'I've got the money here but I can't give any of it to you because your hands are tied up behind your back. You're lying on your own hands. How did you let that happen?'

Lane was finding it harder to keep talking as she rubbed her hand around her slick tight clit. 'Oh yes, you let me handcuff you and bring you out to these dykes you've never met. And they drove you to the middle of nowhere and fell on you. Well, they gave me twenty quid each for you. Do you think that's fair? You probably think you're worth more than that, but I would have let them have you for nothing because you deserve to be fucked, you need it and I very much need to see it done. Do you understand?'

Somehow – and Lane loved her more than ever at this moment – somehow Carol managed to moan her understanding, a deep moan that seemed to come from her cunt. At that moment Lane came, shouting out like an animal in great roars that drowned even the sound of 'Lover Boy' on the stereo. She fell forward on to the floor and lay there for a few seconds heaving before she hauled herself over to Carol's breasts and buried her head where Hawk's rough head had been so recently. She could smell and taste the other woman's hair wax on her femme's soft tits as she licked them.

Ash was working her fingers in Carol, and Lane sucked a tit into her mouth and felt the way Carol's whole body changed, giving in more and getting ready to come. So Lane still knew her best.

Laurence left Hawk kissing Carol's mouth and moved to take the other tit into her mouth. Never before had Lane sucked on one tit while someone else sucked the other. Like adult twins, suckling, as they kneeled on the outstretched leather of Carol's wide-open coat.

Then their lips were drawn to each other while their wet faces still rubbed against Carol's breasts. Lane was rubbing her own crotch and she realised she was going to come again just as she heard Ash groaning in climax and recognised that Carol was close to coming herself. They were all covered in sweat and moving without any self-consciousness to pleasure themselves. Whether they pleasured each other was secondary right now.

Ash was moving away from Carol and Lane drew her mouth from Laurence's and fell down between Carol's legs, longing to bring her off. But she had only just caught one heady mouthful of her lover's hot cunt-musk when Hawk hauled her away.

'We paid!' she reminded Lane as she threw her across the van. Falling badly, Lane cursed, but she knew that Hawk was in the right. Lane could lick out Carol any time, but these women only had tonight, and they wanted what they'd paid for.

In seconds, the lower half of Carol's body was bucking up and down while Laurence held down the upper half and kissed those breasts and those lips. Ash had slumped to the floor; Lane was too bruised from the encounter with Hawk to move.

'Watch this,' said Hawk. She teased Carol, first licking her till she nearly came, then stopping and pressing down on her hips with big strong hands so that Carol couldn't move or get any more satisfaction. Finally Hawk unzipped her leathers and pulled out a white rubber dick almost the size of her forearm. 'Here we go, babe,' she said roughly as she started to move the massive fuck-weapon around Carol's wet labia.

Lane watched, knowing she could not stop this woman from fucking her lover with this giant tool. Laurence was watching rather than kissing, and Carol was able to speak. 'What you doing?' she murmured. 'Who is it?'

'Gonna fuck you, that's all. I'm big though, babe. I mean, really.' And Hawk scooped up Carol so she was sitting and pulled her on top of the dick, slowly but surely pushing into her. Carol groaned, then screamed and wrapped her arms round Hawk. Lane felt hot angry tears welling up in her eyes for the closeness she could only watch as Hawk pushed herself in and Carol simultaneously let herself down further on that cock. Then they were moving together as only Lane was supposed to move in Carol, and in seconds Carol was screaming out because she had taken the whole damn thing into her cunt and was close to bursting.

Then it was over. Carol's orgasm was so intense that it brought Hawk to the edge at the same time and they rocked in the centre of the van while the tape ended with a rousing chorus of 'We are the champions'. Lane almost laughed at the weirdness of that, feeling like both champion and loser at that moment, watching another woman take her lover where she should only go with Lane.

'Not finished with you,' said Hawk as she continued to move in Carol. She lay back, pulling the blindfolded woman down on top of her. 'Laurence! Fuck her arse, like you like doing to the girls.'

'No,' Carol moaned, exhausted and close to tears now at this fresh threat, the one she truly dreaded. Lane watched mesmerised as the wetness spread from the bandanna to her femme's flushed cheeks.

Laurence unbuttoned her Levi's but Lane finally spoke up. 'No.

No one can fuck her arse. It's not included in the deal and that's final.'

She was half-surprised to see that Laurence looked over at Hawk and Hawk shook her head. 'Fuck my arse, then!' said the big gang leader. She rolled over, rolling Carol under her, and pulled down her leather trousers to reveal her studded black leather harness and her big expanse of arse. To Lane's amazement, Hawk did not pull out of Carol but stayed in there while Laurence mounted her in much the same way that Matthias had recently mounted Lane.

But Lane could only watch for a minute before Ash crawled over to her and pushed her sticky fingers into Lane's mouth so that Lane could taste her own lover's juice once more.

'You know what they say?' Ash whispered provocatively at Lane.

'What?'

'When the red van's rocking, don't come knocking!' They laughed gently and their lips met once again and Lane remembered how much she had enjoyed their first kiss just a short time ago. The other woman had small, soft lips but a pressing need and a top's hunger. She pushed Lane down on her back and bent to suck that black cock into her mouth.

'Hey, I'm starting on this one, don't be long!' she called to her friends.

Lane struggled under the small woman but had underestimated her strength. With one hand on Lane's abdomen, Ash was holding her down. 'You haven't paid for me,' Lane said, realising how weak it sounded as an excuse. But she could not let these women overpower her. That was not part of the deal.

She couldn't help but be turned on by the sight of Ash's head moving up and down as she sucked on that dildo, but Lane was exhausted from coming again and again, and from the emotions whirling inside her.

'Please don't,' she begged even as her hips started to buck in rhythm with Ash's sucking. She hated herself for begging as only a bottom should beg. Now they would treat her as a bottom and she would deserve whatever they gave her.

They were very close to the other women and Lane could smell the cunt and shit smells of their fucking, the sweat of all five women in the enclosed van. Ash levered herself over Lane's cock. 'First I take, then I give,' she said as if it were her motto. Then she lowered herself on to that cock. Lane watched helpless as the black rubber disappeared behind the bushy hair into that neat cunt. Ash was kneeling on Lane's hands, taking from her, as promised.

Meanwhile the shouts from Hawk were loud and furious: 'You fucker! Fucking my arse! Get out, you bastard!'

But Laurence took no notice, saying only, 'Just doing what I was told to do, fucking your big arse.' Carol, trapped and blind-folded under both of them, let out soft moans. Lane could just see her if she twisted her head round, and it was this vision that made her look afresh at Ash. She realised that her best and worst fantasies were coming true right there and yet she was not immersed in them, not fully.

She told herself to give in. And it worked. As Hawk yelled and bucked next to them, thrusting deeper into Carol with that dangerous cock so that Carol was screaming again, Lane said to Ash, 'Kiss me, you bitch,' relishing the fact that she was both fucker and bottom at once. And Ash responded by bending down and pulling Lane towards her till they were both sitting up. They kissed passionately and Lane saw the woman's fingers travel to her clit to bring herself off while they fucked.

'That's it,' Lane told her, 'touch yourself.'

'Don't tell me what to do,' came the snotty reply. 'I'll take what –' She broke off to come, whooping like a bird as she gripped Lane to her and pressed her hips down to fill herself with that cock.

'Got a live one,' she called to her friends, who were disengaging. Lane heard the squelch of dildos leaving orifices and wished she had a video to watch again later in more detail.

But she didn't have long for such thoughts. Suddenly they were on her, stripping off her clothes as if it had been rehearsed.

'Make the other one watch,' said Ash.

'Yeah,' Laurence agreed, pulling the bandanna from Carol's eyes to rest round her neck and pushing her up against the wall of the van.

'Shut your eyes,' Lane ordered, and Carol did.

'No. Fucking open them,' Hawk demanded, and Carol did.

Then the big woman was on Lane, pushing her on to her back, raising her legs in the air and lubing her arsehole.

'No!' Lane exclaimed, desperate, thinking of the size of the cock she had seen entering Carol.

'Yes,' Hawk replied firmly. The others were holding Lane, one pulling hard on her nipple rings while the other held her head still. Then they lifted her arse from the ground and slid the suitcase under her so it was a few inches from the floor of the van, to allow easier entry to Hawk.

The screaming started before anything had really happened and continued as Hawk pushed the mammoth organ into Lane's tight, wet arsehole. Someone was sucking on her nipple, someone was telling Carol to watch, someone was entering her like she'd never been entered before, spreading her insides apart as they plunged in there.

'Touch her clit,' said Hawk. As Laurence worked on Lane's nipples, Ash obeyed, sliding a finger between the leather of Hawk's harness and Lane's bush, to reach for her clit.

Lane was crying tears of pain and lust as the smaller woman worked her clit and the big woman fucked her. She heard herself murmur: 'Take me there.' At the same moment she remembered that Carol might be watching and would certainly be listening. She felt humiliated that her femme should see her overcome like this. And then she came.

'Where did you find them?' Carol asked her later, in bed.

'That's not for you to know,' Lane replied. She thought back over the evening. There were things she would have liked to joke with Carol about, but it wasn't right to start telling her what had happened in the club. Carol still didn't know where they came from. Yes, she would find it funny if Lane told her about the stripper who had fucked herself with a sausage and then fed it to one of the women in the audience. But she didn't need to know. And she certainly didn't need to know which member of the audience had undergone that particular trial.

Still, it had brought a raucous crowd gathering round, including three women who looked ready for anything. Lane had exchanged obscene chipolata comments with them, then suggested it might be time for a wazz 'n' whizz break in the bogs.

Nothing hooks women like free drugs, she thought, as she wrapped her arms round Carol. Where would she hook the next lot?

'Who will you get next time?' asked Carol, sleepily. 'Do you think you could just stop any dyke you see and ask them if they want to fuck your femme? Why don't you try it?'

Lane nuzzled her head against Carol's neck. 'Thing is, Carol, I'm in charge. Don't forget that.'

'How could I forget that, after tonight? Although there was that little incident of a certain bulldyke fucking you up the arse with a gigantic dildo while her pals held you down. But I expect you were in control of that too, eh?'

'Oh yeah,' smiled Lane. 'I set that up beforehand. It was all agreed. Surely you don't think I'd give in to anyone otherwise?'

'You? No, you're far too butch,' Carol replied, before biting hard into Lane's shoulder.

SIX

Special Tutorial

Sometimes a person gets in too deep and even as she does so, she knows exactly what she's doing.

Carol knew, even as she was getting ready to go back to Marg's. Since the last incident in that house two weeks ago, she'd had plenty of time to work out that what she had done was Wrong and Bad, even within the decadent moral universe that she seemed to be living in lately. Once your lover starts taking you off blindfold and barefoot in a grubby van with strangers, to watch them fuck you, then it's hard to keep track of right and wrong. But whatever else happens, you do not fuck your students.

Carol was walking over to Marg's. It was still light, a warm spring night and the grimy roads of north London were busy. In her head was the speech she gave Dave Caraway in May 1994, which she still knew word for word – perhaps because so many people had repeated the best bits to her at the time and ever since.

'You do not fuck your students, Dave. Or rather, *you* do fuck your students and *we* don't like it. It's an abuse of power, it's disrespectful, it fucks them up, it's sexist. But you know all that, don't you, as a sociologist? Let me tell you what you don't know. The rest of us –' she waved a hand at the dozen or so colleagues sitting and standing in stunned and delighted silence around the seminar room into which she had lured him. 'The rest of us want you to stop fucking your students. That's the ones we know about

57

and any other ones that you may somehow have hidden from us, and any other pretty and devoted girls you may have lined up for the future. Stop it, or we're gonna tell on you.'

And then she had dropped the threatening tone and stuck up two fingers at him, waving them in his face. And Dave walked out in an attempt to retain his dignity, which was in fact splattered all around the room, dripping down on the laughing and cheering faces of Carol's pals.

Blank it out, forget it, she told herself now. Anyway, it's not the same thing, because he's a man. Not the kind of argument which had won her a PhD, but it would have to do because (having gone the long way round to avoid passing Lane's house) she was outside Marg's and she was not going back until she'd given every one of the girls inside just exactly what they needed from a more experienced woman.

It was all she could do to ring the bell of Marg and Amy's flat, because she was visualising the two of them naked: Amy sitting on the edge of that table with her light brown legs spread around the tattooed arse of her pale flatmate. And she was picturing what she had done to them. Carol's knees were weak, her head was swimming.

Marg opened the door in a swirly, orange and yellow T-shirt, cut-off shorts and DMs. 'Dr Maitland! Come on in.' The smell of student house brought Carol back down to earth. Musty, unswept hall leading to that joss-stick scented flat.

The door to the flat was open and the living room was full of young women drinking from cans and mugs. Someone was working away at a bong. Amy was sitting on the sofa and this time she smiled openly at Carol and said, 'We weren't sure you'd come. No pun intended.' Carol smiled back at her, regaining her poise. 'How could I resist?' she asked. She looked around at everyone. As promised, none of her tutorial students was there, but there were one or two she recognised from lectures. A few stood out as those special kind of women that Carol would call real one-offs.

Even at first glance, the girl in the opposite corner of the room made Carol take notice because she looked back at the lecturer with a nod that was both respectful and seductive. And it helped, of course, that she was on the butch end of the spectrum, a black girl with short locks and baggy sports gear.

Marg handed Carol a glass of red wine, not one of the grotty mugs that the girls were drinking from. 'Kind of a special tutorial tonight, huh, Doctor M?'

'Yes, a very special tutorial, Marg. There's a lot to learn.'

'Wanna meet everyone?' asked the Californian. Carol realised that neither of them was nervous. They were on some higher plain now, going ahead with a dangerous plan.

'Yes,' she replied, noticing that the room had grown quiet with expectation.

'OK. Let's start with the wild ones. That's Becca and Deville there, they're a couple. Becca's the one with the tits.'

'Hey! Do you mind?' The cry of protest from the blonde girl had a distinct upper-class pitch. Carol's original Merseyside accent might have been tamed by London and academia, but she would never sound like she'd been to Cheltenham Ladies' College the way that this girl did. She certainly did have tits, this girl, and a tight lacy top showed them off nicely. Her lover, Deville, was grinning. Demurely dressed in a neat button-down blue shirt and dark jeans, she still managed to look as devilish as her name with that grin.

Marg pointed Carol round the room, at those with traditional names – Gemma in her crop-top, flared trousers and fat trainers, Sheila with her mane of dark hair and hint of make-up – and those with butch nicknames, like Red who wore baggy combats and a long-sleeved grey T-shirt, and skinhead Billy. These girls were all varying shades of white, from sunbed tan to pale-as-Marg.

The girl with the bong was too stoned to meet Carol's eyes with anything but a blank stare and a giggle. She was an attractive young black woman in shorts. She was light-skinned, with the legs of a footballer. It was that muscle around the knee that always got to Carol. Footballer's knee. The girl was called Leila. She handed the bong to Carol.

'I've never used one.'

'Put your lips round the top and suck, then draw it into your lungs. Not difficult,' said Leila.

Carol followed the instructions and felt her lungs fill with the warm pungent smoke. She spluttered as she breathed out and glanced around to see if they were laughing at her, but they weren't. Just looking. But that intriguing girl in the corner had still not been introduced so Carol went up to her with the bong.

'Want a go?' she asked.

'Yeah, sure. I'm Dee.'

Why hadn't Marg introduced her? Was she afraid of Dee's solid confidence? 'Hi, Dee.' Carol let herself flirt as she handed over the glass bong, her fingers brushing Dee's deep brown hand as she looked into her eyes. The younger woman gave a slight smile, the smile of the one who always stays in control. Well, thought Carol, we'll soon see who's in control.

There was a tension in the air but it was still not exactly a nervous tension. Carol thought that what she was picking up was the excitement of a bunch of young women who had some sexual experience but knew that tonight would be different, exciting. They were chatting among themselves while she leant against the wall with Dee. Then Marg banged her mug against the coffee table to get everyone's attention.

'We're going to start soon,' she announced in her relaxed Californian accent. 'I'm going to hand over to Dr Maitland, so get yourselves in the mood, girls. First, fill your glasses for a toast.'

The girls crowded into the kitchen to get more beer and wine. Dee fetched a bottle and filled Carol's glass for her. Then everyone was packing the room again and Marg was saying: 'Raise a glass please for tonight's very special tutorial with Dr Carol Maitland!'

They all cheered and knocked back their drinks, some calling out, 'To the Special Tutorial!' others, 'Dr Maitland!' Carol felt that this was a group unfamiliar with ritual, since they couldn't even make a toast properly. Instinctively, she took over. She now commanded the room and all the girls were looking expectantly at her.

From her corner, she began to speak. Although the material was somewhat unconventional, her voice was just the same as if she were chairing a seminar or lecturing to a small group of advanced students.

'Tonight we will do whatever we want to do. But be aware that I am in charge and you should ask me before you do anything for yourselves. What I envisage is that I will take care of your needs. There are more of you here than I expected, so it may well be that I have to delegate some of the tasks to some of you girls.'

At this point she looked at Dee, pointedly. She was unsure who else might be up to the task. Certainly not their hosts, Marg and Amy, who were both too passive to service anyone else.

'Before we start the main business, I need to be sure that what goes on tonight is private and between us. No one may repeat what has happened to anyone, not even her best friend or her girlfriend or boyfriend. Do you understand?'

One or two replied, 'Yes, Dr Maitland.' This was not good enough for Carol. She snapped into a strict voice that she had not used since she taught in schools, years ago. 'Girls! Kneel down in front of me!'

They all obeyed the unconventional request. 'Good. Now, take off your tops.' She watched, holding her breath, as all the girls did just that. She counted them – there were ten. She wondered if Marg and Amy had deliberately picked out this nice round number of women? Although Becca seemed to look at Deville for permission, and skinhead Billy looked as if she would rather keep the camouflage of her baggy shirt than reveal her breasts, all the girls did take off their tops.

Becca wore nothing under her see-through blouse and her large breasts burst out as if they had a life of their own. Deville took off her button-down shirt and kissed Becca's breasts. But Carol clapped her hands.

'No! I don't want anyone to do anything like that yet. I thought I made that clear,' she said sternly. Deville looked startled but she nodded and knelt down again. Becca stared at Carol as if she were looking upon a goddess.

Meanwhile, Dee was taking off her baggy black and red T-shirt to reveal a plain black bra-top, that looked as if it were made for sports. Carol admired Dee's full figure and dark skin; Gemma's small naked breasts; Sheila's red lacy bra that showed off some cleavage and was just waiting to be undone, and Leila's tight vest. Marg and Amy were kneeling next to each other. Marg had taken off her T-shirt and the top half of the tattoo around her belly button was visible. Amy wore the same cotton sports bra that Carol remembered clearly from last time.

Now that everyone was silent, Carol realised there was music playing. Some kind of grungy pop was banging along in the kitchen and some of the girls were moving almost imperceptibly in rhythm with it. She looked at them all. She herself was still fully dressed in a flimsy red blouse over a lacy black bra, with a full black skirt, stockings, and ankle boots with a side-zip. She was more vulnerable tonight, in fact, than these young women, because she was the only one who stood to lose her job through what they were about to do together. An idea came to her, a kind of swearing-in, and she spoke before she could censor herself.

'Good. Now everyone reach out your right hand and take hold of the nipple of the girl next to you.' Becca and Deville were giggling but everyone else just did as they were told without so much as a smirk.

Now there was a chain of girls in front of her, linked finger-to-nipple. On the end, Gemma was pinching Sheila's nipple through that red lace. Carol felt the blood pumping to her cunt as she surveyed her girls. 'Good, now repeat after me: I will not reveal . . .'

In unison, the girls repeated, 'I will not reveal . . .'

'What takes place tonight . . .'

'What takes place tonight . . .'

'To another soul.'

'To another soul.'

'Good. Now you may kiss each other. I mean, really kiss each other. Everyone to kiss everyone else in the room, including your mistress of ceremonies. Before each kiss, please say, "These lips that kiss yours will never betray our Special Tutorial".'

And that was when she knew that it was really going ahead as planned. Billy tugged on the nipple she was pinching, which was Leila's, and pulled the other girl closer to whisper the vow in her ear. Then they were kissing like lovers, Billy's hands delving straight away down the back of Leila's trousers.

Carol stayed standing and waited, hoping that Dee would quickly come to her. She did not have long to wait. Dee stood and wrapped her arms round Carol, saying quietly and seriously,

'These lips that kiss yours will never betray our Special Tutorial.' Their tongues met even before their lips did, sliding together. Dee's full lips were soft and they pushed at Carol's. The older woman longed for her and knew that it would not be possible to be in control all night. And as she felt Dee's hands on her breasts, she realised for the first time that no one was here who didn't desire her. What had Marg and Amy said to these women? Presumably, question one would have been: 'Do you think Dr Maitland's sexy?' And what did they all expect tonight?

'I want you,' Dee said urgently. But then she broke away from Carol and moved towards Sheila. All around Carol, young half-dressed women were making the same vow to each other and kissing each other passionately as if they had to do it, as if they needed this. Carol remembered her own student days, when drunken parties would often end with friends falling into bed or rolling across a living room rug together. She had slept with both men and women back then, giving herself whenever she felt desire.

'Dr Maitland.' This was Marg, next to her now. 'My lips will never break our vow.' And Marg kissed her as if pleading with her, and Carol knew the girl would need to be whipped and fucked by her again tonight.

When everyone had kissed everyone else, Marg disappeared into the kitchen and brought in the boombox. She put on the Pulp album that Carol had heard before at Lane's flat. With its songs of seedy sex, this male presence seemed strangely appropriate; and even the poster of the naked woman was now just part of the ambience.

'Tell me what you want – your greatest dreams of perfect sex,' Carol said to the girls. 'Line up here and tell me.'

Once again, Dee was first. 'I want to fuck you,' she said, straightforwardly.

'Then you will,' said Carol. 'But first I will need you to fuck some of your friends.'

'Yes, Dr Maitland.' And Dee dropped back, so that the next girl, Gemma, could come forward.

'I want someone to lick me out.'

'Do you want me to do that, Gemma, or do you want one of the other girls to do it?'

'Whoever you say, Dr Maitland.'

'Then Dee will lick you and I will watch. Did you hear that, Dee?'

'Yes, Dr Maitland.'

'Good. Who's next?'

Marg, as expected, said with a mixture of shame and desire: 'I want you to whip me, Dr Maitland.' And Carol told her to go and get the whip.

One by one they told her that they wanted to fuck or to be fucked with fingers or a fist or a dildo, or that they wanted to be fucked and sucked at once, or to be tied up and made to watch others having sex, forbidden to touch themselves. The fantasies were predictable and Carol wondered if anyone wanted anything they were scared to ask for. Was it possible that none of the ten girls wanted to piss on someone or to make love in the street?

Perhaps the kind of girl who went to an orgy with a lecturer from her own university was not the kind who wanted outrageous sex. Perhaps they wanted to be safe. But that was one thing she could not guarantee. She didn't feel safe; she felt dangerous and endangered, her cunt setting the theme for her whole body: hot, wet, pulsing.

She went to work, supervising what was needed to set up everyone's fantasies. 'Dee,' she began, 'please strip Gemma. Billy, tie Sheila to that chair and leave her there. Make sure she cannot touch herself. Marg, I'm still waiting for the whip. And Amy, I want you to lie naked on the floor. Red will fuck you.'

Then she took Deville and Becca on one side. 'I know you are lovers. Becca wants me to put her face down over the table and invite other women to fuck her, without telling her who they are – to humiliate her as they do as they please, and say whatever comes into their heads about her.

'As for Deville, she wants to fuck Becca while everyone watches. So I have decided that Deville will be just one of the women who fucks Becca. I wanted to explain that because if you, Deville, cannot watch Becca being fucked by other women, then you cannot have your own fantasy either. Do you understand?'

They both nodded, although Deville's face was straining with a mixture of emotions. Carol took her to be a possessive woman but didn't care. She led Becca by the arm to the dining table that stood against one wall and asked Marg to tidy away the mugs that littered it. Then she turned Becca around and pulled down the girl's short skirt. Her blonde hair reached down over her pale back. She was wearing a thong.

'I'm going to pull your thong to one side,' Carol told the girl. 'Then I'm going to lay you over the table and get these women to fuck you. Do you understand?' Becca nodded but Carol repeated the question: 'Do you understand? Answer me.'

'Yes, Dr Maitland,' she replied in that upper-class accent.

Every time that one of the girls used this formal response, Carol felt her face grow hot and her fanny swelling.

'Good.' She reached between the girl's soft buttocks and prised out the black thong, pulling it to one side and then touching her wet pussy. The girl shuddered. 'Good, you're ready, aren't you?' Carol asked, much as Lane sometimes asked her.

'Yes.'

'Very well.' Carol looked around to see who was free to fuck Becca. Deville was looking expectantly at the lecturer but she shook her head. No way was Deville to be first. 'Billy,' she called, 'as soon as you've finished with Sheila, please come over here.'

She watched as Billy pulled off her own thick leather belt and lashed Sheila to the chair. She remembered that the butch had asked to use her cock on someone, and decided to warm her up on Becca. Perhaps Carol would take Billy inside her later.

As Becca lay helpless across the table, Carol moved to Deville and started to kiss her. Deville's hair was the cornfield blonde that comes out of a bottle. It was short and spiky and Carol rubbed her hands through it. 'Soon you will fuck Becca,' she whispered to the butch girl. 'But I want you to wait.'

Then she left Deville and moved over to where Red was preparing to fuck Amy. 'Don't force her,' she warned the big woman, who was unzipping her combats and pulling out a big dildo. 'Lick her first, Red, and get her ready.'

'I know how to fuck a girl,' Red said defiantly.

'Do you submit to my authority, or not? If not, you can leave now.'

Red looked confused. 'What?'

'I thought everyone understood,' Carol said, raising her voice so everyone could hear. 'I am in charge tonight. If you can't submit to me and my instructions, you must leave.'

No one moved. Red looked at her with new respect and said, 'I'll do what you say.' And she knelt between Amy's legs and started to lick her cunt. Amy moaned, her hips jerking from the floor.

Carol knew she could safely leave them. 'Leila,' she said to the girl with the football legs. 'Sheila already looks desperate. Look at her, poor girl, having to watch from that chair, tied up, while everyone else gets ready to fuck each other. I think you and Deville might need to tease her a little, so she doesn't feel left out.'

She watched as the two girls went over to kiss Sheila. Then Deville pulled Sheila's tight red pants down to her knees, trapping her further. 'Oh, yeah,' moaned the girl, pleading for more.

'Don't touch her,' warned Carol. Instead, the two tormentors kissed each other, standing inches from the prisoner.

Carol moved around the room as she might move around a workshop after breaking it up into small groups. The girls might need prompting, might need help.

But what she most wanted to see was Dee licking Gemma. Wherever she was in the room (which seemed increasingly smaller as more and more went on, on its dhurrie rugs and Indian-print throws), she was watching Dee and Gemma. First kissing, then running their hands over each other, taking off the remains of each other's clothes. Carol had fantasised that Dee would keep on her trousers, just as Lane usually did. But Dee and Gemma were completely naked now and it was a beautiful sight. On a rug in front of the fireplace, they were touching each other's breasts and kissing deeply.

Carol listened to what they murmured to each other and was surprised that it was not as romantic as the scene suggested. 'Want me to lick you out, girl?' Dee asked in a mean voice.

'Yeah, lick me, you bitch. You know what to do.'

'Going to get you sitting on my face and stick my tongue in your pussy. Going to suck and bite on that clit till you're crying.'

'No,' Gemma moaned, running her hands over Dee's broad arse.

'Oh yes.' And, as she spoke, Dee lay back on the floor and cupped her hands round Gemma's smooth bottom. 'Come here, girl,' she said urgently. 'Sit on my face, like I said.' Somehow Dee hauled Gemma towards her and then the white girl was sitting on her face, just as instructed, her knees spread either side of Dee's head.

Even as Carol watched this scene, Deville was prowling over to them. Left without any action – and apparently not keen to watch as her girlfriend was fucked across a table by another woman – the girl chose to join this pair. She knelt next to Dee, who didn't see her there, and reached a hand between Dee's legs to stroke her pussy. Dee's legs spasmed in response but she didn't stop tonguing Gemma, even as Deville slipped two fingers into her damp cunt.

Now Marg was approaching Carol with the whip, her head hanging low. 'Where have you been?' Carol asked angrily, as Marg held out the whip, placing the handle in her lecturer's palm. 'I asked for this a long time ago.'

'I'm sorry, Dr Maitland. It was in my room, and when I was there, I was so turned on that I had a wank.' She was trembling.

'You did what?' Carol looked at her in fury and felt herself flushing red. She wasn't acting now; she felt how she imagined a sadist might feel and it was empowering and frightening.

'I know I was wrong. I know you'll have to punish me.' She was also carrying a sports holdall, which she now handed over. It was open and inside were various dildos and harnesses.

'Why didn't you give me this before?' asked Carol.

'I forgot.'

'We agreed that you would provide the necessary materials for the tutorial. You have not kept your word, Marg. I certainly will have to punish you.'

So, as Gemma and Dee built to a joint climax on the floor just a yard away, Carol ordered Marg to pull down her shorts and crouch on the floor.

Carol was in the centre of the room. All around her, young women moaned and shouted in every stage of arousal. But as she raised the whip over Marg's naked, tattooed arse, she knew that this would change the atmosphere. Sure enough, she lashed out at Marg and released a scream from the girl that stilled the room. For a minute, everyone watched as Carol sliced the whip across that pale bottom and heard Marg scream and then say, 'Thank you, Dr Maitland!' One or two girls actually screamed, as if they had been lashed themselves. Others groaned with desire.

Delving into the leather bag, Carol selected a knobbly blue dildo, which she now aimed at Marg's cunt. Without warning her, she slid the toy into that wet pussy. Even as the girl welcomed the rough rubber dick inside her, Carol lashed out again with the whip and heard her scream.

Now the other girls were returning to their fucking and sucking, which was heightened by the whipping. But not everyone carried on as before. Two girls were even now kneeling either side of Marg, pointing their naked arses in the air, waiting their turn under the whip.

Carol didn't wait. She didn't even care who they were. Fired up and almost afraid of her own viciousness, she just had time to remember the safe word that Marg had chosen last time. 'I show no mercy,' she warned, addressing herself to the naked arses before her, 'unless you shout "Emergency!" Do you understand?'

'Yes, Dr Maitland!' they chorused. And the whip came lashing down.

Carol was resting after the strange exertion of the whippings. But then, from the cries of passion around the room, one became clear as a bell, separate and desperate. It was Becca, pressed across the table, with the slim marine-style Billy inside her, fucking her with her strap-on in heavy thrusts that rocked the table. Was Becca crying as Billy said, 'Take it, you posh bitch. You need to know how it feels, don't you?'

The lecturer nimbly climbed over a threesome of girls who were clutching at each other as the sweat dripped from their shiny bodies. They chanted together, 'Yes, yes, yes.' She went up behind Billy and wrapped her arms round her.

'Think she needs it that hard?' she asked Billy, grabbing at her tits and sliding a hand down and inside her flies to touch her clit, just below the base of the dildo. Carol's fingers were trapped between Billy's wet clit and Becca's damp arsehole, and she could smell them both.

'Yeah, she fucking needs it, Dr Maitland. That's why I'm giving it to her.'

'Why does she need it that hard?'

'Because she's got this wet pussy that must have been fucked a thousand times, but she doesn't know what it's for. Doesn't know it's for someone like me to fuck and screw till I come.'

So, Becca was getting what she had wanted, to be fucked and humiliated, and the moans that came from her made it clear she was enjoying it. Carol had been mistaken in thinking it was too much for Becca. Close up, she could see the girl thrusting her hips towards Billy, wanting more and more of this harsh lovemaking.

'Fuck her, then,' said Carol, pulling off her own skirt. She stood behind Billy, thrusting against her as Billy thrust into Becca.

'I know you have to fuck me, you bastard. I know I deserve it,' Becca was moaning.

Carol's knickers, stockings and suspenders were clinging to her with hot sweat. Was Deville watching as Billy fucked her lover? The very thought made Carol wetter still.

'Billy, as soon as you finish her, I need you to turn right around and give it to me,' Carol ordered.

It was only seconds before that instruction had made these girls so hot that they came. First Billy was writhing to a halt, then she was pushing a hand under Becca to rub at her clit while she thrust twice more in her, expertly, and heard Becca's cries build to great sobs of gratitude.

Immediately Billy pulled out, turned so she was stood between Becca's legs, leaning back into the prostrate girl's cunt and arse, and delved into her pocket, breathing heavily. She wiped off the dildo on the shirt tied round her waist, then rolled on a condom and pulled Carol to her. After hitching down all Carol's underwear with both hands in one ripping movement, she bent at the knees and entered her, staring fiercely into her eyes as the hard cock burst past the lecturer's cuntlips and into her soaking quim, which had waited so long to be fucked tonight and was finally getting it from this lean, mean obsessive.

She grabbed at Billy's head, but the girl pulled away. 'Kiss me,' Carol said. She meant it to sound like an order but it sounded like a desperate plea and Billy refused.

'Don't want to. Just got to fuck you,' she grunted.

How had this young woman, not more than twenty years old, learnt this tough behaviour, like a butch of the old school? Carol felt taken over by her, not wanting to be fucked by someone who didn't care enough to kiss her.

'No!' she moaned in protest, tossing her head violently from side to side. As she did so, she saw Deville leering at her. Deville, who was coming towards them, pushing her way behind Billy to get at her lover from behind.

Billy gave way just enough for Deville to get in there. Deville didn't speak to Becca – who was still face down on the table with her legs hanging down, not quite reaching the floor – but ran her hands over her lover's arse, playing with the string of the thong, pulling it across one buttock, then letting it slap back in Becca's crack. Her fingers moved to that crack and she teased Becca's arsehole, then pushed a finger in there, while the fingers of the other hand moved to her lover's cunt.

Becca moaned in pleasure and anticipation as a second finger worked its way up her arse, but still Deville stayed silent so that her lover would not recognise her voice, would not know who the stranger was who fucked both her holes at once with slow determination.

At the same time, Billy was fucking Carol with nothing like that slowness, fucking her in hard thrusts that made Carol's knees buckle so that Billy had to hold her up with her hands on Carol's arse. 'You like that, don't you?' she said in a deep, controlled voice, and Carol could only groan in response.

Even as she fucked Carol, Billy was eyeing Marg, who felt pulled towards them. She stood behind Carol and wrapped her arms around both her and Billy, so that the lecturer was enclosed between two of the students. Marg was rubbing her crotch against Carol's arse as Billy pumped her dick in that wet cunt.

Behind Billy, Deville slid all her fingers into Becca and heard her scream, then pushed further and formed a fist in her cunt, all the while working her arsehole. Becca shouted: 'Shit! No! It's too much!' But then she moaned, 'Oh, yes!'

Deville fucked her slow and hard.

Carol was barely aware of what was going on around her as all the women started to join the group. She only knew that the sheer force of Billy's cock in her was bringing her to a dazzling height of feeling, where her whole body was Billy's and she had lost all control. She came then, hearing herself scream, and suddenly Billy was kissing her and moving even more firmly inside her, touching her own clit, pushing her tongue deep into Carol's mouth, and then coming like a man, with that thrust that Carol remembered from men, that final emptying thrust deep in her cunt.

The girls held Carol still. But Marg was kissing Gemma, and Dee was waiting for her turn with the lecturer. Deville was silently bringing Becca to orgasm and it was Becca's cries of release that made everyone heat up again. Their kisses became more passionate, their mouths moving from one woman to another, so that Carol now found herself still held by Billy but being kissed by Dee; the woman she had wanted so much but now had no energy for.

As Deville collapsed on top of Becca, she was pushed away by Leila.

'Hey,' said Deville, who almost fell off the table. 'What are you doing?'

'It *was* you,' murmured Becca, sounding both affectionate and quietly pleased with herself for recognising her lover. 'I thought it was you.'

'What do you think I'm doing?' Leila said to Deville. 'I'm going to fuck your girlfriend.'

'I don't think she needs any more,' Deville said threateningly.

Carol heard this and remembered she had set herself up as responsible for this whole night. If a fight broke out, was it down to her? But there was no way she could move, held in a standing position by these women but drained of all energy and feeling, only able to let Dee kiss her.

'You want someone to fuck, fuck me,' said Deville, provocatively.

Leila pushed a hand down the front of Deville's boxers. 'Sure?' she asked, knowing it was too late for a change of mind. Becca stirred and sat up to watch them, and they joined her on the table, all kissing each other as Leila's fingers worked their way into Deville's cunt.

It was only when everyone was so exhausted and sated that they lay on the floor, some sleeping and others passing a joint from hand to hand, occasionally kissing the recipient on the mouth or sucking on a breast, that Carol regained her sense of her own will.

Two things bothered her. Firstly, Dee had not fucked her. At the start of the evening, she had wanted Dee more than anyone, but somehow it hadn't happened. In fact, Carol had not held on to her power, had not ensured that what she wanted came first. She vowed to herself that the next tutorial would be more controlled.

And secondly, the nagging feeling that she had gone too far was pulsing away in the back of her brain. Now that she gave herself time to think clearly, she realised what was wrong. Previously, no one had actually fucked her. She had fucked Amy and Marg last time, but they had not fucked her. So, in Clintonspeak, she had not broken the pact with Lane. The Big Deal said she mustn't let anyone fuck her, not the other way round. Now, however, she had definitely been thoroughly fucked. What if Lane found out? After all, she lived in the same street! What if the Prof found out? Or anyone at college?

Although some of her girls were actually asleep, she knelt up now and made her announcement: 'Girls! Gather round in a circle. Hold hands for our closing ceremony.' It was time to repeat their vow.

SEVEN

What Do You Do?

'Aren't you sick of people asking you what you do for a fucking living?' Lane asked Jack as they took refuge in the kitchen.

'I don't mind. I just make things up. I just told an architect that I'm an interior designer. He gave me his card in case we can "work together".'

'Meaning?'

'Well, what do you think it means?'

'I think it means he wants you to bring the wallpaper, actually, Jack.'

'Oh, so naive. I love you for it, sis.'

Lane filled their glasses and saw Carol appear in the doorway.

'There you are,' said the older woman. 'Kitchen as usual. Funny how you're so at home in the kitchen at other people's parties, but in your own flat, you don't seem sure where the toaster is.'

'Wanna drink?' asked Lane.

'Don't I always?'

'Well,' said Lane, pouring red wine for Carol, 'it seems that our friend Jack here has been lying about his boring old graphic design job and instead claiming he's a decorator.'

'An interior designer, please, sweetie!' he protested, *Ab Fab* style.

'Jack,' said Carol. 'If you're going to lie, couldn't you say something interesting? I sometimes say I'm an airline pilot.'

73

'Why?' asked Lane, scrunching up her face to indicate that Carol was making life unnecessarily complicated.

But Jack talked over her: 'I'm not lying actually. I have rearranged a few interiors in my time.'

He looked meaningfully at Lane, who just said, 'Ouch.'

Carol suddenly looked left out. Lane draped her arm round her. 'Want to dance, babe?' she whispered in Carol's ear.

But Carol shook her off, muttering, 'No, thanks,' and wandered off.

'What did you bring her for?' Jack asked peevishly.

'Because she's my lover, my partner, remember?'

'She's not your fucking partner, actually, Lane.'

'That's exactly what she is, actually, Jack. My *fucking* partner. What are you getting at?'

'Partners don't let each other fuck around. Partners live together, in harmony, forever.'

'I'm not going to be lectured by a sarky queen about mono-gamy, so fuck off. Anyone would think you were jealous.'

At that moment a cute man came up to Jack, who hooted with recognition and gave him a bear hug.

'Hey, sis, meet Graham. Grey, this is Laney.'

'And what do you do?' asked the stranger.

'I fuck girls,' Lane replied, deadpan.

'What, you're an escort?'

'If that's what you want to call it.'

'So you're an expert on lesbian sex? Brilliant.'

'What?'

'Well, thing is, I'd really like to know what exactly lesbians do in bed.'

Lane laughed and Jack flushed. 'Graham, don't go there!' he implored.

'I know it's a cliché,' said the man, 'but I can't help it. No one will tell me. It's not like dykes talk about their sex lives the way that we poofs do. I've never overheard a girl talking about what she's been doing with her latest floozie.'

He was looking her right in the eye and smiling. Flirting, basically, with his twinkly blue eyes. Lane looked around to see if a certain person was hovering in the door, a person who liked to tease her about flirting with gay men – claiming, for instance, that when one of their gay friends had come to dinner recently with his new boyf, Lane had spent all evening gazing at said boyf. 'I don't mean to do it when you're there,' Lane had protested. 'And I don't believe I am doing it, actually. I didn't fancy that boy, I just thought he had nice eyes.' And Carol had said, 'Well, you never look at me like that.'

Now this guy was definitely giving her that cheeky flirty stuff that nice gay boys were so good at. But that's normal, Lane told herself, gay boys flirt with dykes because it's safe all round. What went on between her and Jack was highly unusual. Wasn't it?

In a sudden burst of honesty, Jack revealed, 'Graham knows about us, Laney. He's just a very good actor.'

'Ha! Tell that to Equity, Jackie.'

Graham, it turned out, was one of those actors who had a fair bit of work but was waiting for his big break and still didn't have his card.

'So, why were you pretending not to know who I was?' she asked him.

'Well, it's not very ladylike, is it, to approach a lovely butch dyke one doesn't know, and say, "So, you fuck boys, let's do it, girl!" '

Lane looked from one to the other.

'Have you set me up here, Jacko?'

'I'm as intrigued as you are, sis.'

'Well,' Lane said, addressing Graham, 'you may have got the wrong end of the stick, so to speak.' She rolled her eyes at her accidental double entendre. 'Because it's more that boys fuck me.'

'Oh.' Graham seemed unfazed. 'Well, see what category this falls into. What I've always wanted, what I've never had . . . I'd love to lick you out.' He looked slightly nervous but quite unashamed.

'OK. Want to watch, Jackie-boy?'

She was interested to see his response. Would he be as grossed out as she suspected? Sure enough, her friend was trying not to show his shock and disgust.

'Er, I don't think that's appropriate, sis. We have our own

special relationship to consider.' And he grabbed a bottle and practically ran from the kitchen.

'Have you fucked my girlfriend?' asked Carol.

'What, in the last five minutes? Well, I suppose it wouldn't be a record.'

Carol was not put off. 'Have you fucked my girlfriend – ever?'

'Sorry, I didn't realise she was your girlfriend. I thought she was mine.'

Carol looked him in the eye. 'Not funny.'

'Don't ask what you don't want to know,' warned Jack, suddenly serious. 'I suspect that if you did want to know, you might be asking a certain other person, rather than me.' And he walked away, leaving her to sip on her drink and wonder why she'd ever got into that deal with Lane.

In fact, now would not be a bad time to have a little discussion with Lane about the state of play. About how, if they came to a party together, it might be nice to spend some time together.

Feeling justifiably indignant plus a little sorry for herself, Carol pushed her way from room to room, searching for Lane through the noisy dance room and the chill-out zone that had developed in the front room. Not there, and not in the kitchen.

Carol made her way upstairs, past the queue for the toilet and into the bedroom where they'd left their stuff, which was now buried under other people's bags and jackets. Here, two people she knew by sight were snogging like teenagers and ignored her.

She tried the door of the next room. It swung open. Lane was standing in the centre of the room, naked from the waist down. A man was kneeling between her legs, licking her out. Lane was guiding his head with her hands. Her eyes opened when she registered that someone had come in.

'Carol! Fuck! Hiya.'

'Yeah, right, hiya.' Staggered, furious but titillated, Carol just stood there, watching how Lane continued to push this man's head very slightly this way and that.

Carol walked up to her and stared her down. Then she took

hold of Lane's face and kissed her fiercely. 'You bitch,' she said to Lane. 'You fucking bitch. Kiss me.'

They couldn't get close because of this sex-slave guy who was devotedly licking away on Lane's cunt. But they could kiss with that love-hate passion made of fury and lust.

Lane pulled her mouth from Carol's and said, 'I'm going to come now and I want you to remember that this made me come. Sometimes, this is what I need. I haven't made you do it before but I will, babe, I will . . .' The word turned to a kind of hum and she was clutching the curly head of this guy while staring into Carol's eyes as if that's who was doing it to her.

Lane led Carol downstairs by the hand. 'There's a bit of business I need to do,' she told the older woman. 'Then I'm taking you home. I'm sorry if I've left you out of things tonight, babe.'

Carol laughed harshly. 'That's one way of putting it.'

'Wait till I get you home, you won't feel left out then.'

'If you think you're fucking me when we get home – if you even think we're going home together . . .'

Lane cupped Carol's pixie-like face in her hands and kissed her with love and desire. 'That's exactly what I think,' she said. 'Now come with me while I sort out this business.'

She led Carol into the chill-out zone where a large, dark woman in a leather waistcoat was lazing on a sofa, chatting to a friend, getting stoned.

'Hey!' Lane greeted her. 'All right?'

'Yeah. You all right?'

'Yeah, cool. Thought you might like to see who I was talking about,' she told the woman, pointing to Carol, who was chatting to someone else. 'That's her. What do you say?'

The woman appraised Carol, looking her up and down. 'Yeah. She'll do. Pretty little thing. Bring her to mine, like we said. OK?'

'Yeah. See you then. Come on, Carrie babes, time to go.'

Carol turned to her. 'Aren't you going to introduce me to your friend? I had this weird sensation like you were talking about me.'

'You'll meet her soon enough.'

★

How angry was she? Hard to say. Furious about some things: that
Lane encouraged her to come to the party when she wanted to
stay in, then went off with that prick, Jack. Furious that Lane and
Jack could fuck with impunity because Carol had agreed to the
deal. Furious, for fuck's sake, that Lane should have some weird
guy licking her out while Carol was searching the party for her.
And what was going on before they left, with that hefty woman
on the sofa? Were they sizing her up?

But all the time, bubbling under the surface, was the knowledge
that she was herself in charge of those orgies, which seemed so
unlikely and kinky in the light of day, but which were so
liberating. What right did she have to be angry with Lane when
she was secretly being unfaithful to her on a grand scale? At least
Lane was being fairly honest about her adventures.

They were in the back of a taxi on their way home and Carol
had still not decided if she would spend the night with Lane. But
that look that Lane kept giving her, that look that said exactly
what Lane wanted from her. It was hard to resist.

Lane was holding her hand and then she let go of it to stroke
Carol's thigh and run her hand under the short skirt of Carol's
dress, finding the top of her stockings. Now that hand was stroking
its way up the bare flesh between stocking and knickers. Carol
moaned.

'What knickers have you got on?' Lane asked in a deep, quiet,
urgent voice that made Carol quiver.

'The dark-red ones with the rip.'

Lane slipped her finger into that rip. It was along the seam
where the gusset met the front. Carol squealed. Lane's warm finger
slipped down her wet clit and gathered juice from her cunt before
sliding back along that clit.

Carol leant back into the seat and gave herself up to Lane as the
driver sped along Green Lanes, apparently oblivious to what was
going on behind him. They didn't have long before they would
reach Lane's flat. Lane whispered, 'Going to make you come now,
Car. Just think of this. Just think of me touching your wet clit
without even having to pull off your pants because you're so dirty
that you wear knickers with a big hole in them so that anyone can

slip a finger in there and touch your clit. That's what you want, isn't it?'

'Yes.'

'Yes, I know it. Everyone fucking knows it, you slut. Anyone else touched you there tonight? Want me to ask the driver if he wants to touch you there, huh? If he wants to get in the back of the cab and touch your wet clit? Do you think he'd be as nice to you, as good to you as I am?'

'Don't know.'

'I know. I know he wouldn't. He'd just have his way, whatever he wanted. Maybe stick his cock right through that hole in your panties while I sat here and watched. 'Cos let's face it, that would turn me on. So I couldn't stop him, could I? Not if I was watching.'

Her finger moved expertly, tightening as the bud of Carol's clit tightened, moving faster as it swelled to a hard nub. 'Don't let anyone know you're coming, you slut, just me and you will know, that's all. Else that driver will know you're a slut and he'll make us get out and walk because no cabbie will have a slut getting brought off in the back of his car, you know, not unless it's him doing it.'

'I know,' said Carol, her voice a quaver. 'Oh, yes, yes, oh, you bitch. Do it to me!' The blood was tingling right through her body, her nerve endings all alive with the tension, and Lane played those last few seconds to perfection, taking her to the height and keeping her there, so she was bucking against the seat back, rolling her groin against Lane's hand, making the smallest noises she knew how to make even though she needed to scream out with it.

'Where is it you want, darlin'?' asked the driver, turning round. Carol slumped back, glancing at Lane, whose hand was still in her knickers.

'Take a left just before the next bus stop, please, mate.' She turned to Carol and gave a sudden short stroke to that recovering clit, making her whole body jerk again. 'Coming in?' Lane asked.

EIGHT
Make Her Beg

It had all been explained to Carol but now she was playing up, which was no big surprise.

'Look, Carrie, I'm not going to listen to this shit actually because we're going to Granta's house and whatever happens will happen and you fucking know it. So what are we arguing about?'

'We're arguing about how you've got all the power,' Carol replied.

'And you hate that, do you?'

'No.'

'So?'

'So, I just want some things to be negotiable. I don't like the way you just turn up and expect me to come out and be fucked. What if I've got plans?'

Lane laughed. 'Listen to yourself. You can't have it both ways. I know you think of an adventure as being something spontaneous where you're not in control. Lucky for you, I've sorted you out so you get all that with no effort on your part, and now you're complaining because – what, because you wanted to watch a video?' Lane could hear that her voice was too mocking.

'Don't be so childish.'

'*I'm* being childish? Well I don't care because in about half an hour I'm going to have you every which way I want, and that will be quite adult enough for one week, thank you.'

'Well doesn't that sound appealing? Mmm, I can't wait to be had. Hope it's really seedy. I'm glad I don't fancy that woman you were selling me to at the party, or else I might enjoy it too much.'

'This is really entertaining, Carrie. I wish I could be as sarcastic as you – oh, I just did it!' Her voice softened. 'Now sit down, you daft cow, and listen to me. I want to tell you something.'

Carol sat down on the sofa. The days were getting longer and the light still flooded in the tall windows of her flat, showing up the highlights in her curly hair. She was sulking.

'Listen,' said Lane, 'I love you. That's why we made this deal, isn't it? Because we love each other and get turned on by each other. But you seem to be getting more and more annoyed about it all. So if you've had enough, then we can stop. I don't have to go with guys all the time and I don't have to find strangers to fuck you all the time, not if you don't want.'

'It's not that. I mean, it is that but I don't want to stop, not really. But I'm getting edged out, like I'm a plaything.' But she was looking around the room, not at Lane.

'Is there something else?'

'No.'

'Only you're acting funny.'

'Am I?'

'Yeah. Like you don't want to say whatever it is.'

'No. I've said it.'

'OK. Maybe I have been too into it all. The Big Deal. You know, getting off on it but forgetting it's not real.'

'Oh, it's real.'

'Well, yeah. But there's more to me and you, isn't there?'

'Yes.' Carol smiled weakly to show that she was agreeing to make up. But she still looked distracted and unsure. Lane sat down next to her and put an arm around her. Carol was stiff at first but then she rested her head on Lane's chest. 'What do you think this Granta will want to do?'

'Wait and see,' said Lane. 'But, you know, if you get freaked, I'm there.'

'That's what's worrying me,' said Carol.

'Oh, you'd rather be alone with her?'

'No, that is not what I meant. I just can't trust you to hold off from some perverted fantasy that involves using me as your sex slave, that's all. But I expect I'll survive.'

Lane shook Carrie playfully. 'You making a joke of it all? This is a serious matter, I'll have you know.'

'How serious?'

'This serious.' Lane blew on Carol's neck, which was guaranteed to make her gasp, then kissed her way up to that beautiful mouth that she had kissed so many times. Their lips met for a second, then Lane drew back and just looked at Carrie, letting the slow pulsing lust show in her eyes.

'Save yourself,' she told her femme. 'You're wanted elsewhere.'

The door to the house was open. Carol hadn't seen such a thing in London since she stayed in a squat, about ten years ago, where it said on the door that anyone was welcome. You had to agree not to have a job if you were going to live there, so you'd be at home if neighbours or strangers wandered in the door for friendship.

Somehow, she didn't think that Granta's house operated on the same setup. Lane seemed unfazed by the open door and shut it behind them. She led Carol down the hall, holding her by the arm. Lane was in jeans but Carrie was wearing her tight leopard-print trousers and a low-cut black lace top which showed her bra. The clothes pressed tight to her body in the warm spring evening.

'Where's this Granta, then?' she asked Lane, with false bravado.

'Just be quiet and come with me. No more questions tonight. Tonight you can give up thinking and analysing and just give in to us.'

Against her better judgement, Carol's body was already doing just that, giving in to Lane, who had seemed so annoying and self-centred back at the flat, before they made up, and who was now behaving even more arrogantly. Like she was Carol's pimp or owner.

When Lane kissed her at the flat, Carol felt her cunt grow wet with need. Even her trousers were wet now and she was ready for anything.

It was dark in this long hallway and Lane seemed to have been here before. She led her downstairs to what must be the basement but then down again, to the bowels of the house. They came to a big iron door and Lane swung it open. It creaked. She pushed Carol inside.

There was Granta. She stood in the centre of the small dungeon. That's what it was, a dungeon. Carol had heard of such places but never seen one. Granta was a big, tall woman, quite dark-skinned, maybe Asian, with thick eyebrows and long thick hair, shaved at the sides. She was wearing black leather trousers and a harness on her top half which surrounded her large breasts, emphasising them and pushing them forward. Her voluptuous body was powerful and Carol felt drawn to her but afraid.

'Hiya,' said Granta, her deep voice edged with a Midlands accent. 'I'm glad you came. I've been thinking about you, Carol. Lane says you're a good girl who does as she's told and takes what she's given. I hope that's true.' The tone was firm but not formal.

Carol looked away.

'Is it true then?'

As Granta asked again, impatient, Lane shook Carol's arm and said, 'Answer her.'

'Yes. I do as I'm told. Lane gives me to people and I have to do what they want.' Carol felt the spotlight was on her. It was embarrassing and sexy.

'Good. Do you know my name?'

'Yes, it's Granta.'

'Now listen up. You're only to speak if I speak to you, and then you say, "Yes, Granta", or "Yes please, Granta". D'you understand?'

'Yes, Granta.'

'If I ask to do something to you and you're thinking, no way, then you say, "I am sorry, Granta, that is not allowed." OK? There shouldn't be anything else you need to say. Do you get it?'

'Yes, Granta.' She got it, all right.

'Good. Lane, come here. You can kiss her before I start on her. That's something I'd like to see.'

Lane stroked Carol's face with what seemed like regret. She bent to kiss her, one hand in Carol's hair, the other on her arse, pulling her close, stroking her.

The kiss buzzed through Carol like a static shock. Every nerve was already on edge. She knew that Granta would ask to whip her tonight – that much was clear from the implements that hung from the walls which were becoming visible through the gloom. But she would not say yes to that.

Lane sometimes spanked Carol once or twice on the bum, but that was more like playing. There was no way that Carol could tolerate the kind of beating that she had herself inflicted on Marg at the tutorial. But danger was in the room with her here, she could see that from Granta's clothes and demeanour, from her firm, confident voice. Where she and Lane played with power, Granta owned it. Carol had to remind herself that Granta had given her an escape route, she was allowed to say no.

Now Lane stood back and Granta came to kiss Carol, who almost flinched at being passed from one to the other. But it was a reflex action that belied her excitement as the big woman pushed her tongue into her mouth. She tasted faintly of beer and cigarettes but it did not bother Carol. The taste reminded her of her first kiss, with a boy on a campsite, when she was a girl. She remembered feeling enveloped by him. Now Granta was pushing her hands under the back of Carol's top.

'I want to see you in your underwear. In your bra and knickers,' she said.

She pulled the top over Carol's head and then unbuttoned the waist of the leopard-print trousers. She pulled the tight trousers down. 'Kick off your shoes.' Carol did and the trousers were pulled off her.

'Good.' The woman surveyed her. Carol knew that her black lacy underwear would be a turn-on, but felt self-conscious about her rounded stomach. She caught herself having this thought and realised how ridiculous it was. This woman, who was big and proud herself, wanted her no matter what.

'Lane, I'm going to need you to help me out here.' Granta led Carol to a strange contraption. It was made of wood and leather and seemed to have been adapted from a vaulting horse. Then Carol noticed it had steel clasps on it and leather straps, and it was surrounded by a wooden frame with more attachments hanging from it: long thin leather straps with metal clamps and rings hanging from them.

'Bend over.' Carol followed the order, bending over the apparatus. Then Granta slipped the steel clasps around Carol's wrists and tightened them roughly until Carol protested.

'It's too tight.'

'What?'

'It's too tight, Granta, please . . .' She remembered the rules. 'I am sorry, Granta, that is not allowed.'

'Be careful how you speak to me,' warned Granta. Now she was strapping Carol to the body of the horse with a thick piece of leather, and then moving to her legs. Carol sensed Lane moving close as Granta pulled Carol's legs apart and strapped her ankles to the apparatus. She was now in such a position that her arse was thrust in the air, her legs wide and her crotch exposed.

Granta spoke to Lane: 'I like to tease them in this position for as long as it takes before they beg. They usually beg, even though they've been told not to speak – even if I punish them for speaking! Will she beg, do you think?'

'Yes. She'll beg.' Lane's voice was cold and clipped and it sent a shiver through Carol. Did Lane even care about her? But Carol was distracted by the feel of Granta's large hands pulling at her pants, pushing the cloth down between her arsecheeks and grabbing at the flesh.

'Mmm, nice arse. Lane, take the other end for me.'

Carol's head was lolling over the edge of the contraption. She smelt the reassuring scent of Lane's Tommy aftershave and her lover knelt by her, took her head and supported it. Then they were kissing as Granta slowly teased Carol, rubbing her hands over her bum and then slipping a finger over her sex for just a second before running it down her thigh or up the crack of her arse.

'Oh, please!' Carol heard the words escape from her own mouth before she was even aware of having thought them.

'Asked you not to speak,' Granta said, matter of fact. 'Don't do it again, please, Carol. You are here for my pleasure, not your own. To fulfil me, like a whore.'

Carol moaned and Lane whispered to her. 'She's paid me, babes. To use you however she wants.'

'I want to whip you now, Carol,' said Granta.

'I'm sorry, Granta,' Carrie responded, breathless, 'but that is not allowed.'

'Oh, then we'll have to see what else we can dream up, won't we? I'm disappointed. Your arse is so round and ready for the whip. Perhaps I'll have to bite it.'

Granta waited a second and Carol knew that she could refuse once more, but she was fired up by the suggestion and braced herself for the pain to come. Still, she screamed when Granta sank her teeth into the soft flesh of her buttock.

'Ow! Shit! Lane, help me!'

Lane kissed her again. 'Quiet now,' she told Carol. 'If you don't say no, then you must accept it without making a noise. I thought you understood.'

Granta bit harder into the other butt cheek and Carol knew it was her punishment for crying out. She was having trouble adapting to these rules, where silence was required and where she was unable to move, pressed against the sleek leather of the strange apparatus, her arse presented like the dish of the day to her hungry tormentor.

'Come and look at this,' Granta said to her co-conspirator. 'Look at her red arse. Look at the bite marks. Fucking beautiful.'

'Fucking gorgeous,' Lane agreed, her fingers brushing over the sore flesh, making Carol flinch again.

Lane, it was clear, was in her element. She came back to stroke Carol's head as Granta's attacks became more vicious. Lane's hand was on her own dildo as if she could arouse herself by touching the thick rubber. Then she was suddenly shoving that cock into Carol's mouth just as Granta's fingers closed on her prisoner's cuntlips, pinching them together in time with the bites she was giving in quick succession to one arsecheek and then the other.

Carol could only just make a groaning sound of pain and urgency from the back of her throat, as her mouth was filled with her lover's cock. Lane slipped a hand under Carol's trapped body and wrapped it round one breast.

The cold edge of Lane's voice was warming up now as she said, 'You're doing well, sweetheart. Now just take what you're given. I'm here with you.'

The words were strangely at odds with the rough way Lane was pumping her mouth with that thick tool. The taste of rubber and the pinching and biting at her rear were almost too uncomfortable to be pleasurable, yet Carol was wetter than she had been for a long time. She could feel her juices dripping down her thighs and she longed to be fucked.

Finally, Lane withdrew, to push her own fingers into her own crotch, ever the self-servicer.

Carol's mouth was released and she begged, 'Please, Granta, fuck me now. I need it!'

'Shut up!' said Granta. 'I told you not to speak.' Then, to Lane, 'She's begging already! She can't take much, can she?'

'No,' admitted Lane. 'I never said she could. She needs fucking all the time.'

'What an arse she's got on her, though. I don't want to stop chewing it. I might carry on doing that while I fuck her. When I fuck her – I'm not ready yet.'

Carrie moaned at Granta to fuck her now.

'What was that? Did she speak when I told her not to?'

'I think so,' Lane replied.

'She'll be punished for that. The nipples, I think.'

'No!' Carol moaned, her mind reeling with thoughts of what Granta might do to her.

Lane came back to her and gently brushed away the tears before kissing her with both softness and passion, her hands in Carol's hair. Carol gave in to it, letting Lane's tongue play with her own, feeling the corresponding throbbing in her cunt. But at the same time, Granta was reaching under Carol's tits, which were pressed against the horse. She pushed her hands inside Carol's bra and pinched both nipples at once.

'Did you speak out of turn, slut?'

'Yes, Granta,' gasped Carol.

'Then I have to use the clamps on you.'

Carol heard clanks as Granta ran her hands through the various leather and metal attachments that hung from the contraption. She chose two and then a cold pain was biting into both Carol's nipples, a pain that seemed to run straight through her nerves to her cunt and make her juices flow even as she was squealing with that pain.

So this was what it was all about. Carol had never reached this point of giving in to the pain and feeling the pure lust underneath it. She was under Granta's spell now and didn't have to do or say anything, only take what was meant for her.

'She's crying,' said Lane.

'Please,' begged Carol, 'please fuck me, Granta, I'll do anything.'

Without speaking, Granta tightened the straps that held the nipple clamps. Carol screamed in pain.

'I'm ready to fuck her,' Granta told Lane, as if Carol had not made a sound. 'See if she's ready.'

Lane kissed Carol again and said, 'Be good for her, babes.'

Then she got up and stroked Carol's backside. She pulled the scrunched wet briefs out of Carol's crack and touched her soaking cunt lightly. 'She's really wet. She needs it.'

Carol moaned at that touch and longed for Lane to fuck her, to touch her clit and fill her up. But she knew it wouldn't happen. Granta was going to fuck her now.

'Take off the panties.'

Lane followed the instruction and rolled them down to Carol's knees so they were stretched wide across her open legs. She couldn't get them off because of the ankle restraints that kept Carol's legs spread wide.

'Rip them off!' ordered Granta, and Lane did just that, tearing through the lace.

Carol heard Granta unzip her leather trousers and felt the warmth of her as she came near. Then she felt the large woman pressing up against her and was surprised that she felt safe. She was giving herself up to someone who knew more than her about the link between pain and pleasure, someone twice her size who needed to fuck her.

'Are you ready to take it?' Granta asked, her hand pressing on Carol's burning arsecheek.

'Yes, Granta.'

She felt a big cockhead pressing against her open cunt. Too big. 'No!'

'You just said yes.'

'I didn't know you were so big, Granta.' Granta came round and showed her the dildo, grabbing Carol's head and holding it next to her mouth. It was a long, thick black thing, curved and scary.

'You just said yes, you slag. You know what happens to prick-teases, don't you?'

'No!'

'No, you don't know? I'll tell you, they get fucked twice as hard.' And with that she pushed the dildo into Carol's mouth to show her how big it was. Carol gagged as her body stretched and the clamps pulled brutally on her nipples.

'Get it? That's going in your cunt now, slut.' And Granta drew out and moved behind Carol. 'Watch this,' she told Lane.

Again, the cock pressed against Carol's entrance as Granta held her by the arse. Then it was slipping inside her wet pussy, sliding up with ease even though it was too big. It seared through Carol as a hard ache. It was only because she was so wet that something so big had got inside her and she cursed her own juices for allowing the invasion.

But as she heard Granta shouting, 'Take it you slut, take it!' she felt the leather of the big woman's crotch rubbing against her arse and knew that the worst was over, the woman was fucking her with her full length now. Carol's cunt had accepted the sex rod and now she felt not pain but satisfaction at being so full. Was this how it was for Lane when Carol fisted her? Something too big inside you, stretching your cunt, filling your insides as full as they can be.

'God, I love watching that. I love watching you fuck my femme,' Lane told Granta. 'Carol, babes, you are so sexy. You just need to be fucked. I'm watching you being fucked and it is good.'

Carol recognised the horniness in Lane's voice and knew that Lane would need to fuck her when this insatiable creature had finally finished with her.

As Granta thrust into her, Carol's clit pressed against the upholstered leather of the contraption with each movement. Her nipples were tight in their clamps, her body stuck with sweat to the horse, her arse stuck in the air as Granta stroked it. What must she look like to Lane, trapped like that, humiliated?

'You need it, don't you?' asked Granta.

'Yes, Granta.' It was all she could do to answer. Granta's groans grew heavier – was she touching herself? Carol pictured the woman pumping her, fingers in pants to bring herself off as she pressed against her captive's reddened arse. Strapped to the apparatus, full of cock, Carol came violently, shaking and screaming with the intensity of it.

'Oh yes!' shouted Granta, fucking her harder so that Carol's orgasm was filled with thrusting and bucking, the big woman coming now inside her. Then Granta fell forward, groaning and pushing, covering Carol and pressing her into the horse.

Suddenly Lane was grabbing her lover's head again. 'Got to fuck your mouth.'

'No!' Carol was emptied, exhausted.

'Yes, I've got to fuck your mouth while I touch my clit. I have to do it and you have to take it.'

'I know.'

'Good, do as you're told!' And Lane pulled her dick from her jeans and pushed it into Carol's mouth, one hand on the back of Carol's head and the other on her own clit. 'I should have done this before,' said Lane, talking in that obsessive voice that only came out when she was fucking Carol. 'Should have fucked you at both ends but I needed to watch Granta's cock going in and out of your wet cunt. I needed to see that and I'll never forget it.'

And she came right then, shouting out obscenities but stroking Carol's head with that perverse gentleness that had come and gone from her throughout this ordeal.

'I kept thinking you wouldn't be up to it,' Lane said when they were back in the refuge of Carol's bed, which seemed a thousand miles from Granta's dungeon.

'If you wanted it, then I wanted it.'

'That's a very sexy thing to say, but I don't believe it.'

'So you think I want to have some giant munching away at my arse while I'm strapped immobile into position?'

'Shit. I'm sorry.'

'You're sorry? What for?'

'I dunno. Exploiting you.' They both laughed.

'Did she pay you?' asked Carol.

'Yeah.'

'How much?'

'Twenty.'

'Twenty quid? Are you joking? You bastard! You sold me for twenty fucking quid?' Carol slapped her and Lane started pummelling back until Carol resorted to tickling and Lane had to roll right out of the bed to save herself, shrieking.

Carol's eyes were alight with victory. 'You big sissy! Can't stand a bit of tickling, eh? How would you be if someone strapped you down and chewed your arse?'

'I'd cry. Oh, isn't that what you did?'

'Ha, ha!'

'It was heavy though, wasn't it?' Lane said, climbing back into bed.

'Yeah.'

'Yeah. I don't think I could do it every week.'

'Well, you'll have to find some vanilla girls for next time, then, won't you?'

'Carol, there's only so many dykes in London. Sooner or later we'll run out and we'll have to start over.'

'You're just not looking hard enough. I could produce half a dozen horny young girls tomorrow if necessary.'

'What, your students?'

'Maybe.'

'You'd fuck your students?'

'I didn't say that. I just said I know where the horny girls are.'

Lane was kneeling over her, hitting her with the pillow. 'Would you fuck your students?'

'Ouch! No! Get off me.'

'I should hope not. 'Cos that really would be kinky. Jesus!'

'Turn the light off. I am wiped out. I feel as if a giant took me to her den and had her way with me while my big butch girlfriend just stood by and wanked herself.'

'Ah, poor baby.'

'Yeah, well, funny how nothing difficult happens to you on these little adventures.'

'Oh yeah? What about in the van?'

'What, with the Chick Van Dykes?' This was their nickname for the gang, and it made them laugh every time. 'Who was handcuffed and blindfolded? Who was fucked by whoever wanted her and didn't have any option? Was that you?'

'No, I'm pleased to say it was you. But they did turn on me at the end.' She yawned.

'That is only to be expected if you go touting round the clubs for sex addicts. Where did you get them from anyway? I've never got to the bottom of that.'

But Lane was falling asleep, seeing visions of a stripper brandishing a giant chipolata.

NINE

Size Queen

What Jack and Lane had shared, that night with Matthias, hung between them like a weight. That was what was in the air at the party. They had talked on the phone as well, but not about that. Just chatting, as if they could only tackle it in person.

Now he was on his way over to her flat and she knew that the next part of her training was about to take place. It was like a secret fire in her, what went on between them. There was no way she could tell anyone else, least of all Carol, about it, or how Jack and Matthias had made her into their boy that night. She wanked about it, she thought about it, it made her horny at times and at other times it ate away at her, burnt away, because she needed to be treated like that but it took something away from her. It took away her womanhood and it scared her.

The masculinity they had given her was a kind of power, but it was not the same power that she felt when she fucked Carol, or when she sold Carol to other women. The men had used her, the way she used Carol, but without the love she had for Carol.

Was there another kind of love, growing between her and Jack? Lane felt like everything was running out of control these days, even though she wanted what Jack gave her and she wanted what she had when she brought other women to Carol. Her desires were taking over her life.

Tonight she had prepared for Jack by packing her dildo in her boxer shorts and dressing in combats and T-shirt like him. She had rolled some joints and worried over what CD to put on. Now there was a drum 'n' bass compilation blaring out of the speakers and she was smoking the first of the spliffs.

When he finally rang the doorbell, she jumped. She buzzed him in and waited while he climbed the stairs to her studio flat. When he was there, sitting on a big red blow-up armchair, she had to speak.

'Jack, how are you feeling? You know, about you and me?'

'I can't talk about it.'

'Why not?'

'I've got a fucking great hard-on, Lane. I need to fuck you.'

She felt both turned on and a bit disgusted with him. 'We can't just go on like this and never discuss it,' she said.

'I think we can. I can.'

'It's too weird.'

'You have to be trained, that's all there is to it. There's nothing to discuss. I know how to train you and I'm doing it. Tonight you'll learn how to fuck a man.'

She gasped. It *was* what she wanted. He was what she wanted. So what was there to discuss?

'How will I learn that,' she asked, 'if *you* fuck *me*?'

'You're learning all the time. Get your pants off.'

She handed him the joint. She had drawn the curtains, although it wasn't yet dark, and lit the room with candles. The beat of the music was carrying her now as she undressed in the dim light. She took off her trainers and unzipped her trousers, pulling them off. Jack was watching her every move as she pulled down her checked boxers. He stared at the big dildo and leather harness.

'I've never seen one,' he admitted.

'What, a girl with a cock?'

'Yeah.'

'Do you like it?'

'Yeah. Take your top off.'

She did. She watched him marvelling at her body and her cock and she wanted him.

This time, it was quick. He undressed to his tight T-shirt and Calvins, then pulled out his hard dick. He told her to roll on his condom. His cock filled her hand. She was going to lie down on the bed but he pushed her to the floor.

'I want you, Lane.' Then they were on each other, her hands moving under his T-shirt as his moved on her back. He pulled her close and kissed her, their mouths as keen as each other, their lips and tongues pressing for more. The metal in his tongue was as shocking as ever.

He stroked her breasts and it felt strange for a man's hands to be there. Then he had her on her back and he pulled her legs apart and pushed them up in the air so he could get in there. Her arsehole was exposed to him and he was kissing her breasts as he played with that hole, his fingers, wet with lube, already impatient to get in there.

'I really want you,' he told her.

'I want you in me.'

It was different this time: they were full of lust for each other but he was treating her as both woman and man, and she felt like both at once. He seemed to be all over her, so much bigger than her. The first finger was working her hole, gliding in and playing in there as he sucked on her breast – teasing her nipple ring, catching it in his pierced tongue – while his other hand grabbed her dildo.

'I need to fuck you,' he said. His voice was breaking up with that need and she gave in to him, her whole body straining with the need to welcome him inside her. His finger slipped from her arse and his cock pressed against that hole.

'Fuck me,' she gasped.

He leant into her, pulling on the leather harness round her hips, and she bent her legs back over her belly. His cock plunged inside her and she shouted out. 'Shit! You're so big, Jack, it hurts. Christ, it hurts!'

'I know.' He pushed in further, though, and she fought against it, trying to pull away from him, kicking at him, even as she longed to accept him. But he didn't give up and she was grateful to him for fucking her, for pressing his length into her till his balls were pressed against her rear and the frown passed from his face. She shut her eyes and just let him fuck her.

It was a few short minutes before he came, but minutes that she would play over and over in the days that followed, wanking herself furiously with a buttplug up her arse that could never replicate that feeling of Jack. Of Jack's cock pumping inside her tunnel, churning up her insides while they both shouted out.

'Got to fuck that arse,' he shouted, while she yelled only, 'Yes!' and 'Fuck!' and 'Jesus!'

Then he was coming inside her in great thrusts, kneeling over her and holding her arms down by her sides so she couldn't move. When he finally let go he was still inside her and she reached beyond her cock to touch her clit and bring herself off, but he snatched her hand away.

'Now you fuck me, Lane.'

'What?'

'You heard.'

He slid out of her, eliciting a long groan from her till the head of his cock burst out of her and she was empty. He only had to move a few inches to position his arse over her erect sex rod. Now he rolled off his condom, throwing it on the floor and wrapping his hand around his own softening member.

'Hold your cock,' he told her. She wrapped a hand round the base of the rubber tool.

'Now I'm going to sit on your cock, Lane.' He did just that, sitting down hard on the thick head so it rammed inside him. He bellowed but even as the sound left his mouth he was lowering himself further, taking the whole of her dick into his gaping hole.

'Yes!' he shouted.

Lane was speechless. She was finally fucking him but it felt like he was doing it all himself.

'Give it to me!' he demanded, and she regained herself, pushing her hands up his briefs to grab hold of his firm arse, and grinding her groin into it so she was really fucking him with the full length of her dildo. Already his prick was hardening up again. As she thrust inside him, the pressure built on her clit and she knew that she would come in him.

She was enjoying it now, although it was far from her fantasies of being in control of a man. Jack was holding on to his power even as she fucked him harder. She couldn't come until she knew that she had him, and her voice was sure and steady but loaded:

'I'm going to come in you and I want you to come for me. I'm fucking your arse now, Jack, going to make you come.'

He groaned and sat down harder on her cock, shutting his eyes and seeming to give in to her. The power surged through her and her clit was near to bursting.

'That's it!' she shouted, pumping in him as the climax built in her guts and charged to her head and her cunt at once. She thrust against his arse and the surge passed through her cock and into his guts and then out through his cock until he was coming all over her in great jets of jism that spattered across her breasts.

They shouted out together like one being with one orgasm and he fell forward and she wrapped her arms round him and kept moving in there in cruel thrusts that made his spunk pump across her stomach.

Jack bit into her neck and she screamed, her whole body in spasm once again. She grabbed his stubbled head and kissed him fiercely, biting his lip, and then they were rolling across the floor, locked together at the mouth and arse, their teeth and his tongue-piercing clashing as they drank the last dredges of lust from each other's mouths.

Eventually Lane guided Jack into bed. She was exhausted and wanted to lie there with him. But when they fell into each other's arms, the sweat drying on their bodies and every muscle relaxed, she thought of Carol. She had never taken anyone to that bed except Carol.

'How do you think of me?' she asked Jack, trying to dispel thoughts of her femme.

'What do you mean?'

'Well, Matthias wanted me to be a boy, and you went along with that. But tonight it didn't feel like that.'

'No. Matthias is a bit of a perv, isn't he? I mean, I see quite a bit of him and we usually fuck and he has all these pervy fantasies and I just go along with them. I let myself be a bit of a perv too, you know? But, left to my own devices, I know there's more to it if you actually connect . . . Is this bollocks?'

'The only thing that's bollocks is you making out that Matthias is some kind of bad influence and you're a little angel. But I know what you mean.' She considered. 'I can't tell you what's going on between me and Carol –'

He interrupted her: 'You mean you won't.'

'Yeah, I won't. Because it's about me and her, not you. I don't tell her about you either. It's a strain for me but it's like living two lives, they don't mix.' She heard her own clichés and wondered if there was anyone who knew what she really felt like. 'Anyway,' she continued, 'I know what you mean about connecting or not connecting, that's all. Calling me a boy got me really randy, but you might as well call me a piece of shit because it's not exactly a compliment, is it? To call a girl a boy?'

'No. But if you like it –'

'I don't know what I like any more, Jack. I can barely get up and go to work and act normal any more. I look around and I think: Is everyone doing weird shit with their mates on the weekend? Is everyone getting strangers to fuck their girlfriends?'

'You what?'

Lane stiffened. 'Uh, pretend I didn't say that, OK?'

'Only strangers?' he asked, alert.

'I told you, I didn't say anything.'

'Yes you did, girl. You said that you're getting strangers to fuck Carol. Little old uptight Carol.'

'Uptight? Is that what you think of her?'

'Well, look at how she was at the party, having a go at me for "sleeping" with you.' His tone was pure bitch.

'That wasn't uptight, that was the jealousy of a passionate woman,' said Lane. 'Jesus, Jack, I can't believe you think that. She's wild.'

'She's wild? I don't think so. She's an academic.'

'Let's drop this. It's not going anywhere.'

'It might be.'

'Believe me, it's not,' she insisted. 'Drop it. Tell me about my training. I want to go to sleep in your arms with you telling me all the dirty things I'm going to learn from you.'

'Don't forget what I'm learning from you, Laney.'

'What like?'

'Like how to be fucked by a woman with a big dick.'

'Do you like it?'

'Yeah. I'm a bit of a size queen. That dildo's bigger than most guys, you know.'

'No bigger than you.'

'Well I don't think we'll resort to the tape measure tonight.' He stroked her head. 'Aren't you tired, anyway?'

'Yes. But I've never had this conversation before – the "who's bigger?" conversation. It's like being a gay boy.'

He laughed. 'Oh, so you're a boy again now? God, you're changeable.'

'Dyke's prerogative.'

Lane woke, confused, the smell of Jack in her nostrils. He was snoring next to her. She pulled on shorts and a T-shirt and went out to buy bread. Outside, everything was normal. People were on their way to and from the Cypriot grocer shops on Green Lanes, having not just fucked their gay friend. She went to the supermarket to enjoy the anonymity and not have to speak to any shopkeepers.

By the time she got back, Jack was in the bathroom, emerging just as she was taking the croissants out of the oven. The water was still dripping down his naked chest and he wore a towel round his waist. He looked at her with those dark eyes and she saw all over again how handsome he was.

'Bacon and eggs for me, please!' were his first words.

'No chance, mate. We can go out and have a fry-up if you want, but there'll be no cooking in my kitchenette. It's a matter of principle.'

He slumped on the bed and turned on the TV with the remote. The *EastEnders* omnibus was on, underlining how late they had slept. The light was flashing on the answerphone but Lane was ignoring it.

Suddenly Jack said, 'Have you ever met Derek and Coby?'

'Dunno. Boys?'

'Boy and girl. They're both bi. I just wonder if we might go and see them today.' There was something mischievous in his tone and she looked at him as she handed him a croissant and a mug of strong coffee, feeling oddly like a housewife.

'What are you up to this time, Jackie-boy?'

'Oh, nothing,' he teased.

'I'll come with you but that's all.'

'Like you came with me last night?'

'No, exactly not like that.'

A plan was forming in Lane's mind and, if this couple were all right, then it wouldn't be long before she was carrying it out.

TEN

Get in the Car

'Jack introduced me to these friends that live near me,' Lane said, looking not at Carol but at the spliff she was rolling in front of her.

Carol had already guessed that Lane had been with Jack recently. When they originally struck the Big Deal, Carol had somehow imagined that Lane would come back from her encounters glowing with a masculine sexiness. In reality, there was a subtle shiftiness about her.

So Carol knew at the start of the evening that it wouldn't be long before the next adventure was proposed or sprung on her, to make up for the gender-bending exploits. But she didn't expect quite what came out.

They were sitting at Carol's kitchen table over their cleared plates. She'd cooked salmon and vegetables; Lane had brought the supermarket lemon tart and a bottle of Cava. They were comfortable together, full and a bit drunk and Carol wasn't sure she wanted to hear what Lane had to say.

But she was going to.

'This couple – Jack's friends,' Lane began, still not meeting Carol's eyes. And she might well look away because, admittedly, Carol was none too chuffed to hear Jack's name again. 'I wanted to ask you what you think about getting together with them.'

'For?' she asked.

'Like you don't know, babes. For sex.'

'Why are you asking?'

'Because it's not exactly what the Big Deal was about. I said I'd bring women to you, but – well, they're a man and a woman.'

'A straight couple?' Carol didn't like the sound of it.

'They're both bi. They're nice.'

'Nice? That's not going to hook me.' She looked at Lane, waiting for her to look back. 'Don't evade, Laney. Tell me what's going to be hot about it or I don't want to meet them. Any giants?'

'What?'

'Well, so far you've come up with two very big women among your willing volunteers.'

'Is that a problem?'

'Oh no. I like big women.'

'Well, these two aren't giants,' said Lane.

'I suppose you fancy them both?' Carol asked her.

'Yeah. But you might, too. The guy's got lovely curly hair like your plumber that you're so fond of. He's slightly hippyish but masculine too, you know?'

'Uh-huh. And the girl?'

'More woman than girl, I'd say. They're probably early thirties, and they're sort of alternative, and she's sexy. I mean, she's not butch or femme or even dykey, really. She's just – she's a bit like Jo, actually.' She named a friend of Carol's who was straight but could never find a bloke who met her standards.

'OK. Now we're getting somewhere. What makes you think they want a foursome?' Carol allowed herself to soften.

'Because they only fucking said so, didn't they? Basically, Jack thought – well, never mind.'

'He thought he'd take you round there and you'd all have some fun?' Now Carol was annoyed.

'Well it didn't happen, Carrie, because it's not what I wanted. You know, it's you that's special.'

'What?'

'You're my lover, not him.'

'I shouldn't need telling.' Carol wasn't sure whether she was reproaching herself or Lane.

'No, but you do, don't you?' Lane looked a bit ashamed of herself.

'And why do you think that is?'

'Because I haven't been clear with you. Jack's my friend.'

'And he fucks you. Or do you fuck him?'

'Do you want to know?'

'No.' Carol knew she could stop this now, before they were fighting, and for once she did just that. 'OK, look, you haven't done anything that I haven't already said is OK, so I'm going to have to trust you, aren't I? Trust you not to get in too deep, not to threaten our relationship.'

'Yes.' Lane looked steadily at her, with a mixture of relief and admiration. 'You're gorgeous, do you know that?'

'If you say so. I suppose you've already told them we'll do it.'

Lane grinned. 'So? I can tell them no. I'm asking you, aren't I?'

'What would happen, if we all got together?'

Lane shifted in her chair, switching into that sexy butch persona that she could turn on like a light. Why couldn't she maintain it all the time? But then, Carol had always liked a bit of uncertainty, some vulnerability in her butches – and in her men too, come to that, in her straight days.

As Lane prepared to seduce her with their joint fantasy, Carol felt a little lurch in her stomach. This wasn't just the excitement of knowing she would be turned on by the story; it was the knowledge that whatever Lane said now, it was not only a fantasy or a prelude to this evening's sex. Whatever she said, they would do something similar with these strangers very soon.

Two nights later, when Carol was on her own for the evening, she heard a car pull up outside and then the doorbell. She wasn't expecting anyone and went to the door thinking it would be someone who'd buzzed the wrong flat.

'Hello?' she shouted through the door.

'Hello. I've got a note for you.' It was a man's voice.

'Who is it?' she asked, suspicious.

'Cab. Got a note for you.'

She put the chain on the door, then opened it. It was dark out. On the doorstep was someone she recognised straight away: the taxi driver who had taken them back from the party, the night Lane brought her off in the back of the car.

If he recognised her, he didn't show it. 'All right?' he asked. 'Got this for you.' He handed her an envelope with her name and address typed on it. She turned away to open it, bewildered and nervous. The cover of the card inside was an old erotic photograph of three women and a man entangled together. Inside, a word-processed message in a typeface that mimicked cursive hand-writing: *For a night of love, get in the car.* That was all.

'I'll just be five minutes,' she told the driver.

She ran to her bedroom, face flushed, heart pounding, to change her clothes.

Lane was making conversation with Coby and Derek but her mind was on Carol. Eventually, she told them about the note and the taxi. She wasn't sure if it sounded sexy or silly so she glanced around the room instead of at her audience, her eyes darting over all the stuff they'd brought back from their travels. She was staring at a collection of erotic carvings as she concluded: 'So, hopefully, Carol should roll up in the car any minute now, ready for anything.'

'That is cool!' exclaimed Derek, throwing back his curly head and giving a kind of gurgling chuckle.

'So,' said Coby from her giant suede beanbag. 'We are all sitting here with what might well be called stonking hard-ons, waiting for someone who might never turn up? Who might have been lying in the bath enjoying her night in and decided not to answer the door?'

'Well yeah,' Lane admitted. 'But we mustn't lose faith.'

'Faith in what?' asked Derek.

'The Lurve Gods that watch over us,' she replied before cracking open another beer.

'Got a photo?' Coby asked.

'You what?'

'Got a photo of Carol? Better than nothing.' They all laughed; the doorbell sounded. They all laughed again.

'Great,' deadpanned Lane as she felt the beginning of the hiccups bubbling under. 'I'm really glad I went to all that trouble, now that Carol's turning up – probably in her underwear – to meet some really sexy pissed people. It's all going really great.' But then she reverted to laughing and hiccuping.

Derek let Carol in while Coby gave Lane a series of shocks designed to get rid of the hiccups.

'Stop it!' It came out as 'St–hic–it!' And it had no effect.

Coby had so far jumped Lane, booed at her and put an ice cube down her trousers. Now she stood over Lane, who had collapsed on the floor cushion, and pulled up her own top to reveal her beautiful naked breasts.

Lane's hiccups were cured. And she was suddenly more sober. She beckoned Coby to join her on the floor. Coby had big brown eyes, cute 'n' lived-in face, dyed reddish-orange hair in a 'Rachel' cut, tight T-shirt with a spiral on it, short skirt, bare legs and plimsolls. Fashionably ironic or ironically fashionable? Why worry, when her red lips were moving in on Lane's?

There was something juicy about Coby. Fruity and juicy. Lane reached her hands under that top and tried to control her breathing as she took hold of Coby's large, soft breasts. She was on top of Coby now, sliding a knee between her thighs. But where was Derek? What had happened to Carol?

She didn't have long to wait for an answer. As she nibbled her way down Coby's neck, blowing lightly along the wet skin after each little bite, enjoying the way Coby's big thighs tightened around Lane's knee every time, she heard footsteps come down the bare wood floor of the hall and then deaden on the big woollen rug.

Lane knelt up. 'Hi,' she said to Carol.

Derek had his arm round her waist. Weird shit, man. That's what you get. Carol was wearing a little black dress. Not a formal one, but a sexy one. 'Hi.' She looked nervous and a bit surprised. But she rallied: 'I see you started without me.'

'Do join us,' laughed Coby. She reached a hand out to encourage Carol to drop to the floor. She did. They greeted each other for the first time, with open mouths that met in a flash of passion.

'I've got to see this!' said Derek.

'Oh no you haven't, honey,' replied Coby. 'Didn't you start

something in the hall that hasn't finished yet?' She stroked Carol's hair.

Derek looked confused. 'Well, yeah.'

'Well, yeah.' From the floor, Coby raised a trimmed eyebrow at her partner.

'I thought . . .'

'Listen, you clit-tease,' said Coby, 'whatever you thought, whatever you planned, forget it. Do whatever happens.'

Lane had the distinct impression that Coby was rather more experienced than Derek. She pressed her knee firmly into Coby's crotch to remind her where they were up to. It got her attention. Coby wrapped her arms round Lane's back and pulled her down on top of her.

Derek sat down next to them and Carol wrapped her arms round him. Now they could all watch each other, if they got a chance. Lane caught a glimpse of Carol straddling Derek where he sat, and shut her eyes, the vision emblazoned on her brain. Even as a pang of jealousy shot through her, she knew she would be wanking to that moment in weeks to come.

Lane unzipped her jeans and felt inside, her hand wrapping around her dildo. 'Do you want this?' she asked Coby as she pulled out the black cock and let it press into Coby's thigh.

Coby looked surprised. 'I can get that from Derek. I want your special expertise,' she said. 'I bet your fingers are good. I bet you know how to lick a girl out till she's screaming.'

'Oh, how can you tell?' Mock-suave.

'Sixth sense.'

'Well, you could well be right, Coby. Shall we find out?' She felt hampered by her clothes and pulled off her T-shirt, chinos and pants before she reached under Coby's skirt and gasped as she touched smooth naked flesh. The woman wasn't wearing any underwear and her pubes were shaved. Lane dived down there for a better look. She pushed Coby's short skirt up round her hips and exposed the smooth white flesh of her belly and cunt.

Lane had never seen a shaved pussy before and she couldn't take her eyes off the exposed pink flesh. It was wet with juices which Lane longed to taste. But first she slipped a finger between those wet cuntlips and watched Coby's eyes open wide in delight, then close. She was making tiny noises the way that Carol sometimes did.

And meanwhile, Carol was making big noises. Lane looked up and saw Carol riding Derek with both grace and urgency, her eyes closed and her mouth half open. 'Yes, fuck me!' she was saying to him between groans. He pulled her mouth to his and kissed her while he fucked her.

Lane felt fired up with excitement. To watch her femme riding this guy while she herself was about to lick out Coby's smooth pussy – it was almost too much for her. But she took the chance to kiss Coby's smeared red mouth and, as their tongues played together, she regained her sense of purpose.

She pushed up Coby's T-shirt and rubbed her face over those large, pale breasts, licking and kissing, holding them in her hands. It was like a surfeit of breasts. She couldn't stop herself from going, 'Mm-mmm!' as she sucked on one of Coby's pale nipples. Then she sucked more and more of that breast into her mouth. At the same time, she pushed a hand back between Coby's legs and trailed two fingers over her bits.

'Lick me out!' Coby bent her knees and spread them wide. She took Lane's head in her hands and hungrily pushed it down. Lane licked Coby's soft cunt, one hand on her mound, marvelling at its smoothnesss, the other hand in a more important role. Lane was playing with Coby's cunt with her fingers at the same time as licking it.

Then she heard Derek coming in Carol and Carol's own groans building to climax. Lane couldn't help but raise her head to watch. As Derek gripped her tight, Carol rubbed at her clit. When she came, she was gasping strangely, as if she couldn't believe it.

'Hey!' said Coby. 'I need you to lick me out. Don't you want to?'

'Oh yes,' murmured Lane. 'I want to. You taste so good. I want to lick you out till you come.' She bent back to her task, licking Coby's clit and working two fingers in and out of her small cunt.

'Somebody kiss me!' Coby cried suddenly. 'Carol, come and kiss me!'

The pair to their right peeled apart and Lane thought she heard the sound of Derek's cock sliding out of Carol's cunt. Then, to her surprise, just as she saw with her peripheral vision that Carol was bending over Coby's face, Lane also felt Derek behind her and his hands on her arse.

'Can I fuck you, Lane?' he asked in a deep, slow voice.

She pushed her naked arse further into the air to show her assent. But how could he possibly fuck her so soon after fucking Carol? He was stroking her arse, pulling at her harness and moaning.

'Can I fuck your arse?' he asked.

Again, she thrust her arse towards him. But she also knew that Coby was building to climax. As she heard Derek unwrapping a condom, she moved her tongue in smaller circles on that tight bud.

Sure enough, his hard cock was now pressing against Lane's arsehole. Lane had a flash of what they must look like: the two more feminine women kissing as Lane burrowed naked between the legs of one of them, whose man was preparing to fuck Lane's arse.

She could hardly breathe in her excitement, with her mouth and nose pressed into Coby's wet flesh, full of the musk and salt of her. But Coby was somehow managing to hold out and Lane realised she would have time to enjoy Derek's cock up her arse while she licked out his girlfriend.

'Have you done this before?' Derek said suddenly. But it wasn't a real question, just a kind of soundtrack for his own benefit. 'Have you taken a man's cock up your arse? Right up there?' Although he had none of the roughness of Jack at his worst or the kinky Matthias, Derek was clearly as turned on as anyone had ever been by the sight of Lane's arse.

As he pressed into her, she opened to him and let him push his cockhead past her opening in an easy glide. He appreciated it. 'Yes!' he shouted as he entered her with his slim cock. It delved deep with ease and she enjoyed the way he plunged right up her tunnel without hurting her, filling her up.

Now Carol had started talking to Coby between kisses: 'Shall I stroke your breasts while Lane licks your clit? Do you like that?'

The sound of her lover's voice made Lane's movements more urgent. Coby's hip movements seemed more controlled, more focused. Lane wrapped a hand under Coby's arse and held tight to the soft flesh as she licked hard. Derek's thrusts were building inside her. She needed to bring Coby to climax before his agenda took over.

Gently, Lane took Coby's clit between her front teeth and bit it, letting the woman know that she now meant business. Then her tongue and that clit were like one piece of muscle, slipping round each other as Coby groaned and bucked beneath Lane. She was pushing herself against Lane and Lane's fingers slipped so deep into her that they were punching against her cervix and Coby was coming. Lane felt it building in Coby's taut muscles and then bursting from her, along with a jet of piss or juice that took Lane by surprise, even as she was gulping it down.

As Coby's body jumped and quivered with the intensity of that slow-building orgasm that had finally burst forth, her partner was pumping Lane's arse. 'Coby!' he said. 'It's so good when you come. It's good to watch.'

At the same time, he gripped Lane's thighs harder as if he was talking to her. But then, they were all one now, all locked together in passion. Lane rested her head between Coby's legs, mouth still open, her own lips meeting Coby's cunt lips. Carol was resting at the other end, her head on Coby's soft tits.

Derek pumped Lane's arse and she moaned and groaned like a girl. No need now to be anyone's butch. He was loving it and so was she, feeling his cock smoothly thrusting in her tunnel. He moved a hand to her clit and she moaned in gratitude. Then, suddenly, Carol was pulling Lane's head from between Coby's legs and kissing her, licking up the sweat and juices that were all over Lane's wet face, then kissing her mouth and murmuring, 'I know I have to watch while he fucks you. I know I can't touch. But I just have to kiss you.'

And Lane came, before Derek, so that he had to hold on to her and keep on thrusting in her arse while she bucked back and forth against him, screaming with the release.

ELEVEN

Acting Out

'How come you got off with him the minute you arrived?' Lane seemed more than curious – fascinated almost but trying to keep it hidden.

'Lust at first sight.'

'What happened?'

They were sitting on the bed at Lane's, half-dressed, with the TV on, discussing their exploits from the previous night. Carol smiled, remembering the moment when Derek had opened the door. 'He just looked at me and went, "Hi, Carol, come in!" as if he'd just won the lottery. And I said –' she put on her seductress voice '– "Well, hello, Derek," and handed him my jacket. He threw it over the banisters and I went, "Aren't you going to kiss me hello?" and we were off.'

'Go on,' urged Lane, slipping a hand under Carol's top, reaching inside her bra. 'Tell me why you were so quick to give yourself away.'

Carol allowed herself a second to gasp at the arousal she felt whenever Lane touched her breasts. But she had a story to tell. 'I was already randy from getting that note from you and getting in the taxi and coming here, not knowing what to expect. So I was ready for him, or for anyone.

'He pushed me against the wall. He's quite a gentle person, isn't he? But he knows what he wants. He pressed his whole body against me and as he kissed me I could feel his hard-on pressing into me here.' She placed a hand on her lower abdomen.

'What, here?' asked Lane, teasing her by placing her own hand lower still, on Carol's mound.

'Oh, I'm not sure now,' Carol replied, joining in the game. 'It might have been a bit lower.'

'What, here?' Lane placed her hand in the crotch of Carol's knickers and pressed her palm lightly into the wet cloth, pushing it against Carol's opening cuntlips.

'Yeah, that might have been it,' moaned Carol.

'And you were kissing this man?'

'Yeah.'

'Did you think about me?'

'Yes. I thought that you were in the house and you might not be pleased with me. I know I'm not supposed to let anyone fuck me unless you're there, unless you want them to do it.'

'That's right. Were you a good girl?' Now Lane was playing with her, teasing her nipple and her cunt at once by stroking each with a fingertip. The slinky feel of her own juices being spread around her sex by her lover was almost too much for Carol, but she knew she had to answer the question.

'Yes. When he went to touch my cunt, I told him we had to go and find you.'

'What did you say?'

'I said . . .' Carol thought quickly. What did Lane want to hear? 'I said, "I want to feel your cock in me but Lane has to be there. Lane decides who can fuck me."'

'Oh, good girl!' Lane was moaning now as if someone was touching her instead of the other way round. Carol loved the way her butch was so turned on by touching her and talking dirty with her, and by the thought of Carol with Derek. 'And what was it like when he did fuck you?' Lane slipped her thick dildo out of the flies of her boxer shorts and knelt over Carol. 'Did it turn you on?'

'Yes.' Carol pushed her hands under the back of Lane's white T-shirt and stroked her back, longing for that cock. 'He fucked me and I was watching you too. And I saw you look at us while you fucked that woman. Were you pleased with me?'

'Yes.' Now Lane had hardened, gone stone. She was in her

head and, somehow, she was in her cock. It was a transformation that always made Carol buzz from head to toe with anticipation for how her butch would take her. Lane continued to speak as she pulled Carol's knickers away from her sex and slipped her fingers in there.

Carol moaned and listened to her words: 'Sometimes I have to fuck you and sometimes someone else has to fuck you. That's just how it is, babes. Right now, I have to fuck you, but it's OK if you want to think about him, because I'm going to be thinking about how you rode him. Are you going to ride me now?' As she spoke she lifted Carol's arse with her strong hands.

'Yes.'

'Yes what?'

'Yes, Lane, I'm going to ride you.' She moaned with desire. 'Fuck me, please, fuck me!'

'OK, if that's what you need. I think it is.'

Lane manoeuvred Carol into position. Lane was sitting on the bed and Carol was to sit on her cock, pressed between Lane and the big cushions that served as a headboard, which would offer some protection from the hard wall. Carol knew this was where Lane wanted her and she regretted it because it meant she couldn't move properly, that Lane had too much control. But she had no choice. Lane was sliding the shaft of her cock around Carol's wet sex, making her beg again: 'Fuck me!'

'That's what I'm going to do.' Lane looked at Carol and slid the tool into her soaking cunt and cried out as hard as Carol did. They held each other with a tight and steady grip as Lane worked her way inside Carol until the whole of that long cock was in there. Carol felt it stretching her cunt wide and delving to her depths. She was full. She moaned and kissed her lover, but Lane kept her mouth shut, baring only her clenched teeth to Carol's lips and tongue.

'Can't kiss you now. I have to concentrate on fucking you.'

'Please, kiss me,' Carol whispered urgently.

'Why should I?'

Carol moaned. 'Please!' She tried again to kiss Lane but still met her hard, ungiving mouth.

Lane was now fucking her with an almost grim determination,

holding Carol's arse so she could exaggerate their synchronised hip movements by pushing her bottom up and down. Eventually Lane reached for Carol's clit, making her cry out. But the hand moved away again.

'Put your finger in my mouth,' ordered Lane. 'Your clit isn't wet enough. All your juices must be trapped in your cunt.' The femme did as she was told, shutting her eyes as Lane slavered over her finger, making it wet.

'Good,' she said. 'Now touch yourself, just for a second, to make your clit wet for me.'

Carol touched herself and couldn't help but keep her hand there, rubbing at her swollen, wet nub. She looked beseechingly at Lane, but she knew from experience what the reaction would be.

Lane snatched away Carol's hand, furious. 'Was that a second?' she asked. 'Was it?'

'No.'

'Look at me. What's the matter with you?' She gave a sudden thrust inside Carol as if to snap her back to obedience. At the same time she was groping on the bed for something.

Suddenly, the leather handcuffs were in her hands. Carol put her hands behind her back, knowing that it would only anger her lover further if she resisted.

'OK, you know what happens now. I have to cuff you just so I can bring you off without you trying to do it yourself.' She was reaching behind Carol and cuffing the first wrist, pulling the soft leather tight and doing up the buckle as she had so many times before.

As her hands were caught tight behind her back, the longing and the knowledge that it would eventually be fulfilled were coursing through Carol, but she also felt the relief of being Lane's captive, of having no responsibility except to satisfy Lane's need to fuck her.

'Why must you do these things?' asked Lane. But she was almost smiling now with the power she had taken for herself, and Carol took the opportunity to kiss her. This time, Lane leant right in to her and took her mouth as she was taking her cunt, pushing her tongue in deep and keeping it there, letting Carol play with it for an instant and then biting on her lip.

She held Carol by the chain that linked the cuffs, pulling on it so that it was forced into her lover's hipbone. They were pressed together, but then Lane pulled away and pushed up the front of Carol's top, grabbed her bra and tugged the lace down to let loose her breasts. Hungrily, Lane sucked a tit into her mouth and moaned as she fucked Carol more vigorously. She slid a hand down Carol's body, pausing to play with her bush of hair. Then a finger slipped down to that swollen clit and Carol cried out as Lane stroked it with something between love and ownership.

Carol was trapped now. Lane's cock thrust in her while one knowing finger moved on her straining clit. Lane let the breast fall out of her mouth and kissed Carol, pushing her back against the wall. With her hands trapped behind her, Carol returned the kiss.

Then Lane pulled her tongue out of Carol's mouth. 'Who are you thinking about?' she asked. 'You thinking about how he fucked you? But he let you ride about, didn't he? He didn't trap you like this.'

Carol moaned, unable to speak, the orgasm building inside her.

'Did he fuck you like this?' asked Lane, not wanting a response now, Carol knew, just wanting to talk to the very end. 'Who's in you now? Who have I given you to? Shut your eyes. Can you tell who it is?'

It was anyone, everyone. It was Lane and it was Derek and it was every guy and every butch she'd ever looked twice at. Carol could see them, queuing to fuck her.

'They're all waiting,' said Lane, as if she read her mind. 'So don't take too long because you'll be doing this a few more times tonight.'

'Oh, no!' cried Carol. 'You bitch! No!' And she came, like a taut string snapping inside her, the orgasm flooding through her in wave after wave as Lane refused to let up. Instead, Carol's cunt was fucked and fucked and her clit was stroked in the same quick rhythm.

Lane had her arms round her and was saying, 'It's OK, you see? It's all OK.' The sensation was so intense that Carol had no thoughts, only a sense of climbing higher than what had seemed to be the summit.

She had been pressed so tight to Lane and pushed so hard against the wall that when Lane finally let her finger go limp on that throbbing clit and loosened her grip on Carol ever so slightly, the relaxation in Carol's muscles made her moan again, because it was like falling through air. But Lane didn't let her go; didn't stop as if her work were done, like some of Carol's past lovers. No, she kissed Carol's head, her cheek, her mouth, her eyes; she murmured to her again and again that it was all OK, that she was a good girl. She continued to fuck Carol in long, languid movements that stirred her up, and to slide a finger over her clit every minute or so, which Carol felt as a jolt through her slowly unwinding body.

'Let me go,' Carol finally asked, meaning that Lane should release her handcuffs. The butch understood. But first she pulled off her own T-shirt and rubbed her smaller, pierced tits against Carol's, which were still half-trapped in the tight bra. Lane moaned and was still rubbing their tits together as she reached behind Carol to release the short chain that held the cuffs together.

'Now you're free,' said Lane, her breathing quick and heavy. 'But only free to do what I want.' Suddenly, she stood up and positioned herself in front of Carol. She pushed her dildo into Carol's mouth. 'Suck on that first, then on my clit. I told you that I wanted you to do that soon. When you walked in on me with that gay boy, I told you that I needed that. But I don't get it from you unless I make you do it, do I?'

Of course, Carol could not speak. She was shocked and excited by this turnaround. Just when she thought that she could rest from the powerful orgasm that had racked her body, she was instead full once again. But this time it was her mouth, the mouth that longed to be kissed gently, now being bullied into action as Lane's sex toy. What did Lane feel as Carol sucked her rubber dick? She did it with the same dedication she would have given to a man's dick – more, because she would never have put herself at the mercy of a man like this, or accepted his cock forced into her mouth so selfishly. She wrapped her hands round Lane's bum and sucked on that cock that tasted so strongly of Carol's own juices. The cock that had given her so much just moments before.

'Enough,' said Lane. She pulled out of Carol's mouth and took off her boxer shorts. She held her cock close to her body then took Carol's head with a strangely menacing gentleness and pulled it into her crotch.

'Lick me out. Lick my cunt and my clit. Then I'll touch myself. When I do that, you stop. Then all I want is to look at you. Do you understand?'

'Yes.' The smell of Lane's cunt, the dripping wetness of it, was so strong that Carol could already taste it, before her mouth had touched it.

'For fuck's sake, Carrie, I can't hear you. Don't make me push you. What did you say?'

'Yes!' From between her butch's spread legs, Carol gave her reply. Then she had no option but to go where Lane's hands were holding her, to lick her way over that salty, gaping cunt and slip her tongue into the opening, sucking away. Soon Lane pulled Carol's head up by a fraction and jutted her clit into Carol's mouth to be nipped and licked. But somehow, whatever Carol did would not be enough for her melting stone-butch girlfriend, who could never seem to let herself come in Carol's hand or mouth.

Now Lane pulled away and, looking down on Carol, folded her hand into her crotch, the middle finger touching the clit, the heel of her hand pulling up on the flesh of her mound to make her clit tighter still.

'I'm watching you now,' she warned. 'Let me see your breasts properly. Hold them for me.'

Carol pulled off her top and let her breasts completely loose from her bra, which was still done up. Looking at Lane for approval, she rubbed at her breasts, presenting the nipples for Lane to see, first pinching them erect, then licking a finger and rubbing it over one nipple. She was in tune with the moans of her voyeur lover.

'Yes,' groaned Lane. 'Oh yes, you are such a fucking slut! Look at you now! Touching yourself, just for me.' Her voice was breaking. She stared at Carol's breasts and then shut her eyes tight and came, pushing her cock back into Carol's mouth at the final moment. The thrusts of her butch's climax knocked Carol's head back against the cushions. She held Lane tight around her arse, but it was only seconds before Lane pulled out with quivering knees and fell down on the bed.

'Such a good girl,' she murmured.

'Why do you call me that?' asked Carol, meekly. 'If I'm a slut, how can I be so good?'

'You're my slut and my good girl. You do what only a slut would do, and you do what you're told.' Lane's mouth found hers and they lay down together.

'Is there anything you wouldn't do?'

'You know what I wouldn't do. Do we have to talk now? I'm so sleepy.' Carol had thought they were both dozing off, but then Lane got up to get a glass of water and livened up.

'I just want to know.'

'Well, you do know.'

'So say it.'

'I won't take anyone or anything up my arse. I don't want them whipping me. That's it really. The rest is just to do with whether it feels right, whether it's done with respect.'

'Respect? But I was calling you a slut just tonight, as usual.'

'Yes, and you call me that with respect. Not at the moment when it's said, maybe, but from respect in our relationship. Now can we drop it? I don't want to have to define everything. You fucked me. It was good. Let's sleep.'

'It's like you're hiding something. I don't know, the way you gave yourself to Derek like that, it wasn't like someone who's only just being introduced to sex with strangers. It was like someone who'd do anything.'

'Anything? Some tame sex with a liberal long-haired guy in his own back room? With his girlfriend there?' But Carol was on shaky ground, fearing Lane's suspicions. Even though she half believed her own lies, there was a nagging voice in her head telling her to get off the subject before Lane somehow sniffed out the fact that, yes, Carol was able to have adventures without her, and was doing just that with her own students.

'You're being defensive,' was all that Lane said. But Carol had a feeling, even as Lane pulled her femme's head on to her chest and yawned, that they would return to this conversation before too long.

TWELVE
Want to Know a Secret?

How things had changed. Lane half regretted the Big Deal because it seemed to be draining power from Carol. Lane was no longer her butch toygirl. Instead, she was almost Carol's master. And what was the secret that Carrie was keeping from her? Lane was becoming more and more convinced that there was something.

When Lane's friend Annie called and chastised her for having been out of touch for weeks, Lane gratefully took the chance to go and visit her in Brixton.

They were slumped in Annie's living room now. There was a kind of ritual to their meetings and Lane was pleased to slip back into it. Annie lay on the red sofa with her furry multicoloured cat, named (Bit of) Fluff. On the coffee table in front of her were a pint glass of squash, another glass filled with red wine, and a full ashtray with an active spliff in it. There were two slices left of the pizza they had ordered earlier. Lane, meanwhile, had made her usual comfortable seat from the big brown armchair and pouffe.

'You were absolutely right,' were the reassuring words she now gave her friend, in response to a long anecdote about a sandwich shop. Annie had told the man she only wanted butter if it really was butter, not margarine, and a row had ensued. 'You didn't do anything wrong. There's a difference between picky and precise!' Lane insisted.

They caught themselves, looked at each other and laughed, because as usual it was the minutiae of life that fed their conversation – and picky was exactly what they were. They both loved to seize on the little things and dissect them. It was a part of Lane that Carol found foreign, but it had served her well at work, letting her move from straight design to the wonderful world of the webpage. She now ran not only the company's own website but those of dozens of clients. And at the end of each working day she completely stopped thinking about work, because her sex life had become more hectic than anything that happened during the day.

As for Annie, the legal profession was now benefiting from her precision and sense of justice.

'How's things with you and Carol?' Annie asked, flicking idly through the dozens of TV channels at her disposal.

'Oh –' Lane was stoned now. Truly stoned. She rarely got like this except with Annie. More than anything, she wanted to tell her the whole deal. It was only a few weeks since the deal was struck but it seemed like a curtain had fallen across Lane's life that day and that, from on this side of the curtain, it was hard to look behind it. Hard to remember that she used to share almost everything with Annie. Now, she had these secrets and they were hammering in her head, trying to get out.

'Thing is,' she began, 'there's kind of a lot of stuff happening for us.'

'What like?'

'Like this deal we made. About sex.'

'What?' Annie was grinning at her, trying to guess what it could be about. Lane looked at her friend, lying there in her faded purple combats and T-shirt. Annie had fair hair with natural highlights, floppy on top and carefully sculpted at the sides. Her big brown eyes and open face were so familiar. Would they cloud over when Lane told her everything?

Lane took a deep breath, realising how stoned she was. 'OK. This is all secret, right?'

Annie nodded, intrigued.

'Well, I had sex with Jack, so –'

'You what?' Annie sat up, making Fluff leap off her with shock and indignation. Everything was always new and surprising to Fluff, who seemed to have the memory of a goldfish.

'I had sex with Jack. Oh come on, Annie, it's been on the cards for quite a long time.'

'On the cards? What are you talking about? Would you be surprised if I slept with Jason?' Annie was practically bouncing up and down, like someone whose pal has gone bonkers and must be brought back to reality.

'Umm.' Lane scrunched her eyes in mock contemplation of this ludicrous proposition. Jason: cute and clever, gay and black, was certainly as eligible as Jack. But for fuck's sake, *Annie and Jason*! No fucking way.

'What's the difference?' asked Annie.

'The difference is that Jack and I have fancied each other for years. I guess I forgot to tell you that. Ever.'

'Yes. It seems that way.'

'So, Jack and I had sex.' She paused, but Annie only grunted and huffed, already starting to get her head round it.

'Anyway,' Lane continued, 'I told Carrie about Jack, because she'd kind of guessed and things were getting weird between us and I thought it would be better to be honest.'

'And was it?'

'Yes, in a way. We made this deal. I can shag blokes if I bring other people to have sex with her.'

'Jesus. This is a bit of a turnaround. I thought you were into monogamy these days.'

'That was *last* season, dahhling!' Lane drawled in her *Ab Fab* voice.

'And now what? Have you brought any of these "people" to have sex with Carol?'

'Yeah. A few. There were these women who had a van –' She realised Annie was hoping not to get too much gory detail. 'Anyway, it's happened. A few times.'

'And how do you feel?'

'Weird. Sometimes I think I love Jack, you know, like a lover. Other times, he's just the cute guy who's initiating me into the secret ways of his tribe. When to kiss and when to drop your kecks. That kind of thing.' Annie laughed.

Lane went on to explain she'd wanted to have sex with gay men for a long time, and that Jack was willing and able. It was almost starting to sound normal.

'OK,' said Annie. 'I get the idea. But how do you actually feel?'

'Erm, fucked up.'

'You don't look it, particularly.'

'No, I'm glowing from excess sex, I dare say. But things are weird now with me and Carol. I know I should have seen it coming and all that. But the worst thing is that I think she's having some kind of affair.'

'What?'

'She's being secretive. She snaps at me if I ask too much. Sometimes she seems angry about the whole deal, as if I forced it on her. But if I suggest we give it all up, she doesn't want to. The weirdest thing was when I asked if she'd have sex with her students.'

'Carol? She wouldn't, would she? She's too ethical.'

'I don't know. I really don't know any more, Annie.'

'So talk to her, properly.'

'I don't want to know.'

'Why not?'

Lane thought about it. 'If she's having an affair, then she's betraying our deal. Why would she do that? It doesn't show much respect for me, does it? I mean, if we didn't have this deal, if we had a relationship where the worst thing you could do was to sleep with someone else, then it would be understandable if she didn't tell me what she was up to. But the way things are between us, she knows she should tell me. The only reason not to tell me is –'

'What?'

'Well, there's this other bit of the deal that I can't really tell you about. It's too personal. But basically, if Carol has sex with anyone else, then she has to let me do something specific, something she doesn't want.'

'That's terrible. You get to do what you like and your only forfeit is to have more sex – to bring people to have sex with your girlfriend, and join in. But if *she* gets up to anything then you, what, punish her?'

'It's not like that. She agreed to it. She agreed because she wasn't going to sleep with anyone else. She said she didn't want to.'

'So you have all the power?'

Lane grinned sheepishly. 'Well, you could see it like that, but she doesn't.'

'Yes she does. Of course she does. That's why she's not telling you what she's up to, if she is up to anything. Because she wants something for herself, some power. And because she doesn't want to tell you everything. And because if she did tell you everything, then you'd punish her.'

'So you're on her side?'

Annie shook her head, exasperated. 'No, I'm just saying the whole thing is transparently unfair. OK, she broke the rules, but they were completely loaded against her.'

'Which is what she wanted.'

'Why? Why would she want that?'

'Because she wants me to be in charge, always.'

'Carol wants you to be in charge? In your dreams.'

'Well, you haven't seen us having sex.'

'No, I'm pleased to say that I haven't. Just because Carol might like being the femme in bed, doesn't mean she doesn't want any power. For god's sake, Lane, she's a powerful woman, she's usually got the upper hand over you. The rest is fantasy. Where have you gone? It's like you can't tell fantasy from reality any more. You've always said that Carol was more in charge than you. Have you forgotten?'

'No.' Lane was shocked at herself. Why did it need Annie to tell her all this, which was so obvious? Perhaps it was true that she was starting to confuse real life, real relationships, with the strange dynamics of the Big Deal. Or was Annie just exaggerating because she was envious of them and didn't like to think it could be all right?

Lane asked her: 'Do you want to join in?'

'Join in? And end up like Sam, Jilly and Rose?' Annie named three friends whose fuck-buddy antics had turned sour when love reared her beautiful head. 'That's really nice of you, thanks a lot, Lane! For fuck's sake, keep things separate.'

'Yeah. You have a point. Maybe I shouldn't have told you, anyway. It's like betraying Carol to be telling you all about it.'

'So you were going to keep it all a secret and spend all your spare time fucking people who are mostly strangers, instead of chilling at your mate's house?'

'Yeah.' They laughed. It was good to be together. It was enough. They put Lara on the PlayStation and raided tombs. Who needs insane sex when you can manipulate the lithe, half-clothed body of that animated feist-fest?

So why was it that, on the way home, Lane called Jack and asked him to meet her in Russell Square?

THIRTEEN
Unfinished Business

Carol looked out of her office window at the greenery of Russell Square, where men apparently fucked each other in the night. She had only had sex there once in all her years of working at the university, and that was with Al, years ago. But they didn't wait for night.

Right now, her final tutorial student of the day didn't seem to be coming; he was twenty minutes late. She started putting her marking in her bag but there was a knock at the door. Seemed like she would have to go over Peter's crappy essay with him instead of going home and opening a bottle of wine.

'Come in!' she called irritably.

The door opened, but the face that appeared was not the pasty, unshaven face of Peter Mallow, but the healthy, deep-brown and smiling face of an attractive young woman. It was a couple of seconds before Carol had fully computed who it was. The very sight of this woman made her blush as the sensations of lust and danger flashed through her in diluted form. Only then did she consciously think: Dee from the Special Tutorial.

She gathered herself. 'Dee! Hi! Come in and sit down.'

Dee shut the door and looked around Carol's office, with its packed bookshelves and ageing computer, and the big windows overlooking the square.

'What can I do for you?' Carol asked, wondering if the girl

wanted some professional help. But something in the air suggested otherwise. For a start, Dee had not sat down. Carol, who was perching on the desk, felt somehow embarrassed and awkward.

'It's more what I can do for you, Dr Maitland,' said Dee. Her deep voice was confident, with a hint of north London. She was wearing similar baggy sports clothes to last time, but she'd done something different to her hair. Carol distracted herself by staring at the short locks.

'Er, what's that, Dee?'

'Look, if I'm out of order, you just let me know, all right? But I thought there was some unfinished business between us, know what I mean?' Dee was looking straight at her, with the same control which had dazzled Carol at Marg's flat.

'Yes, I think I do know what you mean, but this is hardly the place, is it, Dee?'

But Dee was coming towards her. 'Why not? Don't you want me? I know what you like and I'm wearing it, know what I mean?'

Carol glanced at Dee's crotch. Yes, she knew what she meant, and even through those sports pants she could see the bulge. It was difficult to argue with Dee. She was using a kind of insistent playfulness at the same time as looking steadily and with a focused desire at Carol: at her face, her chest, her legs in their tailored trousers.

'Dee! Someone might come in!'

'So lock the door.'

Carol took her keys from the pocket of her bag and handed them to Dee. They both knew she was handing over control. As Dee locked the door, Carol could only stare, her nerves on edge and blood pumping to her cunt in anticipation.

Dee turned from the door and came back to her. She placed a hand on each of Carol's shoulders and looked at her, as if to steady her. 'OK, Doctor M?'

'Yes.'

'Have you got a first name?'

The lecturer laughed. 'Carol. Or Carrie.' What made her say that? Only Lane and one or two close friends called her Carrie.

'Carrie? I like that.'

'Oh, corny!' Carol laughed awkwardly. How had she allowed this to go so far? She took off her glasses and held on to them nervously.

'Hey! It's OK. We're cool. Come here.' Dee leant in and kissed her. A buzz went through them both and Carol remembered the urgency she'd felt at the Special Tutorial, how much she wanted Dee. It all came back to her as she pressed her mouth to Dee's, letting the girl's tongue delve deeper.

At the same time, one of Dee's hands moved from Carol's shoulder to her breast, stroking gently over the thin fabric of her summer blouse. It was open at the neck and Dee undid another button even as she kissed Carol harder. She slipped a hand inside and under the lace of Carol's bra. As Dee's fingers brushed her nipple, Carol shuddered with desire. She opened her legs and Dee shifted round to stand between them, pressing her crotch into Carol's.

'This way round's kind of boring, don't you think?' asked Dee. 'Turn around, Carrie.'

Carol stood and turned her back on Dee, then moaned as the young woman pushed her down on the desk and started to undo those tailored trousers. She pulled off Carol's shoes and trousers and stood between her legs. Then she grabbed Carol's arms and pinned them to the table.

'Is this what you want, Carrie?'

'Yes. Oh, yes! Fuck me, Dee!'

'OK. You don't know how much I've been thinking about this moment. Planning how I'd fuck you over your desk. And here we are, babes. Fucking A!' And Carol felt the familiar threatening thickness of a big dildo pressing at her cuntlips.

'Fuck me!' she cried again, as Dee wasted no time in pushing into her, while still holding her down. She knew they should be quiet, that there might be colleagues working in the adjoining offices who would hear them. But that just added to the excitement that was making her cry out.

Dee forced the thick cock inside her and Carol's cunt opened gladly to it, as wet and ready as if they had been flirting for hours instead of minutes. Pinned to the table, at the service of this girl she barely knew, Carol was close to ecstasy. There were no curtains at the window and, although they were on the second floor, she had the strange impression that they could be seen from the street, that even now people were watching the handsome young butch taking Carol from behind.

'Oh, that's good!' moaned Dee. 'I knew you'd like a dildo; I saw the way you took it from Billy the other night. I thought, there's a woman who needs some cock. I've got to give her what she wants.'

'Yes! Yes! You're right, that's what I need,' cried Carol, realising that Dee's sexuality was like Lane Lite – a friendlier version of that steely butch style.

But she was too quick to judge, because suddenly Dee ripped off Carol's blouse without undoing it. 'Sorry,' she said even as she did it, 'but I can't reach your tits.' She seemed unable to control her lust for Carol. Even as she spoke to her quite sensibly, she was shredding Carol's clothing and grabbing at her tits, pulling on her nipples with each thrust of that big cock.

Carol was screaming and moaning uncontrollably now. They had both given in to their need for each other. But they froze suddenly at the sound of someone twisting the doorknob.

'Carol?' called a familiar voice. 'Are you all right? What's all that noise?'

'Ignore her,' whispered Carol, waiting for her colleague to go away.

Instead, a key turned in the door and suddenly Petra was in the room. Dee did a strange thing. Instead of pulling out of Carol or even shouting at the woman to fuck off, she simply turned Carol's head to face Petra.

'Busy, are you?' asked Petra, towering over Carol, who was pressed against the desk with Dee inside her.

'You could say that,' panted Carol.

'I'll stay till you're free.' Petra turned and locked the door behind her with her own key, then sat in a chair and picked up a journal.

No one questioned this ludicrous suggestion. There was nothing to be done. Carol was close to orgasm and was not about to send Dee away. Dee kissed her neck and pulled out of her slightly, then plunged back in to the hilt, so that the buckles of her harness were rubbing against Carol's arse. She held on to Carol's heavy breasts and pulled them this way and that as she groaned in time with Carol.

'You are so good to fuck,' she told the older woman. 'I've been waiting for this, God, I've been waiting.'

'I know,' Carol moaned in reply, thinking of the fantasies she'd been having about Dee – and picturing her arrogant friend, Petra, sitting in that chair and watching.

With each thrust, Carol's clit was pressed against the wood of the table and she felt herself move closer to orgasm. But suddenly, Dee's fingers were on her clit and Carol was shouting out with release, coming immediately, her cunt gripping and releasing around Dee's cock.

'Oh, yes!' she cried, filled with cock and filled with shame as she thought of how she was being watched by a colleague.

Dee pulled out of her and rolled her over to kiss her on the lips, on the nipples, in the sweat-drenched channel between her breasts, in her wet bush. Dee dropped to her knees and licked very lightly at Carol's clit while touching herself. It was only seconds before she came, her mouth wide with a muted groan. She kissed and kissed at Carol's pulsing cunt.

'OK,' said Petra suddenly. 'I think it's over now, isn't it? Who's this anyway? Isn't she one of Clive's students?'

Carol sat up and looked at each of them. It was the first time she'd seen fear on Dee's face.

What was it like to have that kind of class power and abuse it the way that Petra so often did? The thin white woman in her impeccable clothes and make-up looked and sounded, in these circumstances, like the keeper of the bourgeois rules. Not for the first time, Carol wondered why she stayed friends with Petra. But then, who was really in the wrong now? Could it be the lecturer who, naked in her office, her clothes in tatters, allowed herself to be fucked by a young female student?

Dee was pulling the waistband of her tracksuit trousers up over her dildo and wiping her face. She touched Carol's face, murmuring, 'See you around, babes,' and had now regained her self-possession enough to send a glare at Petra on her way out.

Petra unlocked the door for Dee and locked it again behind her.

They were alone; Petra in a pure white blouse and subtle checked trousers, Carol in her ripped blouse, her pants twisted around one buttock.

Petra played with the keys as she looked down at Carol. 'I thought you were up to something, Carol Maitland, but I never thought I'd get to see and hear it quite so graphically.'

'You wouldn't have done, if you hadn't let yourself into my room uninvited.'

'I could hear you at the other end of the corridor, for God's sake. Everyone could bloody well hear you. You fool! Look at you.'

Carol got down from the desk and adjusted her underwear. She pulled on her trousers and dug around in her desk drawer for her running T-shirt. As she pulled it over her head, Petra was still tutting away.

'Have you got a point to make, Petra?' asked Carol.

'Yes. I want to know who that was. I want to know what a Special Tutorial is. And then I'll decide what else I want.'

'What do you mean, Special Tutorial?' Carol knew her voice was trembling.

'Just something I heard some girls talking about, that's all. Dr Maitland's Special Tutorial. And I thought, what's that? Just a natural curiosity, you know what I'm like.'

'Yes, I know what you're like. You're a nosy, dangerous cow.'

'Well, that's a very adult way of engaging, Carol. Would it be better if I had this conversation with the Prof?'

Professor Jones was one of the few black men who had got on in the college and also one of the few people in authority there who believed in putting students first, before research and before the egos of his colleagues. He and Carol were allies on many a committee. He was unlikely to be entertained by what Petra might tell him.

'I'll tell you,' said Carol. 'But try and remember we're friends, OK?'

Lane stood outside the office door. It was unusual for it to be shut and she wondered if Carol was already on her way home. But then she heard voices:

'So come to the Special Tutorial.' This sounded like Carol, although not her normal voice, almost distraught.

'Perhaps I will. But will that be enough?'

Who was that? Lane knocked on the door.

Carol's voice called, 'Who is it?'

'It's me.'

'Who?'

'Lane!'

'Oh . . . just a second.'

What could be going on for Carol to be too distracted to even recognise Lane's voice? Lane tried the door but it was locked. Why would Carol have locked the door from the inside? It was Petra who opened it, offering a fake smile. Of course, that other voice belonged to the college cow.

'We can speak again about this,' the cow said to Carol.

Lane looked at Carol as Petra hovered between them.

'What happened to you?' Lane asked her lover, who was wearing a grotty old T-shirt with crumpled office trousers and no shoes.

'Me? We went for a run. I'm just getting changed. Actually, I think I'll have a shower.' She seemed absurdly distracted. She went out, but Petra didn't.

'What's going on?' Lane asked Petra.

'What do you mean?'

'Why are you in the office with the door locked?'

'We were getting changed after our run,' Petra said calmly.

'Where are your sweaty shorts, then?'

'Oh, kinky!'

'Anyone would think the two of you were having an affair.'

Petra laughed haughtily. 'That is rich. Didn't I see you with your young man just a couple of weeks ago? Out on the town all cosy together?'

'Listen, Petra, I'm not messing about here. Something's not right, and I wouldn't put it past you to be coming on to Carol.'

'Well, thank you for being so honest.' The sarcasm poured from Petra like vinegar from a bottle of Sarsons. 'I agree that your lover is rather gorgeous, but funnily enough she is not interested in me. Perhaps you haven't noticed, but I'm not quite as butch as she likes them. Not quite as rough around the edges, either. I don't think wild guesses are going to work on this little puzzle.' She turned on her heel. 'Lovely to see you again,' she added without looking back.

Lane was left to sit in the window, cursing Petra, looking out on Russell Square and wondering whether the excitement of last night, when she cruised there with Jack, was worth the confusion of Carol's strange behaviour. Was one the payoff for the other? Or was it just a coincidence that, since they had struck their deal, Carol had grown more and more distracted?

FOURTEEN
Passing in the Night

It was less than twenty-four hours since Lane had met Jack at the gates to the square, pocketed a handful of condoms and lube sachets, and listened to his warnings about police, queerbashers and HIV.

'Don't stick too close to me,' he said. 'Otherwise, people think you're a couple. It doesn't matter that much but it narrows your market. If you pull, I'll keep an eye on you. If I pull, you can watch or whatever. Play it by ear, OK? But don't go off with anyone!'

'OK.' Even as she agreed, she felt nervous, wondering what she was getting herself into. A dyke in a gay men's cruising ground. Wasn't she asking for trouble? They started to walk through the quiet, unlit square, peering about as their eyes grew accustomed to the dark. Lane's heartbeat quickened further as she caught sight of men looking at her, men appearing and disappearing in the gloom.

It wasn't long before she discerned a pattern to the men's movements. They were either leaning against trees waiting for you to come to them, or walking in a slow but purposeful way in giant circles. She heard noises from the bushes and stopped to listen. It was the sound of branches cracking underfoot. Then she thought she heard a groan.

As she stood on the path, listening, a man approached her and asked for a light. She flipped open her Zippo and they assessed

135

each other in the light cast by the flame. But then he walked on. Had he recognised her as a woman? It didn't seem like it, more like she just wasn't his type. Suddenly, Lane was more interested in passing as a man than in whether she actually fancied any of the guys.

She hurried to catch up with Jack. He was standing on the path, staring at something or someone. As she got closer, she saw that a young man was leaning against a tree returning Jack's gaze.

It was a warm, still night and this man was wearing just T-shirt and jeans. The tight, white T-shirt shone in the moonlight, showing off his fine physique. He was still, except for the toe of one of his trainers, which kicked at the grass. Jack approached him and Lane drew closer. They spoke in voices almost too low for her to hear. She caught a few of Jack's words: 'Whatever you want.'

The man touched Jack's arm but Jack glanced back at Lane and said something. The man nodded and Jack beckoned her over. 'This is my friend,' he said, by way of introducing her. She looked at the man. He was a 90s clone, cropped dark hair, muscled forearms, thin waist. The glimmer of a coloured tattoo curved out of the cuffed sleeve of his T-shirt.

'This guy's active,' said Jack. No name. They said hi to each other. His voice sounded so deep compared to hers and he noticed.

He took hold of Lane and looked harder at her. 'You a girl?' he asked, without expression but with a strong Scottish accent. Lane nodded, her heart beating faster. 'You ever take it up the arse?' Again, she nodded. 'I've never done a girl,' he said, still looking at her.

'She's well trained,' said Jack, as if selling a horse.

'OK.' His mind was made up. 'What's in it for you?'

'She can fuck me,' said Jack. Lane touched her flies. Her fingers met the resistance of her hard dildo, which strained against the canvas of her trousers. On the way to meet Jack, she had stopped off at a tourist hotel to strap on in the ladies and take off her boxer shorts, which might get in the way of any action.

'Whatever,' said the man.

They had not moved away from the path, and now two other men were watching the encounter. As the stranger led them into the bushes, Lane was aware of the other shadowy figures following just a few metres behind. She was scared of what she had committed herself to, and of the other men who might make further demands on any or all of them.

Although she knew Russell Square in daylight, and knew really that there were no areas of bushland where men could lose themselves, she was still surprised when they stopped on the grass between two trees. Could they really fuck each other in the open like this?

The answer was clear as the men took hold of each other's belt buckles and unclasped them. Jack slid down the other man's flies and grabbed Lane's hand. He pushed it into the man's trousers, at the same time undoing Lane's combats and reaching for her dildo.

Lane's hand closed on the man's thick, short rod. It was hard and filled her hand. She was both drawn and repulsed by it. She didn't even know him and now she had his dick in her hand. But she had no time to think about it, as Jack was pulling down his own trousers and briefs and bending over the low branch of one of the trees. She took her hand from the stranger's cock and pulled a condom from her pocket which she rolled on to him the way she had learnt from Jack. Then she rubbed on the lube as his head fell back and his mouth opened in a low moan.

He followed her over to Jack. Her hands fumbled to roll a condom over her own rubber cock, but holding it reassured her and she got there. She bent to enter Jack, rubbing her lubed cockhead against his tight hole with one hand, wrapping the other arm round the top of his thigh to steady herself and to cup a hand around his balls.

'Are you ready for this?' she asked Jack, who only grunted in reply.

Warm hands pulled down on her waistband and she gasped as the cold, wet head of the stranger's cock pressed into her crack. 'That's a girl's arse, all right,' he said, grabbing at her buttocks. 'Better make sure I get the right hole!' He laughed to himself.

As she pushed into Jack, the man pushed into her, slowly but firmly. They all groaned as two thick cocks entered two holes. Her hole gaped for him; her tunnel gulped him up in painful spasms. Her whole body was open to the experience that had only been a scary fantasy until this moment: a stranger fucking her in a cruising ground.

'Take it all, show me how well trained you are,' he ordered her in that deep Scottish voice.

The other men were moving in and unzipping their trousers. She was just aware of them taking their places at either end of the chain. She dropped her hand from Jack's balls as one of the men pushed his dick into Jack's mouth, while the other was talking in a low voice, a few feet behind her.

'Can you take this?' he asked the man who was servicing Lane.

Suddenly a sharp shove into Lane's behind told her that the answer was yes. The Scotsman was thrusting harder in her with the force of what was happening to him. They were groaning and screwing in unison now, each man's thrust pushing her forward to fuck Jack harder. He was anchored by the tree branch and his resistance sent a shockwave back through them all, forcing them to buck their hips back before the next thrust.

Lane's rectum was stretched around that thick cock, the sensation coming in waves as it slid back and forth, deep inside her. She had felt that before, but she had never felt it like this, where the force of one man's thrusting inside her was just one half of the equation, which her own cock answered by thrusting into the arse of her prostrate friend.

He was holding her by the hips, pulling her into him with each thrust, and they were all moaning and calling out in low but intense voices as the whole chain of them built towards climax.

'Take it, show me you take it like a man!' she was told again. Lane was full, her whole body pounding, the Scotsman's fierce orders and the illicit shouts of the other men adding to her pleasure, as she pushed a hand past the base of her dildo to touch her swollen clit. The back of her hand pressed against Jack's arsecheek with each thrust.

Jack was still giving head but the lucky recipient was shouting, 'That's it! Shit, that's it!' as if he was close to coming.

'All together!' shouted one of the men, and they all groaned with the thrill of aiming for one perfect simultaneous explosion.

Lane moved one finger expertly up and down her clit as she

fucked Jack and took it from the stranger, all the time shouting 'Yes! Yes!' as if she had no other vocabulary but the vocabulary of need and desire.

'Take it!' shouted the Scotsman again and again as he pounded her guts without mercy, screwing her aching tunnel till she started to wail with the intensity that built in her centre and then shot through her amid the shouts in front and behind. Her finger was vibrating against her clit as she came, slamming against Jack's arse at the same moment that the Scotsman slammed up against her with a short series of shuddering thrusts and a great roar of release.

Their chorus was too loud, she knew that. All her fears of discovery only added to the shudders that ran through her nerves as they all fell forward, the Scotsman collapsing on top of her as she fell on to Jack. Propped up by the tree, he anchored them all for several seconds before he collapsed on the ground, with the domino effect following him, so that Lane was falling, sandwiched between him and the man whose cock still filled her tunnel. She shouted, 'Watch out!'

They all shouted, but they couldn't help but pile on top of each other. To her internal battering Lane could now add the pain of a well-built man falling on top of her. Squashed between him and Jack, she shouted, 'Get off me! For fuck's sake!'

A silence fell. 'Is that a girl?' asked a gruff voice.

'Fucking dyke, innit?' replied his friend. 'Jesus! They're everywhere these days.' Then, to Lane, 'You want to watch yourself, love. Not everyone's so understanding as us, you know?'

The two friends were standing, watching the others on the ground. Her Scotsman slowly withdrew his cock from deep inside her. She groaned with pleasure at the pure sensation as inch after inch slid from her hole.

Finally, he rolled off her, keeping an affectionate hand on her bum. 'Nice arse you've got there,' he told her.

'What you doing fucking a girl?' asked one of the other men.

'You should try it some time,' he replied. 'Makes a change.'

'Why, what's the difference?'

'They moan different.'

Even Lane laughed at this. She was still lying on top of Jack, her dildo deep inside him, but he hadn't complained, hadn't even moved. Now he murmured, 'Laney, let me go.'

As she pulled out of him, she wondered at the way he had taken it from her and sucked on some stranger's cock without complaint. There was clearly a bigger submissive side to Jack than she had realised. He moaned, 'Oh, yeah,' as she withdrew.

She rolled off the condom and chucked it on the ground, then kissed his muscled arse. 'You're a good fuck, cuteboy.'

'Hey!' he protested. 'Less of the cute, girlie!'

He rolled over and grabbed her, kissing her fiercely. 'Don't forget who the trainer is here.'

One of the other men said, 'Nothing to see here, Barry,' and they walked away.

'I'll leave you to it,' said the Scotsman. He pushed their heads together and added, 'Lovebirds.' Chuckling, he was gone.

'Laney,' said Jack. 'Let's go home.'

Lane came out of her reverie. Carol was back in the office and the professor was at the door.

'Good evening, Dr Maitland!' he called. 'My secretary *heard* you had someone *in* this afternoon.' Was that a Caribbean inflexion, or some kind of double entendre? Lane glanced at Carol, who looked thrown.

'Professor Jones! Hello! Have you met my partner, Lane Wolfson?'

'Lane! Yes, of course, we met at the awards ceremony last year. Oh, well, I'm pleased to see there's nothing untoward going on here. Although, there's a time and a place, you know, Carol, a time and a place . . .' And he wandered off.

'What's he talking about?' asked Lane.

'God knows. Shall we go home?'

'Yeah, OK, if you've finished for the day. Maybe you'll treat me to an explanation of why this place seems to have turned into Weirdsville.'

'Has it?' Carol asked, but she didn't look at Lane.

FIFTEEN
The Opening Ceremony

All the girls were there when Carol arrived. She nodded at everyone and beckoned Dee into the kitchen.

The younger woman took her hand in a gesture that seemed remarkably generous to Carol, who said, 'Dee, I am so sorry about what happened in my office.'

'I'm not!' Dee was smiling that sexy smile.

'I don't mean, you know, the sex. I mean the interruption. I should have protected you from Petra, but –'

'But there's something about being caught with your pants down that stops you from speaking up?'

'Yes.'

'Don't worry about it.'

'Well,' said Carol, 'I am worried about it, because Petra's coming tonight.'

'She's what?'

'She promised not to tell anyone about you and me if she could come to the Special Tutorial.'

'How'd she even know about it?'

'I don't know. She said she'd overheard something.'

'So she's blackmailing you?'

'No. We've reached an understanding.'

Dee draped her arms over Carol's shoulders and looked at her the way a lover looks at her woman. 'Don't worry about it.'

'Would you stop saying that?' She kissed Dee gently on the cheek.

'I tell you what, I would not jump *her* in her office!'

'Is that what you did, jump me?'

Dee considered. 'What did it feel like from your end?'

'My end hasn't recovered.' They laughed and Dee kissed her, gently and persuasively.

'Do you want us to scare her off? We could come up with something, between the lot of us.' Dee raised her eyebrows.

'No. Let her have things her way for tonight.'

'And have *you* her way?' asked Dee.

'Maybe. I've told her that she can have whatever she wants.'

'Dangerous shit, Doctor M, fucking dangerous shit.'

Carol kissed her, then undraped Dee's arms. 'Enough doom. An orgy is an orgy, wouldn't you say? Let's get out there!'

They returned to the living room just as a bemused Marg was showing Petra into the flat. 'Oh, Dr Maitland! Here's Dr Hill. She says you asked her along.' The girl was straining to speak normally while gurning at Carol. The subtext seemed to be: Abandon Plan A, enemy aboard!

'That's all right, Marg. Dr Hill is joining our tutorial for this evening.'

'Right.' Marg managed to invest the word with its opposite meaning.

'Do you want to talk to me privately?' asked Carol.

'No, you're the boss, Doctor M.'

Petra was swanning about, saying hello to those she knew, introducing herself with rather too much ceremony to those she didn't. She finally took a moment to greet Carol. 'I didn't know what to expect,' she said as she kissed Carol on each cheek. 'But you've got some of the cutest girls on campus here, haven't you?'

'Yes.'

'And you were keeping them to yourself. Naughty!' Then Petra dropped her facade. 'I want you,' she said, under her breath, with convincing lust. 'And I don't want to wait all night for you. What happens here?'

'Everyone has a lot of sex, what do you think?'

'And is there an order of ceremonies, so to speak?'

'We've only done it once. I asked them all what they were into, but we don't need to ask them again because, believe me, I can remember. It's burnt into my third eye. I see it when I fall asleep and when I wake up in the morning. Young women fucking each other like they've only just learnt how to do it.'

'Most of them probably have. They look like first years.'

'Not all of them. But, OK, the average age is probably twenty. So they have less experience between the lot of them than me – or you.' Carol was enjoying herself now. It was like having an ally, a co-tutor.

'Who are they all? I hardly recognise anyone.'

'The blonde girl with the impressive chest is Becca. She comes in a boxed set with the insecure butch, Deville. The girl who brought you in is Marg. She lives here with Amy, who's quieter but knows what she wants. She's the elegant black girl, with the long braids.'

'And the others?'

'Less distinctive. Or perhaps I don't take enough notice of them. I always get distracted by the more unusual students, it's one of my flaws. But there is one girl called Billy who knows how to use a dildo –' Carol mugged, recalling the moment when Billy had thrust inside her where they stood.

Petra was unimpressed. 'Well, if you've nothing planned for your opener tonight, I think I may have the very thing,' she said. 'I've wanted you for a long time, Carrie, you know that, don't you?'

'Yes.'

'How about we show these girls how it's done?'

Carol raised an eyebrow. 'Convince me.'

Petra put her hand on Carol's mound. She didn't lift the short skirt but stretched her fingers across the fabric and stroked down either side of Carol's cunt, flicking her clit with one finger through the skirt. Her aim was precise, her touch just firm enough to get a reaction. Carol started to melt.

She had trouble controlling her breathing as she told Petra: 'You can't kiss me. And you can't have Dee.'

'What, Clive's prodigy? Don't want her. I know where she's been.'

'Thanks, Petra, that's flattering.' Carol walked away and took a seat on a floor cushion, her back against the arm of the sofa, to talk to Becca and Deville. She wondered aloud whether Deville would be up to watching her lover being fucked all over again.

'We all have to grow out of our jealousy,' Deville told her in all seriousness.

'That sounds great in theory,' Carol replied, 'but what happens to your relationship while you're fighting your jealousy?'

Becca shook her head. 'Why are you trying to put us off? Coming here has been really good for us. It's opening us up to new stuff, you know?'

Carol had a sense of *déjà vu*. These girls knew no more than she had known at their age. Was she taking advantage of their naivety? The bong was doing the rounds and when it reached Carol she took the chance to lose some of her worries.

The girls were more relaxed than last time and already the action was beginning, with Billy, Gemma and Amy sitting in a row, their hands down the back of each other's trousers, while Dee and Leila (to Carol's distaste) were kissing on the sofa.

Marg came over to talk to her and Carol asked what the music was. 'Garbage,' said Marg.

'Well, saved me saying it!' said Carol.

'No, that's what the band's called, Doctor M.'

'I know.'

'Oh, right. Sorry.'

'Marg, tell me something.' Carol saw the girl brighten at the attention from her favourite lecturer and dominatrix. 'Why do you like being whipped?'

'Why do you like doing it?' asked Marg.

'I asked first,' said Carol. 'I don't get it. All that pain.'

'OK. When you're turned on, right, it's like this buzz going through you?' Carol nodded. 'So, when you get whipped, the pain's not like normal. It's mediated by the buzz. Plus it kind of *adds* to the buzz?' Her Stateside inflexion turned half her sentences into questions but Carol just nodded again.

Marg's hand was resting casually on Carol's thigh as she asked: 'What do you get out of doing the whipping?'

'I'd never done it before I did it to you.'

'Yeah, you said. Kind of an honour for me, then.'

'I wouldn't say that, Marg. But I was surprised to find that I do like it, I am turned on by it. It's just a bit worrying for me. In every other field of life, I believe in being non-violent if you possibly can. Then when it comes to pleasure, to sex, I end up lashing a girl half my age. Making her scream and getting off on it.'

Marg was smiling. 'Yeah, but as you would say in class, Doctor M, you haven't quite answered my question.'

'Which was?'

'Ah, come on, don't you know?'

'Yes, I know. Why do I like whipping your sweet ass?' (Carol's attempt at an American accent was laughed off by Marg.) 'The power. It surges through me, takes me over. I don't get that normally in sex, because I'm usually the bottom and that's a different kind of power. You should know about that, though.' They grinned at each other, complicit submissives.

But their cosy tête-à-tête was interrupted by the roaming Petra, who bent her face to Carol's and said quietly but firmly, 'Come with me.'

Carol gave a wave to Marg and followed Petra out of the room and into one of the bedrooms. Although she had fucked both the girls of the house, Carol had never been in either of their bedrooms. This one was clearly Amy's: tidy, modern, with French literature and black politics on the bookshelves and a couple of fashion magazines by the bed.

But Carol didn't have long for her inspection. Petra shut the door and said, 'Take off your clothes.'

'What?'

'Oh, come on Carol, we are at an orgy. I don't think it's such an unusual request.'

'We prefer not to call it an orgy,' said Carol. 'To me it's just my Special Tutorial.'

'Yes, with your special girls. I know. And now it's time for a special lesson for them all. I'm going to teach them how to make their favourite tutor come, slowly and tantalisingly.' It still sounded like a threat. As Petra came towards her, Carol pulled her lycra top off over her head. She wasn't wearing a bra and Petra's eyes opened wide.

'I've been waiting to see those tits of yours again,' she said, reaching out a hand and stroking one breast.

Carol moaned, surprised at how turned on she was now.

'What are you going to do to me?' she asked Petra.

The uber-femme kissed her. 'I'm going to use you as a visual aid, of sorts. The lesson is, how to make you come, as I said. And I will employ many skills. Licking your cunt and your clit in slow motion, for instance.'

'I told you not to kiss me.'

The next kiss went straight through Carol in a white heat. Petra's tongue seemed sharp as it slid between her teeth; Petra's fingers tightened on Carol's nipples and then played over the smooth skin of her full breasts.

Carol was wearing a short black skirt over stockings and a suspender belt. When she got dressed for this evening, she had planned that she would keep her clothes on throughout the session and that Petra and the girls would just see flashes of the stockings. But now Petra's hands were on the fastening of the skirt and Carol shuddered at the feel of those hands on her naked waist – and at the thought of appearing before the girls half-dressed.

They were still kissing, their tongues jostling for power and moans escaping from their throats, as Petra let the skirt drop to the floor. She reached down to stroke Carol's mons and a shock went through them both as Petra touched curly pubic hair.

'Oh, Carol!' she teased. 'Where are your knickers? Did you forget to put them on? What will those young women think when they see their role model with no pants? No bra, no pants. It's just not respectable.'

Carol was moaning and her nerves were all on edge. 'Please, Petra, let's go back.' She realised she was begging and tried for a lighter touch. 'You don't want them to start without us, do you?'

'No, I don't. But it's really my decision now, isn't it? You don't look too powerful there, in your stockings. Funny, my view of you has changed lately. I haven't seen you in a full set of clothes for more than half an hour at a time.'

'Take me out there, Petra. I want you to have me.'

'OK.' Petra smiled like a baddie in a Disney film, but at least she was doing it on purpose, this time. 'I'll have my way with you, my pretty one.'

'Yeah, right,' said Carol. But when Petra turned her around and pushed her towards the door, one hand on her naked arse, Carol gasped.

From the doorway of the living room, she saw that the women had formed little groups and were kissing and feeling each other up without any self-consciousness. But it was only seconds before all action stopped and all eyes were on Carol, her bare breasts, her naked cunt and her stockings. She was still wearing her pointed shoes but now she kicked them off, embarrassed. In the back of her mind was this thought: Why are you embarrassed about your shoes? You are being humiliated in front of your girls.

But this was not really a humiliation. These young women were still full of admiration for Carol and it was Petra whom they eyed suspiciously.

'Girls,' said Carol, trying to speak calmly. 'Dr Hill is in charge tonight, as you can see. Please show her the respect that you showed me at our last tutorial.'

Petra was standing behind Carol, her hands on her shoulders proprietorially. They were just inside the doorway, commanding the room. Everyone watched as Petra slid both her hands down Carol's front, over her breasts, over the curve of her belly, over her bush and up and down the inside of her thighs. Petra was so tall that she hardly needed to move except for those hands with their long, manicured fingers and smooth skin.

She tucked her hands into Carol's suspender belt and started to speak to the assembled women in their various states of undress: 'Good evening, girls. You will see that things will be a little different at this evening's Special Tutorial. I am going to show you how to give Dr Maitland what she wants and needs. I am also going to show you what it is that I like. What I feel driven to do to those beautiful women who need to be teased and tantalised to orgasm by the most delicate and careful means. You will find that just when someone moans for release is when you should deny her; that when a woman begs you to fuck her is when you should barely touch her.'

Petra had their full attention as she continued, her voice intense but her breathing apparently normal as she stroked Carol's pubic hair. 'This is the kind of thing you can always start with. You girls may be used to more swift and immediate satisfaction but, believe me, there is more than one way to make a woman scream.'

Deville raised her hand, as if in a lecture. 'Dr Hill?'

'Yes, your name and your question, please.'

'I'm Deville Logan. I'd like to ask you whether we can touch each other while we're watching.'

'Certainly, Deville. But I'd prefer it if you used this time to practise what I'm actually showing you, rather than using your own ideas.'

The girl nodded and the others looked at each other with a mixture of expressions. Becca was blushing. She seemed embarrassed that it should have been her lover who asked such a question. But Marg had already pulled off her shorts and was now pulling off Sheila's skirt, obviously hoping that this girl who had been tied up throughout the last session was going to take a more active interest in this one. Red was so turned on that she started to kiss Sheila even as Marg was undressing her.

On the sofas and rugs, in three groups, the girls looked so sexy and so willing that Carol almost forgot her own position as the evening's demonstration model. But how could she forget, when Petra was holding her round the waist with one arm and playing with her tits with the other?

Carol couldn't control herself: she was already bucking her hips back against Petra's groin and moaning, her head rubbing against Petra's chest.

'I need someone to take my place here while I progress with the details,' said Petra. Carol looked longingly at Dee but the black woman was shaking her head in disgust at Petra's suggestion. She clearly thought that Carol was worth more than this. What she didn't understand was that Carol was on fire, longing to be used by Petra, however she saw fit.

It was Billy who stood up and came to Petra's aid. She left Gemma and Amy to tend to each other's needs and took over from Petra, wrapping her arms around Carol from behind and thrusting against her so that Carol felt Billy's cock pressing into her arse through the denim of the girl's jeans. The lecturer remembered the last time, how Billy had taken her after servicing Becca, had ripped down her knickers to get to her wet cunt. If only that could happen now, but instead she was sentenced to a long and slow build-up that was already making her feel faint.

'I've got you, Dr Maitland,' Billy told her, stroking Carol's naked body as if she owned it.

'Good,' said Petra. 'Keep doing that while I eat some pussy.'

Carol moaned and heard herself beg: 'No, fuck me!' but no one took any notice. She was able to watch the girls copying them. Dee stood up and hauled Leila to her feet, wrapped her strong arms round her from behind and started to touch her neat pubes. Amy abandoned Gemma and fell to the floor between Leila's muscled, footballer's legs. The three black girls were watched by Marg, who was out of her depth. Without any whipping, it seemed, she was lost.

The others were touching each other as their eyes stayed glued to Petra, who was kneeling in front of Carol. The first touch of Petra's mouth to her cunt made Carol groan with relief, but it was ages before the second touch and she bucked her hips so much, trying to get her cunt to come in contact with those lips, that Billy grasped her tighter and pinched at one vulnerable nipple.

'Lick her out!' called Deville.

'Yeah,' said Red. 'Slurp on it.'

'What's her pussy taste like?' asked Deville.

'That's enough!' snapped Petra, turning away from Carol to chastise the students. 'Show some respect!'

Then she resumed her task, licking ever so lightly at Carol's pussy lips; pushing her tongue between them to enter the first millimetre of her cunt, then licking lightly over her clit. As Carol moaned and cried out for release, Petra sat back on her heels and smiled to herself, then reached out a finger to tease a bead of juice from Carol's entrance and rub it over her clit.

'Fuck me, Petra, please!' she cried, but her tormentor laughed.

'No, oh no, Dr Maitland. First of all, let's be professional about this. I don't think first names are appropriate in this context.'

'You bitch,' moaned Carol. 'Touch me.'

'Oh dear,' said Petra. 'That's exactly the kind of language we don't want. I'll have to make you wait now, while you reconsider how you want to address me.' And the brunette stood up and left the room. Billy saw her opportunity and pushed her fingers between Carol's labia from behind.

'Yes, yes! Oh, thank you! Do it to me!' Carol had no sooner cried out than Petra was back in the room.

'What is going on here?' she demanded.

'I'm touching Dr Maitland,' said Billy. 'She needs it.'

'I decide who needs it,' Petra replied sharply. 'Take your seat, girl. Dee! Come up here!'

'No!' said Dee. 'I'm needed here. Do your own dirty work.'

'It takes more than one to control this woman properly,' said Petra, unfazed by Dee's insubordination. 'Perhaps you don't realise that.'

Petra grabbed Carol by the arm as Billy released her.

Carol was wet with sweat, her hair sticking to her face and tears welling up in her eyes as she longed for someone to relieve her from this limbo. Her cunt was swollen and alive with feeling, but it needed to be fucked. Her clit was pulsing each time that she clenched her cunt muscles, but she needed someone to touch it.

And then Marg surprised everyone by standing up and walking behind Carol, gripping her by the shoulders. 'I'll hold her, Dr Hill,' she told the new mistress of ceremonies.

'Why?' asked Carol.

'To see what it's like to be the tormentor,' said Marg, simply. But she kissed Carol's neck to reassure her.

'Bring that chair,' ordered Petra.

Marg picked up the dining chair that was pointed out to her. Once again, Petra held Carol by one arm. When the chair was placed beside her, Petra pushed Carol down into it and Marg knelt behind to hold her down.

As Marg's arms folded under Carol's naked breasts, pushing them up, Petra knelt to pull her legs apart. 'Can everyone see?' she asked.

There was silence for a second, then the girls quietly answered yes.

Petra pulled apart Carol's labia. 'Look at her cunt. It's so wet. I'm going to touch it now,' she said. Carol moaned at the touch and prayed that it would continue. It did. With one finger, Petra played at the entrance to her fanny. With the other hand, she played with the top of one stocking, sliding her fingers under it and along the sensitive skin of Carol's inner thigh, then up to stroke right up to that cunt. For a few seconds, all the fingers of both hands ran along Carol's drenched cuntlips. Her mouth was open and she wanted someone, anyone, to kiss.

'Kiss me,' she begged to the room, her eyes looking first into Dee's. But the strong butch was toying with Leila's nipples and she looked away from Carol. Leila's moans were mounting now and other girls joined her with their own low sounds. Deville had Becca in her lap and was teasing her lover by touching her cunt very slowly while rolling one nipple between the fingers of the other hand.

'Dr Hill,' said Carol, now sunk so low that she was even calling Petra by her professional title, as requested. 'Please kiss me.'

To her surprise, Petra kneeled up to kiss her, but she let her hands slip from Carol's fanny. She kissed Carol on the lips with an eager passion that seemed to contradict her prolonged foreplay and Carol melted into it.

When Petra pulled her mouth away, she ducked back to Carol's pussy and started to eat it with that same passion, moaning her appreciation.

'Can I kiss her, Dr Hill?' asked Marg.

'Yes.'

'Oh, yes!' cried Carol. Then Marg let go of her from behind and came round to kiss her. The girl's small mouth closed on Carol's and then she straddled her by sitting on the arms of the chair. She started playing with Carol's breasts and Carol let all her desperation out in that kiss as Petra finally pushed her fingers into that wet opening and started to pump her.

With the two women fulfilling every part of her, Carol let herself give in to the fucking, her cunt tightening and releasing in time with Petra's quickening thrusts, her clit sending shockwaves through her body with each focused lick.

Now everyone in the room was moaning and crying out but

Carol could only groan from the back of her throat as Marg's kiss deepened again and they were all locked together in a single aim.

Petra stopped abruptly. Marg stopped too and said: 'How long can you wait now, Dr Maitland?' It was as if she was Petra's accomplice and Carol felt betrayed.

'Please, Dr Hill, I need to come,' said Carol.

'I know, but it's good to have the discipline to wait just a minute or two.'

Carol couldn't even touch herself because Marg was holding her arms pinned to her sides. With pleading eyes, Carol tried to persuade her to help, but the girl only grinned in delight.

Petra was strolling around Carol, talking to the girls. 'Everyone, stop what you're doing and just hold it. The time will come very shortly . . .' It was like being put on hold on the phone in the middle of an urgent call, but a lot more frustrating.

Carol and those girls who were also being teased were all crying out, 'Please, please touch me,' but Petra just stood by and listened.

Just as Carol thought it might never happen, Petra crouched in front of her again. 'Good,' she said, and touched her clit with one finger.

'Fuck me!'

'Oh no. Come for me now, Dr Maitland, so the girls can see that you can make someone come with just a single finger on her clit.'

The girls took the hint to continue teasing each other's clits and the moans built together with Carol's. She longed to be fucked but her clit was ready to burst and her whole body was bucking against the hard chair, her arse stuck to the seat with sweat, her legs pushed further apart by the cruel hands of her colleague who was hidden from view by Marg. Marg, who pressed her into the chair and watched the expression of release that was starting to form on Carol's face. The electricity was building into great swirls of energy that grew from her centre and her head and suddenly exploded outward as Petra's finger stroked over the tip of her clit and down one side again and again while Carol screamed louder than ever in her final release.

'Thank you, Dr Maitland,' said Petra, her finger still moving and Carol still screaming. 'Very instructive.' She took Carol's clit between her teeth and sucked it as Carol's legs shook with the force of further spasms.

There were other screams and cries in the room and the familiar racking sobs of Becca, finally brought to climax by her lover.

'Take a break, girls,' said Petra, getting to her feet. She pulled Marg off Carol and thanked her. 'An excellent demonstration,' she said, kissing Carol on the top of her head.

Instead of taking a break, the girls were swapping around to test out their new skills. But Petra said under her breath to Carol, 'I'm going to slip away. I've got work to do at home.' She kissed her perfunctorily on the lips and left.

Carol sat in her chair in her stockings and watched the girls. They didn't need anything else from her, which was just as well because she was drained and sex-lagged and ready for bed. But, unlike Petra, she wouldn't be going anywhere until she'd seen everything there was to see right here.

SIXTEEN
Who's in You Now?

Lane had been waiting for Carol for over an hour now, and the
novelty of having the big flat to herself was wearing off. She
was never as relaxed at Carol's place as she was at home. She
couldn't just stick on a CD and chill, because she didn't like
Carol's music. The only band they both liked was Catatonia and
they'd been overexposed to them as a consequence. Everything
else on the shelf was world music and tape compilations made by
friends.

And tonight, of course, Lane was still worrying over what had
gone on in Carol's office the other day, before Lane arrived. She
hadn't been given any explanation. Instead, Carrie made fun of
her for asking about it, saying she was paranoid.

She was mulling it all over when the phone rang. Given the
faint possibility that it was Carol to explain where she was, Lane
hovered by the machine. But the voice that followed Carol's
outgoing message was a very different one, suave and upper class –
a voice Lane was coming to hate.

'Hi, Carol! I just thought I'd call and clarify arrangements for
the Special Tutorial –'

Those words again. They had capital letters, they meant something extra, that much was clear. But what? There were suddenly
a lot of things that Lane wanted to discuss with Petra. She picked
up the phone.

'Hi, Petra!'

'Oh, hello, Carol.'

How far to push it now? People often mistook Lane for Carol on the phone. She might be able to keep it that way for a few minutes, but then she risked that Petra would say to Carol, 'Lane pretended to be you, answering your phone and asking questions.'

'It's Lane here, actually. I know Carol wanted to talk to you. Something about the Special Tutorial.'

'Oh, really? That's why I'm phoning,' said Petra, all innocence.

'I'll ask her to call you about it, shall I? Remind me what it's all about.'

'It doesn't matter. We just call them STs – our little joke!' And she actually went 'tee-hee'.

'Listen, Petra. What you were saying the other day. If you fancy Carol, I might just be in a position to make your dreams come true.'

'How so?'

'Let's just say that Carrie and I have a little deal. And part of it is that I choose women, special women, to do certain things to her.'

'Really?'

'Yes, really. Now it would give me a kind of perverted pleasure to see you fucking Carol, so if you want to do it, name a date.'

'Is this for real?'

Lane considered. She had surprised herself, but somehow it felt right. To be in control of such an event would give all the power to Lane. Although she was giving Petra what she wanted, she was only doing it to fulfil her duty to Carol and her own voyeurism. Lane felt sure that she would retain the upper hand.

'Yes, it's for real. But if you're not up for it, just forget I said anything.'

'Oh, I'm up for it. I'll come round to Carol's, shall I? Say, Tuesday evening?'

'Yes. One more thing. I'm not going to tell her that it's you. I'll hold her down or blindfold her. It's just part of the whole thing. You are active, aren't you?'

'How could you doubt it?'

'Petra?'

'Yes?'

'Can you stop speaking like that for a few hours? Maybe, not speak at all for the duration?'

'Fuck off, Lane.'

'Only so Carol doesn't recognise your voice, you know. That's all.'

'Believe me, sweetheart, she'll know who I am on Tuesday.'

'We'll see, won't we, *sweetheart*?' They both hung up.

OK, so it was bonkers, but so was everything these days. It couldn't make anything any worse with Carol, who had stopped looking Lane in the eye when they talked. It was something to do with the college and with Petra. And it couldn't be that long before Lane cracked it.

She skinned up. She knew she was smoking too much these days, and over-romanticising herself as a sex outlaw, but it was hard to get back to any sense of stability. Her days at work were no longer rewarding. They were a bit of a haze. The nights when she didn't have any sexual exploits were spent watching videos of *Eurotrash* with her finger twitching between PAUSE and SLOW on the remote. Free porn.

Not that she didn't feel good. She felt high, but separate from real life. How you might feel if you were criminally insane, probably. Her morbid thoughts were interrupted by Carol's key in the door.

'Hiya!' Carol was in the doorway, smiling at her as if nothing was wrong. Maybe they could fix this thing.

'Hi,' said Lane. 'What happened to you?'

'Nothing. Why?'

'Duh! Because you said you'd be here by six and it's seven-fifteen.'

'Did I? What do you want to eat? You haven't started anything, have you?' Carol was on her way into the kitchen area.

'Oh, yeah. I thought I'd cook dinner, given that there's nothing in the fridge and I had no idea what time you'd be here.'

She saw Carol flinch at the sarcasm. 'Let's not have one of those nights, hey? Let's just be, you know, nice.'

'Nice? I thought nice was a capital offence in your book.'

'Well, tonight it's a goal.'

Lane shrugged. 'Oh, I nearly forgot, Petra rang. About a Special Tutorial. What's that?'

Her lover's eyes showed she was caught out but she said, 'Just some extra classes we're going to teach together.'

'I don't believe you,' said Lane. And they headed downhill in high gear.

It was not easy to rescue themselves and it didn't happen that night. In fact, Lane wound up in front of the TV after Carol had gone to bed. The late film was *Brief Encounter*. She did not want to put herself through it but there was nothing else to watch. As usual she empathised with everyone.

But that ending – what a killer. 'Oh, welcome back from Adultery Crossroads, darling, would you like a cup of tea?'

When you've smoked two spliffs too many, the TV can become a god, telling you how to lead your life. It can preach to you that love is bigger than jealousy. It can give you the kind of insight that makes you go upstairs, get in bed and put your arm around your sleeping, cheating girlfriend and whisper, 'I love you, babes, it's going to be OK.'

Lane stopped asking questions. Days went by and she didn't ask a thing. And the atmosphere improved. She considered cancelling the plans she'd made with Petra, but then she would have to go back to the old strategy of recruiting strangers, not acquaintances, to fuck Carol, which had been exhausting. First, they had to be found. Then they wanted to be in charge.

Still, she had to wonder if she'd done the right thing in picking a colleague of Carol's, who admitted to fancying Carol. Lane didn't believe they were sleeping together – Carol only fancied women who were butch, or 'butch of centre' anyway. But the two of them had a secret and they schemed over it together.

Lane had plenty of ideas about what the secret might be: that Petra and Carol had picked out all the students they fancied and put them into one seminar group, for instance. While the students discussed sexuality in Woolf, the tutors would be unsticking their knickers from their crotches by wriggling in their seats.

It didn't matter because tonight she would have the upper hand.

And that's what she was thinking when she went over to Carol's on Tuesday.

'I've planned something special tonight,' Lane said as they ate dinner together.

Carol returned her gaze. 'I thought you might have.' She smiled flirtatiously, then added, 'You're not talking about what you've brought for pudding, are you?'

'No. That is from Marks, mind you. But I was talking about the visitor we're expecting later. I don't want you to know who it is, though. So you'll be blindfolded, in there.' Lane gestured towards the living area. 'And we'll see if you can guess who it is.'

Carol had trouble reacting, as her mind was reeling with the thrill of her butch's plans for her. But she tried not to give too much away, saying only: 'Gives a whole new meaning to the tradition of the parlour game.' She raised her foot under the table and rubbed it in Lane's crotch. 'What am I supposed to say to all this?'

'Thank you will do for now.'

Carrie pressed her foot against Lane's cunt. 'It's someone I know, then? I don't remember agreeing to that.' She couldn't help shrieking as Lane grabbed her foot and tickled it.

'I don't remember saying we'd form a planning group,' said Lane. 'You're lucky I even bothered to tell you there's someone coming round.'

'Get off me!' She managed to kick away Lane's hand. 'Are you charging them a fee, like the Chick Van Dykes?'

'I'm not doing that again. It makes them think they can do what they like.'

'Oh, it's not out of respect for me, then?'

'I didn't hear any complaints about respect when I took you out for dinner on the proceeds.'

Carol laughed to herself.

'What?' asked Lane.

'Just that you're starting to sound like a pimp.'

They had fed each other the chocolate mousse and started on a second bottle of wine when the doorbell rang.

'There's your next john,' Lane said. Their smiles faded. Lane got up and pulled the red bandanna from the pocket of her combats. 'Take off your shirt,' she told Carol, who followed the instruction, unbuttoning the tan blouse and slipping it off as Lane watched. 'And your trousers.' Carrie's hands went to the zip at the side of the brown linen trousers and she undressed to her bra and knickers, both white lace.

Lane cupped Carol's breasts and kissed her, pushing her tongue into the older woman's mouth. As Carol responded, the doorbell rang again.

'I should have prepared you sooner. Stand still.' Lane carefully wrapped the blindfold around Carol's eyes and led her into the living area. 'Sit on the floor.' She looked down at Carol, her curves and her lingerie all so tempting, her curly blonde hair and that bandanna that would stop her from seeing who it was who fucked her. 'Wait there.' Lane went to the door.

'I'm from the agency,' said Petra, bizarrely. 'They said you had someone who needs seeing to.'

'I might have. You'd better have a look and see what you think.' Lane led her into the main room of the flat and Petra stopped dead to gaze at Carol where she sat on the floor.

'Don't say anything right now,' warned Lane. 'This person is the one who may need servicing. What I'm thinking is, you take a look, do anything you can do straight away, and we can have a chat about it all later.'

Petra nodded. She was wearing a black skirt suit, but she quickly took off the jacket and undid a few buttons of her blouse. Lane poured her a glass of wine and Petra sat down on the sofa.

'Our visitor is here,' Lane told Carrie. 'We'll be ready for you shortly.'

What would Petra do? Lane did not have long to wonder. The tall, arrogant woman drank her wine in long mouthfuls with her eyes half-closed. Then she rose from her seat to walk around Carol, appraising her, before undressing herself. She did not look at Lane, but Lane looked at her. She watched Petra strip. First the plain, heeled black shoes were kicked off, then the silk blouse was removed, revealing neat breasts in a black satin bra. Then the short skirt fell to the floor. Lane watched Petra rolling down her tights and gasped. Underneath, Petra wore a black G-string.

Suddenly, Lane could see what was attractive about her. Her slim frame was almost imposing in its sculpted beauty. Petra sank to the floor and took hold of Carol's head to kiss her, making her moan deep in her throat. Lane had the uncomfortable feeling of watching a lesbo flick made for heterosexual men as the mouths of the two femmes locked together.

The tall, dark woman was already running her hands over Carol's back and arms. Lane was fired up with lust and jealousy. She watched as Petra slipped her hands inside Carol's lacy bra and the blonde woman reciprocated by wrapping her arms round Petra and kissing her harder, moans escaping from her.

Lane unzipped her own trousers and slid her hand over her bush, giving herself the promise of more to come. Now the two women on the floor were getting into one of Lane's favourite positions and she longed to push Petra aside and fuck Carol herself, kneeling face to face, her own fingers plunging into that warm cunt. Instead she watched as the dark-haired woman reached inside Carol's lacy pants, eliciting a groan of gratitude.

The pangs of jealousy that shot through her heart only heightened Lane's excitement as she slid a finger to her clit, which pulsed in readiness.

'Fuck me!' shouted Carol, the way she often shouted it at Lane.

Petra's whole body moved in long thrusts as she pushed her fingers deep inside Carol and rocked back and forth to the rhythm of Carol's cries.

Lane rocked on her own hand, her arse pressing into the seat, her finger moving with a firm, swift pressure on her clit, picking up the juices that flowed from her cunt and spreading them over that tight clit. 'Fuck her!' she shouted at Petra. 'Screw her pussy! She needs it!'

'Yes!' shouted Carol in response, excited by the sound of her lover's voice and by the rhythmic slide of Petra's fingers in her cunt.

'Push your fingers in her fanny! She'll take it from anyone –' But Lane's words were breaking up as she gave in to the urgency of her climax and it broke through her body in a huge wave that knocked her back in her seat. She was shouting out obscenities and could see only white lace and black satin as the familiar sounds of her lover reaching for orgasm filled the room.

Lane watched through a blur as Petra, that impostor, kissed and fucked Carrie. It was almost more than she could bear. 'Make her come before I pull you off her!' she ordered. Then, 'Who do you think it is, Carrie? Hey, sweetheart, who's in you now?'

'Oh!' cried Carol, as her body went tense and then shook. 'Who is it? Who is it?' She slumped forward, to be held up by Petra who was kissing her head and her face but not making a sound.

Lane staggered to her feet and knelt beside Carrie, then whispered, 'I'll show you who it is.' She untied the blindfold and said, 'It's Petra.'

'Oh!' This time Carrie's cry was filled with surprise and confusion. 'But how?' She looked between the two women. 'Why?'

Lane laughed. 'Because I liked the idea.' She left the room.

While Lane was out of the room, Petra told Carol to confess.

'Why would I do that?'

It was not difficult to read Petra's motives when she replied: 'How can you live with that level of deceit? It will destroy your relationship.'

'You'll destroy our relationship,' Carol insisted in a stage whisper, as she heard Lane coming back from the bathroom. 'Shut up!'

'Did you know it was me?'

'What do you think?'

As Lane came into the room, Petra started to dress, saying, 'I'll tell the agency that I've finished the job, then.'

'OK,' replied the butch.

When Petra had dressed and left them, Carol was full of remorse. Her love for Lane was overpowering and she beckoned her on to the floor. Desire passed from Lane's lips to Carol's as they kissed.

'Did you like that?' Lane asked.

Carol nodded and Lane said, 'Good, now it's my turn. My turn to fuck you just like that.' And her hunger for Carol was raw as she pushed her hand into those wet, twisted knickers and pressed her face against those breasts.

'God, I want you,' moaned Lane, gently pulling one breast from Carrie's bra and kissing it, licking her nipple and fingering her cunt.

'Fuck me!' cried Carol.

'That's what you said to her, isn't it?' snapped Lane. 'This is just for me now, so I think you can be quiet.' The softness returned as she backed up her point by shutting Carol up with a passionate kiss. Lane's tongue moved around Carol's mouth with all the confidence with which her fingers now pushed their way into Carol's aching cunt.

There were no more words as Lane held Carol tight and kissed her, pumping her cunt and then moving softly over her clit in tantalising strokes. Carol pushed her hands down the back of Lane's trousers, inside her boxers, to stroke her bum. Lane moaned. They moved together for only a short time before Carrie was surprised by an orgasm that built from deep inside her. It was profound and sudden and then it passed and she shook her head.

'What?' asked Lane.

'Nothing,' gasped Carol. 'Stop now, Laney.' She moved her hand from the back of Lane's pants to the front and pushed her fingers in through the flies. Her lover's hips thrust forward and Carol revelled in that moment, knowing that Lane was giving herself up and would not pull away to wank herself as she so often did.

In seconds, Lane was coming, shouting with such an animal force that the shouts pounded through Carol and frightened her. She murmured, 'It's OK, honey, it's OK,' as Lane often did to her, but tears were already springing from Lane's eyes and they wrapped their arms tight round each other and rocked there together.

'What have I done?' asked Lane.

'What have I done?' responded Carol. But neither of them asked what exactly the other one had done, which was just as well for Carol.

SEVENTEEN

Backroom

No amount of adventures with Carol could stop Lane from needing to be fucked by men. And although she wanted to see Jack again soon, she was more driven to go cruising by herself. She felt a bit like a married gay man, one of those midnight visitors to Clapham Common who just couldn't help themselves.

It was partly the sheer physical sensation of being fucked up the arse, which couldn't be fulfilled by Carol because she wasn't into it. And partly the danger of cruising strangers: it was illegal; they might do anything to you; and if they discovered she was a woman, they might well react badly. But to Lane, it was all summed up by the gut feeling she got that night when she and Jack picked up their Scotsman in Russell Square. The excitement and adrenaline rush were unique.

Tonight, she had something new in mind. She had read about the backrooms on the continent and what went on there between strangers, in the dark. And from careful reading between the lines of the gay press, she had gathered that one such backroom was going on illegally in a popular club in King's Cross called Dicks.

She had a couple of beers and a spliff while she was getting ready, trying to control her nerves, which were making her heart beat fast and her stomach churn before she even got dressed for her night out.

★

At the door to the club, Lane nervously adjusted her clothes. To hide her figure, she was wearing baggy camouflage pants and a blue bomber jacket. She looked at the ground as she passed the men on the door. Inside, it was dark and she handed over her money without raising any suspicions.

She followed the crowd downstairs and found herself in a club the size of an aircraft hangar, with fabulous lights, booming music, a huge bar and thousands of men.

Lane had no trouble at the bar, although she was more nervous than ever. The club was absolutely men-only – no female barstaff, no fag hags to be seen. She deepened her voice as she said just one word: 'Becks.' The beer was handed over, at a suitably inflated price.

Looking around from a safe spot against the wall, Lane was able to reassure herself that, yes, she had dressed correctly. Leathers, combats, jeans with a white or khaki T or vest were just about all that anyone was wearing. It was too hot for shirts, although some guys had tied them round their waists. Others – the musclemen – were bare chested, sweat dripping down their firm chests as they danced. Lane's only problem was that she did not dare take off her bomber jacket, for fear that her tits would show. But some of the guys who weren't dancing were still wearing their jackets.

Stop worrying, she told herself, realising she was behaving the same way as she had in her early teens. She used to go to the synagogue youth club and worry that she was not wearing the exact same clothes as the other girls. In retrospect, she was in a kind of drag back then, with her chain-store skirts and the make-up that her mother helped her to apply.

The most excitement to be had at the youth club was a snog with an inept boy in a storage cupboard at the end of the night while your dad waited for you in the car park. But if she played it right tonight, there would be rather a lot more on offer.

It was eleven o'clock and Lane resolved to wait until midnight before braving the backroom. She needed to be sure that everyone was out of it on drink and drugs and would not be thinking too carefully about who exactly they were fucking.

She lit a joint that she had ready in the pen pocket of her jacket. It was not long before a Britpop kind of guy in suede trainers and

V-necked green T-shirt was sidling up to her and smiling. She passed him the joint. He started talking to her but she just waved a hand by her ear to indicate there was no way she could hear him above the music.

'It's not my scene!' he shouted in her ear. 'My mates dragged me here!' Although Lane could hear him, she shook her head apologetically as if she couldn't. She did not want to have to talk to him and risk discovery. He took a couple more tokes and handed back the joint, smiled again and shrugged in frustration, then wandered off.

Already, Lane was thinking that waiting till midnight was too ambitious. She looked around at all the men. There were quite a few she would not mind finding in the backroom. Why not wander in there now and see what was going down, so to speak?

As to where the backroom was, she had no idea. She started by circumnavigating the club, allowing herself a good look at anyone who took her fancy. In this light, they would not notice her lack of eleven-o'clock shadow. A tall man looked back at her as he danced, but then shut his eyes as the music claimed him.

Then a guy dressed exactly like Lane, from bomber jacket to DMs, pushed off from the column he was leaning on to walk across her path. She watched him settle against the wall and tip his head slightly in acknowledgement. He had spiky hair, blond with dark roots, and a randiness played around his narrowed eyes and mischievous mouth. He looked the same age as her and she felt drawn to him. But this was useless. She could not reciprocate because only in the backroom did she have enough chance of hiding her identity.

The guy glanced back at her as he walked away again, this time heading to a dark doorway near the DJ's booth. Lane followed, her heart pounding. The door was marked PRIVATE. He went through it and she was not far behind.

Inside, it was dark and she could not see anyone clearly, but there were dozens of men in the room and, when the door swung shut, their shouts of ecstasy drowned out the music from the dance floor.

Lane picked out: 'Harder, you fucking bastard!' and 'Shit! Yes! Shit!' and 'Lick my balls!' and 'Someone hold his dick!'

Lane moved over to a small group in the centre of the room. She could barely tell the men apart in the dark, but gradually her eyes adapted enough to see that one man was licking the balls of another while he fucked a third who was being sucked off by the fourth. She watched, mesmerised. At the same time, she realised just how many chances there were of someone blowing her cover in lieu of blowing her.

Then the man she had followed was there, taking off his bomber jacket and unzipping Lane's camouflage pants. She reciprocated, suddenly thrown, unprepared, into the anonymous sex she yearned for. The man reached down the front of Lane's trousers and she shuddered with the thrill even as she pushed his hand away, afraid he would get his hands on her dildo and recognise it as less than fleshy. He groped her through her trousers instead.

'Fuck me!' she told him in a deep voice that sounded fake to her.

'No,' he said, 'you fuck me!'

She nodded in consent. He knew his way around the room, leading her over to one wall. Once again, it seemed, leaning against the wall was going to be his favourite position, but with a twist. There was a line of metal rings and straps hanging from the wall. Two men were already shackled up, next to each other. One was being soundly whipped while the other was being fucked from behind.

Lane's date waited for her to grab him, turn him round and lock his hands into the metal rings, then strap a leather belt from the wall around his waist. He spread his legs compliantly and she realised there were leg shackles as well. She buckled him into these and then wrenched down his trousers. He had a lovely tight bum and she longed to fuck him. Although he had said nothing about staying safe, Lane knew to roll on a condom and lube up.

As the screams of the man being whipped seared through her, Lane took care to enter her man carefully. She knew from Jack that her dildo was bigger than an average dick and she did not want to hurt anyone who was in no position to protest. She rubbed her cockhead down his crack and gently back and forth past his arsehole. He was moaning loud enough for her to hear.

With her free hand, she took hold of his cock. It was small and thin, the smallest she had encountered, as yet. It was endearing.

As she stroked his penis, she pressed her cock against his hole. It opened a little, then a lot, so she could press inside him. Power surged through her as she fucked her way inside the shackled man. She was overheating already in her thick jacket but there was no holding back from the lust that surged through her, making her thrust the whole of the dildo deep inside him as she pumped on his dick.

Then Lane felt someone's warm hands on her waist, pushing inside her trousers. She was not wearing underwear and she sensed his pleasure at this in the way he grabbed at her arse. She was doubly thrilled now, letting the dangerous approach continue, feeling a finger pressing into her hole.

As that finger slipped inside her, Lane bucked her hips back to envelop it. And so it continued, with Lane bucking between the finger in her and the arse she was fucking. She needed more and wrapped her thumb and first finger round the base of her cock so the other fingers could tease her clit.

The finger in her arse slipped out, but the man behind her had not given up, as she realised when he whispered in her ear. 'Going to fuck you, I just got to get a rubber on.' He smelt of leather and CK one. He was soon grabbing the leather of her harness to steady her as the tip of his cock pressed against her eager arsehole. It seemed the harness was not arousing any suspicions, just arousing his need, because he pushed hard against her and she grunted in discomfort.

The man she was fucking was moaning now and all Lane's concentration went into pumping his arse and his cock, as the man behind her tried again, more carefully, to enter her tight and inexperienced arsehole.

He moaned as she let go and let him in, feeling his meat filling her up in battering thrusts. Lane was still afraid to shout out, afraid that her voice would give her away, but holding it in just made her more excited, a ball of tension waiting to be released, the pain beating through her along with the thrill of fucking and being fucked by men who thought she was one of them.

Her pick-up was shouting out, caught up in his own fantasy: 'I didn't do it, get off me, I didn't do it!' It was only seconds before he came, thrashing about in his restraints like a man trying to free himself. She pushed twice more into his depths, then came herself – or himself, as the men would think – stifling her cries in case they sounded as different as the man in Russell Square had claimed.

Her whole body shook, sandwiched between two strangers, the leatherman coming deep inside her with great shouts of triumph. They pulsed against each other, all three in the thrall of something bigger, part of the shouts and groans and lashings that still went on around them. Lane stroked once at her clit and her whole body convulsed again.

The man behind her was holding and releasing her arse in time with his lessening spasms of climax. Finally he withdrew, slowly and with long groans. Lane gasped as she was freed from his cock.

Following his example, she pulled out of the other man's arse, holding on to it as she slid out inch by inch, until the head of the rubbered dildo burst from his hole. She quickly rolled off the condom, throwing it to the floor, and tucked away her cock.

Any thoughts of releasing the man from his shackles were banished as two more men approached and tightened the belt around his waist. She thought he said, 'No more –' but then she clearly heard his old refrain '– I didn't do it,' and realised it was part of the game.

Suddenly someone was on her again, this time grabbing her by the shoulders and powerfully pushing her to the floor. He unzipped his flies and forced his fat cock into her mouth before she could gasp for air. She nearly choked as he started to fuck her mouth as if it were his.

Then someone was between her legs, undoing her flies once again. She pushed away the head that was diving to her crotch.

'Hey!' said a familiar voice. The man looked closely at her face in the darkness, ignoring the fact that it was being screwed. 'Picky are you? Who do you think you are?' Then a horrible recognition dawned. 'Lane?'

The man pumping her gob said gruffly, 'Shut the fuck up, mate! He's busy.'

'Not any more,' said Jack, getting to his feet and shoving the man away from Lane. 'He's mine.'

Lane gulped down air. Then a group of men were surrounding them, urging them not to start a fight, and the first guy pushed them away and walked off.

'OK,' said Jack, 'everything's all right here.'

Uncomfortable as it was to be looked after in this way by a bloke, Lane still did not dare to speak. Jack manhandled her out of the backroom and up to a corridor that seemed to be set aside for drug deals.

'What the fuck are you doing here?' he asked her angrily.

'Same as you.'

'You're still in training. I expressly told you not to go cruising by yourself. You don't know how to protect yourself. What were you doing letting that scumbag in your mouth?'

'I didn't have much choice.'

'Exactly. You should not be here, sis, and I'm putting you in a cab right now.'

'I'd rather go back in there with you.'

'No. I'm not going to be your big brother for the night. I've got myself to think of tonight, thank you.'

Lane looked at him apologetically. 'Jack, I do appreciate, you know, the training and everything. Is there anything I can do for you?'

He considered. 'I'd like to learn to fuck a woman; not in the arse –'

'If you can't even say the word, then you probably can't do the deed.'

'Well,' he said sheepishly, 'it doesn't sound right when a man says it, does it? It would just sound offensive.'

'Try it.'

'I want to fuck a woman's cunt.'

Lane grimaced. 'You're right, it's offensive. Anyway, why? You're supposed to be an unreconstructed homosexual.'

He raised that beautiful pierced eyebrow. 'Uh-huh? And fucking you would be what?'

'Just helping out a friend, Jackie-boy.' She put a hand on his broad shoulder. 'But there are limits to that kind of help, and I don't think I can –'

'I wasn't thinking of you, sis. But that girlfriend of yours.'

'What? You and Carol? You're joking.' He did not look like he was joking, though. He had a dirty look on his face.

'I'll see what I can do, Jack, but give me time.'

He nodded. 'You owe me one in the meantime, Laney.' And he frogmarched her out of the club.

Next morning, padding about in her underwear, Lane emptied the pockets of the clothes she'd worn the night before, which smelt of fags of both kinds and had semen stains clear enough for a court of law.

In the back pocket of her camouflage trousers was a business card. JIM HARDACRE, WRITER. She had no idea which of the men was Jim, but she rang his number straight away, before her nerves could get the better of her.

A woman answered the phone and Lane hung up. She was surprised to hear a woman's voice, though that didn't have to mean he had a girlfriend. But more importantly, her hung-over brain was finally realising that she couldn't meet him again, because she was a girl and he thought she was a boy. Simple as that.

Still, there was something to be said for repeat dates. And thinking back on the encounter with Jack in the backroom, she was glad that she now 'owed him one', because that gave her a repeat date of the best kind.

But Jack and Carol? It was hard to imagine. The antagonism between them was pretty clear at that party.

As she thought of the possibility of her two favourite fucks getting it on together, of watching the two of them together, Lane felt her juices soaking into her shorts. She lay back down on the bed and gave in to her fantasy.

EIGHTEEN
Feed that Pussy

'Annie was telling me about your adventures, Laney,' Jason revealed after taking a toke on one of Annie's first-class spliffs.

'Oh, was she?' Lane glared at the snitch, who looked uncomfortable.

'Yes, but she was too discreet. I want detail!' Jason's big dark eyes glinted behind his metal-framed glasses.

'I didn't have any detail,' Annie said in her own defence.

'Just as well!' said Lane. 'I don't remember authorising you to relate so much as a considered précis to Miss Gossmonger here.'

'I'd have sniffed it out,' claimed Jason. 'You are what you fuck. You're turning into a gay man. You're speaking camp like it's your first language.'

'But Lane's always been camp,' said Annie. 'She's certainly more camp than butch.'

'Do you mind?'

The others were laughing at her. 'That's right!' said Jason. 'She's a lesbian queen.'

'I prefer queen among lesbians, but let's not split hairs,' said Lane in her campest voice. 'Seriously though, I quite fancy myself on a queer-hist-doc on digital cybertelly in 2050 –'

She let her voice go both camp boy and retired gay lady as she flapped a hand in the air and launched into an improvised

173

monologue: 'It was so limiting and prescriptive at the turn of the
millennium. As a lesbian, you could be butch or femme, or you
could dismiss it, but there was nothing else. I felt very male, so I
had to be butch.'

A pause to shake her head at the sad memories. 'I can't tell you
the humiliations and petty everyday degradations I endured. My
girlfriend saying my voice wasn't deep enough on the answerphone, my father ashamed that I couldn't hold a power drill. They
thought I wasn't a real butch, you see. It's only now that I can say
proudly I'm a fanny fairy – or a pussy poof, I think the young
people are saying.' She cocked her head, listening to an imaginary
interviewer. 'Muff Mary? Yes, dear! Is that from the former USA?'

She lost it, chuckling in delight at her new comic creation. The
others were laughing like two stoned, relaxed and amused people.
It was a beautiful moment, but Jason just had to spoil it.

'OK, very funny, now spill!'

Lane made a swift decision that she would not tell either of
them about her night in the backroom. But she gave in to Jason's
curiosity and told him about her night in Russell Square with Jack.
Annie occasionally raised an eyebrow as she quietly skinned up,
but it was Jason who whooped and shouted 'No way!' and put his
hands up to his face in scandalised delight.

'Come on, Jason, you've done it yourself. What's the big deal?'

'Er . . . only that you're a girl! What are you doing? Jesus!'

'So to be a muff Mary, do you have to fuck men? Doesn't that
make you bisexual?' This was Annie.

'Me? I'm a dyke. If I slept with a *straight* man, then I'd be
bisexual.'

'What if you slept with a bisexual man?' asked Jason.

Although he was just messing about, Lane felt the conversation
tipping over that crucial edge. And Annie, as she lit up the latest
joint, was allowing herself one of those philosophical little smiles
that always precursed her switching into the pursuit of logic. Two
lawyers about to attack an argument built on sand. Built on an
artificially created beach, actually.

'Jason,' cautioned Lane, who was opting for diversionary tactics,
'don't make me remind you of your own confused gender politics.'

'What?'

'*Who* refused to leave a certain gay bar when the women-only session was starting – not because the staff were being rude and obnoxious but because, and I quote, he *might* be a male-to-female transsexual who had to live as a woman before being allowed treatment?' She stared at the culprit.

'I stand by that argument.'

'We're all banned for life from the only pub with extra women's toilets, and you're proud?'

'There was a principle at stake.' He said it as if he truly believed it – the mark of a man born for the Bar.

'You were taking the piss for the sake of a testosterone-fuelled row, more like. No one who wanted to be a lesbian would have been caught dead in that aftershave.'

'What if I wanted to be a muff Mary?'

'You can't be. They don't exist yet.'

'Well,' Annie told her, 'I don't think you're on much firmer ground than Jason. How *do* you explain how you can have sex with blokes and still be a lesbian?'

'Because I've got a girlfriend. Now, I've got to go and feed the cats at number 63, because Fee and Fennell are away. So you'll have to entertain yourselves by analysing my unique brand of rebellion. Or you could have a look at that bookshelf there, which holds a variety of advanced texts on lesbian gender, and you might stop thinking I'm a freak.'

'Lane!' cried Annie, staring at the clock, which showed it was 11.20. 'Why have you left it so late? You never said you were in charge of their cats or I would have chased you round there hours ago. They'll be starving.'

'No, they'll be fine. They've got this double food container that works on a timer, for when I can't make it. So I set it yesterday just in case I didn't come home. And in the evening I went round and the little buggers had already eaten. They've worked out how to hotwire the fucking thing!'

She went out, laughing, expecting to be back in twenty minutes for more slumber-party mayhem. It was a warm night and a little muggy. She strolled up the road, past the terraced Victorian houses with their windows open and televisions on. Fee and Fennell were an alternativey straight couple; film-makers who had befriended her last year because they liked the wacky planting in her window boxes. Little did she know then that she would become chief cat-minder for eternity. In return, they regularly had her round for sloppy dhal and organic rice, and would hand her a going-home present of a Tesco bag full of home-grown on her way out.

Recently, of course, she'd hardly seen them because her exploits were taking up so much time. They'd had to come round specially to ask her whether she could mind the cats while they went up north in the VW van, or whether she was 'too busy these days'.

She let herself into their garden flat. The cats ran to greet her, rubbing themselves against her legs. They seemed quite happy. She followed them into the kitchen. Glancing at the cat bowls, she saw that they had cheated the timer once again.

'Oh, you bad cats,' she told them in a soppy voice. They purred. And then a much louder noise, like a massive amplified purr, reached her ears.

'What the fuck was that?' she asked her furry friends. They didn't seem to know. It happened again. Fee had told her there were dykes next door. Maybe this was the time to take a look at them.

Lane petted the cats, locked up and headed next door. She rang the bottom bell. After a long wait, a girl came to the door in her underwear, her long hair in a mess. 'Hi! Have you come for the Special Tutorial?'

'Have I what?' Pennies clunked into rusty slots and her vision blurred. 'Yes. Yes, I have,' she managed to reply. 'It's my first time. I'm a friend of Dr Maitland.' A loud purr escaped from the open door to the flat.

'Oh, I didn't know she was going to ask her friends. Cool. Come in. Do you know the kind of thing we do? Only it could be a bit of a shock otherwise.'

The girl laughed nervously and went on wittering, but by now they were in the doorway of the flat and Lane couldn't hear a word. All she could hear was the regular purr generated by a roomful of dykes groaning in rhythm with the thrusts of the two women on the table in the middle of the room. Those women were Petra and Carol.

Lane didn't even have to think before screaming at Petra, 'Get off her, you fucking devious bitch!'

Carol looked up in absolute horror. She was kneeling on the table with Petra fingering her from behind. But Petra barely reacted to Lane's bile and was unfazed by her arrival.

'You didn't seem to mind on Tuesday,' she said coolly, without letting go of Carol's cunt. 'Did Carrie tell you to come along tonight and join the fun?'

'You don't call her Carrie! Do you hear me! Get off her before I knock out your perfect teeth, you bitch! You are fucked!'

Petra laughed. 'I'd like to be.'

'OK.'

The girls were following the scene as if it was avant-garde theatre.

'You!' Lane pointed at Carol. 'You sit there and watch this, you lying cow.' She looked around. 'Where's the phone?'

A naked girl gestured towards the next room and Lane went into the kitchen and dialled her flat. The answerphone clicked in. 'Annie, Jason, get over here!' she shouted. 'I'm next door to Fee and Fennell's. The student house.' She put the phone down and told the girl who'd opened the door to go and open it again. Her fury was turning to a white-hot lust.

'I need lube!' she ordered. She climbed on to the table behind Petra. 'Bend forward!'

Carol was sitting at the table as if waiting for her dinner. Lane ignored her. Someone in black underwear handed over a pump-action bottle of lube. Lane pulled Petra's slip dress up over her hips revealing a white thong which she tugged to one side. She rolled up her sleeve and worked the lube over her hand.

'Did you think you'd get out of feeling the power of my fist?' she asked.

'I wouldn't be so presumptuous,' Petra replied pompously.

Lane pressed her fingers against Petra's wetness and heard the other woman gasp. Hate, lust and jealousy were seething in Lane as she pushed two fingers into that warm cunt. Three fingers, and Petra was rocking back with need. 'Don't ever touch Carol again,' Lane told her as she pushed a fourth finger inside her.

She was meeting no resistance so she pulled out and bunched up her hand, then pushed it into Petra's fanny. At the second set of knuckles, Petra flinched and Lane pulled back almost imperceptibly and started to work on that resistance, sliding back and forth.

'Yes,' moaned Petra, pushing back with her hips and relaxing her cunt muscles enough for Lane to shove her hand in there. They both cried out with the intensity of that moment, but they were interrupted in their passion.

'What the fuck?' It was Jason.

The girls gasped and swore at the sight of a man. 'Is it women-only?' he asked, so breathless that his tone couldn't be discerned.

'When did that ever stop you?' asked Annie. She was looking at the scene on the table with awe.

'Gay men welcome as guests,' Carol piped up.

Lane looked at her. 'Did anyone give you permission to speak?' she asked.

'This is still my party,' said Carol. 'Anyone got any objections to Jason staying?' she asked the room.

The girls looked at each other and at Carol. No one spoke. Annie and Jason dropped to the floor, taking their places in the audience.

'Right,' said Lane, 'where were we? Is that my fist in you, Dr Hill? You don't look so clever now, do you?' Silence. 'Do you?'

'No.'

'No, that's right.' Lane twisted her hand in Petra's cunt.

'Fuck!'

'That's what I'm doing.' Lane bunched her hand into a fist and Petra buckled, shouting in pain.

'Oh, God!' Her head was on the table. 'Yes! Fuck me hard!'

Lane's hand punched against Petra's cervix and she grabbed at one small breast with the other hand, pulling the neckline of Petra's dress down so she could reach naked flesh. She pinched a nipple and they both groaned.

'You sound like you're going to come,' Lane said, taunting.

'I'm going to come from your fist,' gasped Petra, her breathing loud and heavy as she pushed her arse back to let Lane's wrist inside her. She shouted and writhed and then Lane heard Carol's unmistakable groans as well.

'Carol!' she shouted. 'Stop touching yourself. Wait for me.'

Petra was electrified by these words. 'Wait!' she repeated, and she could have been talking to Carol, herself or Lane. 'Wait, wait, wait!' Her arse was rubbing in Lane's crotch and Lane backed off to stop herself from coming too as Petra's shouts ceased to be words and her whole body shook in climax.

Petra rose up to press her back into Lane, who stroked her flat belly and bit into her neck.

'I don't ever want to have to do that again,' she told Petra. 'So keep your clammy hands off my woman.' She pushed Petra back down and slowly withdrew her fist from that pulsing cunt.

'That's enough for you,' she said over Petra's moans of protest. 'Someone else needs some attention.' Lane addressed Carol. 'Do you remember our deal?'

'Yes.'

'Do you remember what we said I'd do to you if you went with anyone else?'

'Yes.'

'And now I find you on the table with this bitch's fingers in you and a room full of students watching, in their knickers. I think that falls within the remit of the deal, don't you?'

'Not now, Lane!' Carol's eyes showed her panic as she froze in the chair.

Lane considered. She wasn't wearing her dildo right now anyway. 'No, not now. You need some time to prepare yourself mentally for what's to come, don't you, babes? Right now, you can lick me out.'

Lane pulled off her jeans and boxers. Petra was slumped on the table and Lane told her to watch. 'See if you learn anything,' she said as she shunted herself to sit on the edge of the table and stretched out her legs, resting one on each of her lover's shoulders.

By now the room had metamorphosed into a crazed orgy of sex and voyeurism. So far, Jason was still a nervous and fascinated onlooker, but Annie had found her niche in a group of girls who were licking each other out. In the sticky heat, most were naked or wore only a bra or a thong, the sweat visible on their backs and bellies.

Lane had never seen anything like it. The long-haired girl who had opened the front door was lying on her back with a skinhead butch sitting on her face and someone else between her legs. The skinhead had all her weight on one knee so she could reach low enough to lick out Annie at the same time as riding the other girl – and so on. Their moans were like music. Lane was starting to understand why Carol was so into her Special Tutorials.

She watched the action, holding Carol's head tight between her thighs and moaning with relief as the escape she needed drew closer. She was stoned from her smoking session with her friends and her sexual responses were more powerful yet fuzzier around the edges, as a fluid warmth spread through her and her skin buzzed.

'Lick me, Carrie, give me what I need!' she murmured to her lover, whose head moved rhythmically in Lane's crotch, her tongue concentrating on that tight clit, which was ready to burst.

'Yes! Just do that! Just do that!' Lane heard herself repeating this mantra as a flooding orgasm overwhelmed her and she pressed her cunt into Carrie's face and shuddered against it for what seemed like minutes.

When she recovered enough to open her eyes, she saw that Petra was lying on the floor, exhausted, watching them with a faint smile on her face.

'What are you smiling at?' Lane demanded.

'You. What do you gain from that? From shoving your snatch in her face when I've just been fucking her, when you've just fisted me. Funny kind of relationship.'

'Not like yours, hey, Petra? Does Anil know where you are tonight?' There wasn't much fight left in Lane, just a bit of bitchiness seeping out of her drained and satisfied body.

Carol stood up and kissed her. The passion between them was as deep as ever. If Carol was nervous about what might happen when Lane demanded her 'payment', she wasn't showing it. But she was far from calm as she stood between Lane's legs, rubbing herself against Lane's naked cunt, needing more.

Lane's hand went to her own mound where she turned her palm outward and let her fingers brush Carol's clit, producing a gasp of need. They kissed and Lane's head bobbed down to meet Carol's in one long kiss that lasted as long as their latest bout of sex.

When Carol came, Lane had forgotten her fury. She hauled

Carrie into her lap and held her, kissing her face and her breasts, murmuring words of love to her. Petra was almost forgotten, but Lane couldn't help feeling a twinge of victory.

Minutes later, a girl approached with a fierce-looking whip. It had a thick handle and three thin strips of leather. She handed it to the near-naked Carol who took it without showing any surprise.

'Kneel on the floor, Marg. You know the position.'

Lane watched as her lover, her femme who was not into pain, wearing nothing but black stockings, whipped the red-haired girl across her tattooed arse. With each lash and each shout from the willing victim, Lane felt more aroused. She would like to see this kind of thing more often. But first she would like to fuck that girl immediately after the flogging.

'Thank you, Dr Maitland!' shouted the girl, between lashes.

Two more girls knelt either side of her and raised their arses in the air. Far from being worn out from the sexual and emotional roller coaster she had already ridden tonight, Carrie seemed invigorated by it, flailing their bare bums in a fury.

Petra had disappeared. Annie approached Lane.

'Well, what have you brought us to, here?' she asked, her eyes bright, and a disbelieving but delighted smile on her face. 'All going on in your street – for how long?'

'Let's not think about that,' warned Lane. 'I've got some short-term plans of my own, now.' She pointed at Marg. 'That girl with the Celtic cross on her arse? I'm going to have her, as soon as she thinks her ordeal is over.'

'When will that be? How long will Carol go on?'

'I don't know. I never knew she was into this! She doesn't like pain, supposedly. But she seems to like inflicting it better than I realised. Where's Jason?'

'He's hiding somewhere. He couldn't bring himself to leave, but he said he needs boys.'

'We could fix that for next time.'

'Next time? Aren't you going to suggest the class is disbanded?'

'No. I'm going to suggest it's broadened. Look at this lot! They're fucking mad for it!'

'That girl you're after,' said Annie, nodding towards the

screaming woman who had red weals coming up on her arse under Carol's whip. 'D'you want to take turns?'

'Oh God, it's almost incest.'

'What, she's your cousin or something?'

'No! You and me in a threesome – it's unnatural.'

'You asked me here,' Annie pointed out. 'What did you think would happen?'

'I wasn't thinking anything. I just saw –' Lane gestured helplessly around the room. 'This! And I knew you had to see it too.'

'Well, thank you for sharing. Now, I think Ms Tattooed Bum is ready for us.' Carol was walking away from the women she had just thrashed, like a blasé dominatrix, leaving them lying on the floor.

They approached the girl, Marg, whose face was wet with tears.

'Hey!' Lane greeted her, cupping a hand around one small breast and admiring the dark tattoos that ran around the girl's belly button and upper arm. 'You OK?'

'Oh yes,' she smiled thinly.

'Then you're ready for some more action?'

'What?' But Annie was already stroking the stripes that criss-crossed the girl's tattoo. As she flinched from the pain, Marg said, 'OK, whatever.'

'Look at this, girls!' Jason was back in the room, with a sports bag. 'Look at this stuff! It was in the bedroom.' He placed the bag on the floor and pulled it open for Annie and Lane to look inside. It was near to overflowing with dildos, vibrators, handcuffs, harnesses and whips.

'Good timing, Jase!' Annie pulled out a blue dildo in a red harness. 'Ever used it inside out?' she asked Lane.

'Show me,' said Lane.

Annie took the dildo out of the harness, then slipped the shiny red plastic straps over the girl's feet and up her legs, pulling them into position around her arse. Marg moaned submissively, almost sleepy with passivity, as Annie tightened the buckles to fit. The tool was chunky but short. She started to work it 'the wrong way' through the metal ring of the harness – pushing the cockhead into Marg's cunt.

The redhead bucked her hips, finally showing her excitement. 'Oh, yes!' she cried.

Meanwhile, the woman to her right was looking at Jason with something like lust. She seemed to be recovering from her beating, and when Jason took a buttplug out of the bag, her eyes widened in delight. It looked as if the boy was going to go with his instinct rather than learn any new tricks.

As he lubed up the implement, the girl knelt on all fours, in the same position in which she had received her lashing. She was presenting her arse all over again. Her head hung low, the long dark hair hanging to the floor in a curtain. She was the girl in red lingerie who had opened the front door earlier. Now, her knickers were pulled into the crack of her arse and her cheeks were striped with red weals.

'Sorry, I can't do this,' Jason admitted. 'I'm too gay.'

'Allow me to take over,' suggested Annie, distracted from the task she had just begun; of stuffing Marg.

The dark-haired girl groaned, 'Please!'

Meanwhile, Marg was panting and wriggling and Lane took over where Annie had left off. She stroked Marg's poor reddened arse and kissed it before embarking on her mission to bring this cute girl to the summit of sexual delight.

'What do you want?' she whispered to the redhead.

'Touch my clit,' begged the girl, her American accent enriching those beautiful words.

'With pleasure,' said Lane. Her fingers slid to Marg's love-switch and she marvelled at how each woman she'd touched tonight felt different. Marg's clit was fleshy and full and Lane teased it with one hand as she pressed her palm against the base of the dildo with the other hand. She was keeping it deep in Marg and letting the girl's muscles do the rest of the work. Lane kissed her spine. But then another woman came over to distract Lane with her kisses and it was all she could do to keep her fingers working away.

'Let me die now,' Lane said between kisses. 'I've had it all.'

'Not yet, you haven't,' said the new arrival, slipping off her bra. 'You haven't had me.'

★

Hours passed before everyone had had her fill. There were moments when Lane thought she would come just from looking, like when two butch young things held a third woman down across the table to be teased by a fourth. One finger moved slowly over the girl's arse and only brushed her cunt before sliding down the inside of a thigh. The girl shouted out for release but she was not allowed it.

And then there was always the opportunity to watch Carrie when she did not know that her lover was looking. Lane quickly saw that there was a special relationship between Carrie and a handsome woman with short locks called Dee. They followed each other around. If one of them joined in with another couple, it was not long before the other was there to make it a foursome.

Meanwhile, Lane found that it was easy to get off with anyone she fancied. The girls seemed to have no boundaries. Just about anything was allowed and the screams that came from them when they hit their youthful climaxes showed the delight of the inexperienced. Every orgasm was like a gift from the gods to them.

But it could not go on for ever. Finally, the room was silent bar the satisfied sighs and quiet kisses of the women who lay around on sofas or on the floor. The Indian throws that had been scattered on the floor in the chaos were now pulled over naked bodies. Lane sought out Carol, who was entangled with Marg in a corner, almost asleep.

'Listen,' she told her femme. 'I want to make some changes for next time.'

'What?'

'Let me talk to them.'

'First,' said Carol, 'we have to do the vow.'

It was Lane's turn to ask, 'What?'

She watched as Carol, naked, hauled herself to her feet. 'Girls, time for our vow,' she announced to the sleepy room.

Lane watched, aroused, as all the girls knelt up as one. They started to kiss each other, murmuring: 'These lips that kiss yours will never betray our Special Tutorial.' One by one they got up and went to kiss Carol, calling her Dr Maitland and making the vow to her. Then they were wandering like randy sleepwalkers around the room, kissing each other. Lane found herself sucked in to the strange ceremony, kissing every girl in the room and repeating the strange promise.

When they were all still once more, Lane made her own announcement. 'Thanks for having me,' she said. 'And thanks for letting me have you! But I have to say, there's a lot of initiative going on here and not a lot of leadership. I'm surprised that Dr Maitland lets you do as you please.' Calling Carol by her professional name sent a strange shiver through Lane. 'Next time, we will have a few more rules and a little control. And next time, I want you to bring a few of your most open-minded gay male friends along with you. We need a bit of entertainment for our pal Jason, and I can think of at least one other man I could bring who would be an asset to our session. OK?'

The girls looked at each other and then at Carol. But she was defeated. She had no bargaining power because of the way the evening had begun, when Lane found her being fucked by Petra. Carol shrugged and the girls looked uncomfortable.

'Look,' Lane insisted, 'just do it, all right? If you want to come here again, then you have to follow certain instructions.' But already their attention was wandering as hands reached for breasts and mouths nuzzled into necks. They were settling down for a night of lazy love. Lane scanned the room for Carol's clothes and gathered them up.

'Come on,' she told her lover. 'The amnesty is over. I'm taking you home.'

NINETEEN
Payback Time

'Shit on toast! Do you know what time it is?' Lane sat bolt upright in the bed of her studio flat, wide awake in an instant, after catching a bleary glimpse of the clock.

'What?'

'It's one o'clock, it's Friday –'

'Is it *Crackerjack*?' Carol's sleepy joke fell flat.

'We've slept half the day, Carrie. I don't know about you but I'm supposed to be at work.'

'I did wake up once but I didn't like what I remembered of my dream. All these students having sex and you were there.'

'Did Petra fuck you?'

'Yes. How did you guess? Did you have the same dream?' Carol continued to tease, but it sounded like there was a part of her that believed it could all turn into a dream if she said so often enough.

'No, it was real life,' said Lane. 'It was real life that I went to feed the cats, heard weird noises, and found my girlfriend being fucked by a colleague on a table, watched by a dozen undergraduates. That really happened to me, despite the fact that this same girlfriend explicitly told me not so long ago that she did not want to have sex with anyone but me.'

Carol was hiding under the bedclothes.

'Well,' asked Lane, 'how shall we play this? It is funny this way. But I could quite get into a bit of anger. Let's see, I have a few things to be angry about, including quite a few lies, wouldn't you say?'

Silence.

'Wouldn't you say?'

'Yes,' squeaked Carol from under the covers, giggly and apprehensive.

'Do you remember making a deal with me, Carrie?'

'Yes.'

'And what was going to happen if you let anyone else fuck you?'

'Don't remember.'

Lane pulled back the duvet and grabbed hold of Carol. 'I think you do remember. You told me last night that you remembered.' A threatening note entered her voice as she pinned Carol to the bed. 'What was going to happen?'

'Was it that you would take me out for dinner?'

'Try again.'

'Was it that you would tell me off?'

'Uh-uh.' Lane shook her head. 'Try again.'

'Was it that you would fuck me up the arse?'

'Bingo! You got it! Genius. Why don't I do that right now?' Lane let go of her femme and appraised her.

'No!' Carol's fear sounded genuine. 'No! Honestly, Lane, I don't want you to.' She got up and started to fill the kettle, as if the discussion were over.

'Hey! A deal's a deal.' Lane jumped from the bed and grabbed Carrie from behind, pressing one finger between her arsecheeks. 'Right up that hole, with the dildo, I think. Before lunch.'

Carol fought her off and swivelled round, dropping the kettle on the floor. Water poured across the red painted floorboards as she stood there in one of Lane's old T-shirts which stopped just above her triangle of pubic hair.

'I'm sorry, Lane,' she said in a tone of deadly seriousness, 'but there is no fucking way that you are going to bugger me. I hate it when you even touch my arsehole. I don't want anything going up there.' She shuddered. 'I shouldn't have agreed to the deal, but I did because I honestly didn't think I was going to have sex with anyone else. But then things happened . . .'

She sank back down on the bed and Lane stood over her. 'What do you mean, things happened? How can it just happen that you end up in an orgy with your students?'

'They're not my students.'

'Well, they seem to know you, sweetheart.'

Carol sighed. 'I went round to Marg's for dinner. And it turned out that she and her flatmate had more than dinner in mind. Then it escalated from there.'

'Fucking hell, Carol, how long has this been going on?' Lane was amazed and angry.

'Not long. It was so exciting and I just got carried along with it.'

'What *about* us?' Lane demanded.

'What about us? You fuck boys whenever you like and get anyone you meet to fuck me. What kind of relationship is that?'

'You agreed to it, Carrie, and you agreed to the conditions.' Lane glared at her. 'You agreed that I would fuck your sweet arse if you messed around, and now you've messed around with . . . Fuck, I don't know how many people.' She blinked and shook her head slowly from side to side, trying to take it all in. 'Have you had sex with everyone that was there last night?'

'No . . . Does it make any difference?'

'Yes. You said you wouldn't go with anyone else. We agreed. So, if you have done, then you obviously don't care about me or being truthful to me. I'd say, the more women you've fucked, the less you care about me.'

Carol laughed. 'That's kind of a double standard.'

'You think it's funny? If you thought we had a double standard when we struck our deal then you shouldn't have agreed to it. You should have suggested alternatives. But, oh no, that's not your way, is it? That's too fucking straightforward. So instead, you let me think that you're being true to the deal, but in fact you're screwing that bitch, Petra. Kind of a doggy name, actually, isn't it? Petra?'

'Oh, come on, Lane, don't start picking on her.'

'No, let's pick on you. Let me present the evidence. First you tell me that you're not going to have sex with anyone else. Then you agree I could fuck you up the arse if you did go with anyone else because, hey, you're really not going to go with anyone else. Then –'

'Lane! It was a stupid deal. It was crazy.'

'So? You agreed!' Lane had the feeling that the facts were somehow slipping away from her and had to be restated. 'You agreed, Carrie! If you go with anyone else, I fuck you up the arse. You fucking agreed!'

'Would that make everything all right, then, Lane? All the infidelities, wiped out by buggering me against my will? Because that's what it would be. I am not going to let you do it. I can't.' Carol's expression was wavering between determination and defensiveness.

A silence descended. They had gone from playful to battling in the ten minutes since they woke up.

'So, what happens now?' Lane asked eventually.

'Maybe we should take a break for a few days. I know I'm breaking a deal, I know that. And if that means that you don't want to be with me . . . Well, like I said, we could have a bit of time to think it over.'

Lane took a tea towel from a hook and threw it on to the puddle on the floor around the kettle. She kept her face away from Carol to hide the strength of feeling behind her words. 'I don't want to do that. I'll come up with something else, OK?'

'What do you mean, something else?'

'I mean, a new clause to the deal.'

'Lane, there's more going on here than clauses to deals, isn't there?'

'Yeah.'

Quietly, gently, Carol said, 'I love you, Laney.'

'Yeah.'

Carol got up off the bed and put her arms round Lane, who was holding the wet tea towel and blinking away tears. 'Hey, hey!' said Carol. 'Come on, hon, it's going to be OK.'

Lane nuzzled the top of Carol's head. 'Yeah, maybe.'

They kissed. The relief of connecting was enormous. Lane pushed her tongue deep into Carrie's mouth and held her close. Their tongues were dancing together, their hands moving under each other's T-shirt. Lane stroked Carol's breasts and, at the same time, pressed her hips against her so their pubes rubbed together and their clits went on full alert.

Neither of them spoke. Instead, their groans of urgency grew louder as Lane pulled Carrie down on the rug in the centre of the room and buried her face in her femme's musky cunt, eliciting a delighted moan. Then it was Lane's turn to moan as Carol started to lick *her* cunt. Their hands were all over each other as their tongues moved from cunt to clit in long, synchronised strokes for minutes before focusing on those small pleasure buds.

Lane licked at Carol's clit and pushed the crook of her finger into that wet cunt, only to jerk as her lover copied her action; entering Lane with a single finger that tucked itself inside her cunt. Lane's other hand moved to Carol's bum, cupping around one soft cheek. Together they licked and stroked, tucked into each other and moving in a single rhythm. Their groans were buried in each other's wet centre as they built to a single climax that exploded between them, making their circle of love shudder and spasm.

They fell asleep like that, each pair of lips enclosing a softening clit.

'Did you get off on that whipping at the Special Tutorial?' Lane asked when they were back in bed with big cups of black coffee. It was evening.

'None of your business.'

'Well, if you don't want to hear my new proposal.'

'What?'

'No, you don't want to hear.'

'Lane, if it leaves my anal passageways intact as the one virgin territory left in the well-trodden kingdom of my body, then yes, I want to hear about it.'

'OK. Suppose that two of your dear students were to whip you at the next tutorial?'

Carol was shocked. 'Where did you get that idea from? I don't like it.'

'Think it over, Carrie. It's on the negotiating table, as they say.'

'As who says? I've never been at a negotiating table where one side had to choose between – what do they call it in the navy – sodomy and the lash?'

But in the silence that followed, Carol tried to imagine what it would be like to bare her backside to a whipping from her girls.

TWENTY
Get Ready

'You're coming to the next tutorial, Jason.'
'Oh, no. I told you, I'm gay. Remember, I was stealing
Playgirl from the newsagent before I'd even kissed anyone.'
'OK, setting aside the implication that I'm not gay, which I
kind of resent, I can safely tell you that you will enjoy the next
tutorial. Because there will be boys.'
'What? That was a girl thing if ever I saw a girl thing.'
'Not any more. And remember my mate Jack?'
'How could I forget him?'
'He'll be there. He's been asking about you, Jason, so now's
your chance.'
'OK, I'll think about it. But all those girls in their knickers, it's
weird! Anyway, you're not gay.'
'I fucking am.'
'You have sex with men, Lane.'
'Gay men,' she corrected him. 'It just means I'm queer.'
'Is that still trendy, Laney? Only it seems kind of passé.'
'Oh, are you a style guru now? Mr Suit.'
'I only wear that for work! Jesus!'
'OK. Now listen, d'you think Annie's cool about what hap-
pened the other night?'
'You haven't spoken to her? I thought you said she was coming
next time?'

'Well, I hope she is.'

'Laney, ring her up!'

'Why, what's she said?'

'Just ring her up.'

Lane said goodbye to Jason and took his advice.

'So, this is embarrassing,' Lane told Annie after they'd said their hellos.

'Why would you be embarrassed? You asked us to come to the house. Did you expect to be embarrassed?'

'I wasn't thinking. I was in a white rage.' She realised that Annie had never heard the full story. 'Petra was fucking Carrie when I walked in.'

'Oh! God, what did you do?' Annie caught herself. 'Silly question. You fucked Petra, of course, as anyone would have done.'

'They might have,' Lane said, defending herself. 'Wait till it happens to you.'

'It can't really, unless I get a girlfriend.'

'Yeah, any news on that front?'

'Well, there is someone I wouldn't mind seeing again.'

'Who's that?' Lane asked excitedly.

'Someone I met at that house. Where were we anyway, the devil's house?'

'Something like that. Some student who Carrie supposedly doesn't teach, but I don't get how that can be true. Anyway, this girl first lured Carrie round there with the promise of free dinner and then it turned out there was more on the menu. Then she started hosting these so-called Special Tutorials. And that's where we came in.'

'Was that the first one?' asked Annie.

'Oh no.' She paused as it all came back to her. 'Can you imagine, all going on in my bloody street, next door to Fee and Fennell! Talk about what will the neighbours think!' She reined herself in. 'Anyway, who is it you fancy? You kept that quiet.'

'You haven't given me a chance to tell you,' Annie pointed out. 'And I didn't notice you phoning me for a debrief after that night, either.'

'You could have phoned me,' said Lane. 'I was embarrassed.'

'So you said. Well, I was waiting for you to show some concern for what you put me through. Including having sex with about six total strangers after months of celibacy. But this one girl, she's called Sheila, she was really nice. The one in the red underwear – when she was still wearing her underwear, anyway. Long dark hair. The one Jason handed over to me.'

'Yeah, I remember that! And she was chief front-door opener.'

'And?'

'And what?'

'What did you think?'

'I think she's attractive.'

'Mm-hmm,' purred Annie. 'But I didn't get her number. I don't know how I'll see her again.'

'Well, I may be able to help out there . . .'

The most difficult person to convince turned out to be Jack.

'Actually, Jack,' said Lane, playing her trump card. 'Jason will be there and he's been asking about you.'

'Jason! Why will Jason be there?'

'Never mind why. Just say yes.'

'OK.'

'OK!' cried Lane, triumphantly. 'Now, get out your diary. The planning meeting is –'

'The what?'

'We're getting together, all the oldies, to plan how we'll deal with the students.'

'You really are bonkers. First you tell me that you've uncovered a secret lesbian orgy where your girlfriend gets fucked by that cow we met at The Corner, then you tell me you're going back there. Then you want me to come too, and then – then you have a planning meeting!'

'Yeah, yeah. It's just crazy,' said Lane, feigning boredom. 'But Carol will be at the meeting and I think it might turn into a kind of rehearsal, if you know what I mean.'

'Yeah?'

'Yeah.'

'But if Jason's going to be there,' said Jack, 'won't I be in too much demand?'

'I don't think you get the idea yet, Jackie-boy. You don't have to choose one or the other. Think cruising, think backroom. We're just wild, crazy kids.'

'Where are you meeting?'

'At Carrie's.'

'Oh, very wild and crazy.'

'Sorry, we couldn't get anywhere else. We tried to book Russell Square but the council refused the sex-party planning-group licence.'

Grudgingly, Jack gave in. 'Give me the details and we'll see if I can spare the time to fuck your girlfriend.'

After she put the phone down, Lane wondered if she should broach the subject with Carol. But perhaps it would be better coming from Jack.

Everyone turned up as agreed and they were halfway through their planning meeting when Carrie came up with her suggestion: 'Put the boys in another room.'

'Why?'

'Because the Special Tutorials are supposed to be for lesbians and for other girls who fancy their tutors or each other, not for men. God, Laney, what's happened to you? Have you forgotten what "women-only" means? Put the guys in another room and you can still go in there with them if you really think they're sexier than women. But no men come in the main room. OK?'

'Yeah, I agree.' This was Petra, who had barely spoken so far.

'Oh, hello, married lady,' said Lane, not hiding her contempt.

'I'm not married.'

'You live with a guy and you're telling me that I'm weird for wanting sex to go on between men and women.'

Siding with Petra, Carol asked: 'Lane, are you a dyke, yes or no?'

'You of all people should not need to ask me that, sweetheart.'

'So don't be so bloody-minded. If you want boy–girl sex, go to a straight orgy.' As Carol spoke, Annie handed her the joint in what looked like an act of allegiance.

'What do you think, boys?' Lane asked Jack and Jason.

'I wouldn't dare have an opinion,' said Jason, all queeny.

'Well I would!' declared Jack. 'If there's going to be cute boys, I'm not sharing them with girls.'

Lane stared at him, mouth agape.

'What?' he asked, all innocence.

'You know very well what,' Lane told him. 'You don't always refuse to share with girls.'

'Enough,' said Carrie as she passed the spliff to Petra. 'We don't want to hear about your outside activities, you two.' She narrowed her eyes. 'But Jason, didn't you come over all queasy when one of the girls wanted you to screw her? Surely you'd rather we kept ourselves to ourselves?'

He just gave Carol a look that suggested he had no reason to tell her anything.

'I don't know why we're having men at the next tutorial anyway,' said Petra. 'The girls are out of control as it is.'

'I'll give you that,' said Lane. 'They're out of control because you don't know how to keep them under control.'

'I had them under my thumb,' said Carol.

'So to speak,' said Jack.

'Can we stop saying "so to speak" and "as they say"?' asked Annie. 'I've got double entendres coming out my ears but we still haven't discussed the real dirt. What are we going to do with them?'

'We're going to service them,' said Carol, confidently. 'The way I serviced them the first time.'

'Was that nostalgia that crossed your face then, sweetheart?' asked Lane.

'No, the pizza's repeating on me,' Carrie shot back. Scattered across the kitchen table were the remains of the takeaway that had been delivered earlier, along with two open bottles of wine and a few empty ones.

The committee were no longer upright round the table. Jason was leaning his head in the crook of his elbow, Lane had her feet on the table. Petra had her legs crossed under her and Annie was rocking her chair on its back legs.

'Anyway,' continued Carol, 'there's something I haven't told you all. This will be the last Special Tutorial. So we have to get it right.' They grew more attentive.

'You mean it's the last one this term?' asked Petra.

'No. It's the last one, ever. Marg goes back to the States at the end of term and Amy's giving up the flat. It seems like the right time to stop, before we're found out.'

'You can't do that,' said Petra.

'I can,' Carol said firmly. 'Try and stop me. You can't. Your threats to tell the Prof about me are useless now, because you're in it up to your tits, aren't you, love? So just enjoy it while it lasts.'

They sat in silence for a few minutes. Petra looked stunned.

Jack had his hands behind his head in contemplation. 'I know what I think should happen on the night,' he said.

'Yes?' asked everyone.

'We get them all into groups according to what they're into. Just give a list of things we want to do to them and see who wants what.'

'OK,' said Lane, 'you start then.'

'OK. Boys who want to fuck, boys who want to be fucked.'

'Are you going to do both?' asked Jason, sitting up.

'And anything else that needs doing, yes. But I'm just giving examples. Come on, let's hear yours.'

'Mine?' asked Jason.

'Whoever,' replied Jack, playing it cool, as if he didn't really care what Jason's sexual fantasies were.

'OK,' said Jason. 'Wank circle.'

'Oh!' said Annie, suddenly animated out of her stoned state. 'Can you have a female wank circle?'

Petra's eyes twinkled. 'We can have whatever we want.'

'OK, I want that.'

'Now we are getting somewhere,' said Carol.

'And what do you want, Carrie?' asked Lane.

'I don't know.' She shook her head. 'I don't want the responsibility of deciding who does what. I have enough responsibility in my life already.'

'But what happened at that first tutorial?' asked Lane, pushing it. 'Didn't you take charge?'

The others were silent, waiting to hear Carol's response, but she only said, 'That's private.' Lane raised her eyebrows but said no more. 'What do you want, anyway?' Carrie asked her.

'I want to fuck all the girls and then go in the other room and fuck all the boys,' claimed Lane.

'Challenge!' cried Jack.

'What?'

'I don't believe you,' he explained. 'I'm challenging your answer.'

'Why?'

'Because there's no way you're going to be active all night, that's why.'

'Oh, let a girl have her fantasy, Jackie.'

The others were developing their themes in their heads. Petra said, 'Let's make a list and one or two of us can be assigned to each group.'

'For God's sake!' said Carol. 'Can't we leave anything to chance?'

'Oh, sorry!' said Petra, sarcastically. 'Was that too anal?'

'As the actress said to the bishop,' murmured Jason.

Annie kicked him under the table. 'Banned phrase!' she told her friend.

'Someone had to say it,' he pointed out.

Everyone was either stoned and floppy or drunk and boisterous. Both, in Jack's case. 'Let's have a rehearsal,' he suggested now. 'And let's try out some new ideas.'

'Such as?' asked Carol.

'Did you tell her?' Jack directed the question at Lane.

'No, I thought I'd leave you to turn on your charm.'

'What is it?' Carol demanded impatiently.

Jack got up and went over to whisper in her ear.

'Here we go,' said Petra. 'Time to state your desires.' She wrote a note on the cardboard of the pizza box, tore it off and handed it to Annie, who looked shocked. Petra caught Lane staring at her. 'Are you going to sit out, Lane? Or have you got a secret desire we can fulfil tonight?'

'There is one thing that's been overlooked,' said Lane.

'What's that?'

'I have a plan for Carol that she's agreed to. I want to see Marg and Amy whipping Carol. They're the ones who started this whole tutorial thing, apparently, so they deserve a little reward.'

Eyebrows were raised all round but Lane went on: 'Carol's never been whipped before, so what we were wondering . . . Would anyone like to help her practise?'

It did not take long for the drunken crew to get over their surprise at each other's requests. Lane was amazed to hear the following deal being struck:

'OK,' Carrie said to Jack. 'You can fuck me if you and Petra whip me afterwards.'

As for Jason, he was clearly waiting for his turn with Jack. He and Lane shared a joint as Annie and Petra moved into the sitting-room area, where they stripped. Annie sat in a big armchair and spread her legs so that Petra could kneel between them and bury her head there.

Jack, meanwhile, rolled on a condom, getting ready to fuck Carol.

'Isn't that freaking you out?' Jason asked Lane.

'No. It's turning me on,' she replied.

They watched as Jack went to kiss Carol and she pushed his face away. 'No kissing,' she insisted. 'I don't like you enough for that, Jack.'

In his sharp white vest and briefs, Jack's strong, broad build was emphasised. His rubbered dick looked oddly vulnerable as he eyed Carol suspiciously. 'Do you want me or not?' he asked.

'Does it matter?' she asked. She had undressed to a blue bodystocking which she now pulled apart at the crotch. She touched herself, looking at him. They were sitting on the floor, her blonde curls contrasting with his dark skinhead; her petite frame almost dwarfed.

Carrie looked across at Lane, who was still sitting at the table. 'What do you think, Laney? Missionary or doggy?'

'Missionary,' Lane replied, her face flushing with her sudden involvement in this scene. 'Let's teach him the traditional way.'

'OK,' Carol agreed. She lay back on the floor, her hand still in her crotch. 'Jack, you have to check how wet the woman is and you have to be sensitive to what she wants.' She looked at him, holding his dick like a lost boy. 'Get down here then, laddie.'

Lane's eyes were wide with lustful fascination as she watched her two favourite sex partners getting it on. Jack's strength and sexual assertiveness had evaporated. He looked cautious and full of wonder as he lowered himself over Carol and groped between her legs. She helped him into her and her hips jerked from the floor as his thick cock found its way inside.

'Oh yeah!' she cried. 'That's it!' Lane noticed that she kept her hand on her clit as he fucked her.

The cute black guy beside Lane was clearly finding it all a bit more difficult than she was. 'What's up, Jase?' she asked him.

'What do you think?' he responded. Lane remembered that she had all but promised him that tonight he would have his chance with Jack. The drink seemed to be affecting him badly: 'He doesn't want me. He wants your girlfriend more than me.'

'Hey!' She passed him the joint. 'Chill, Jase. It ain't over yet, kiddo.' She kissed him affectionately on the cheek, his light stubble brushing her lips, and ran a hand over his cropped, tactile black hair. 'Don't let him have all the power,' she whispered. 'He doesn't want it anyway. Trust me – I know what I'm talking about.'

Jason nodded and released himself from Lane's fussing. His friend Annie was shouting out in ecstasy and he wanted to take a good look.

Lane didn't know where to focus her attentions. Petra's head was still moving furiously between Annie's thighs as the shouts continued. Meanwhile, Jack and Carol had found their own rhythm and were groaning together with each thrust. She recognised from their sounds that each of them was close to coming. Carol's hands were clasped around Jack's tight arse, pulling him into her. Jack's hands were on the floor, as if he were doing press-ups. He seemed to have too much awe for Carol to actually touch her. And that was when it all started to make sense to Lane. As she heard her two lovers reaching their joint climax, as Carol shouted out, 'Yes! Yes!', Lane realised that Jack's disdain for Carol in the past had actually hidden his fearful respect for an older, feminine woman.

Well, he had been initiated into the ways of the femme. Now it was his turn to do someone else a favour. Lane had bought two whips from the lesbian sex shop. She went to find them, up the metal staircase to Carol's mezzanine bedroom. As she came back down, with a bullwhip and a cat-o'-nine-tails, she saw everyone still lolling around.

'Hey! Come on people, prepare yourselves!' she told them from the stairs.

Petra stirred. She left Annie where she sat; legs spread, eyes closed. Jack pulled out of Carrie slowly and hauled her to her feet – before she was ready. She moaned but let him lead her over to the fireplace. Here he placed her hands on the mantelpiece and told her to stay like that. Petra quickly joined him to spread Carol's legs. Thrilled, Lane saw that her lover's thighs were wet with cunt juice.

'Have you done this before?' Petra asked Jack.

'Darling, what haven't I done?' he camped.

Annie stirred and opened her eyes. She stared at the sight of Carol in her bodystocking, open at the crotch, spreadeagled across the fireplace. Jason dragged himself from the kitchen to slump on the sofa and watch.

Lane held out the whips. Petra took the cat-o'-nine-tails, Jack the bullwhip.

'Are you OK?' Lane asked Carol.

'Hold me,' her lover replied.

'I can't hold you,' she whispered as she stroked Carol's blonde curls. 'I have to watch. But I'll be right here.' She slipped her hand inside the bra of Carol's one-piece and cupped her breast, fingers closing on one tight nipple. 'I have to watch,' she whispered again, breathless with anticipation. 'If you want them to stop, just say so,' she said gently. 'OK,' she added for Petra and Jack's benefit. 'She's ready.'

Lane let go of Carol's breast and stood where she could watch the whipping being meted out. Petra and Jack, who had sized each other up just weeks ago outside The Corner, were now partners in crime, both dressed in their white underwear. Jack nodded at the tall femme in her skimpy bra and G-string, letting her know that she could go first. Petra flicked back her black hair and held out the whip.

'I'm going to whip your arse and make you scream,' she told Carol before her practised flick of the whip sent its tails lashing down across that round backside. Carol's agonised cry pierced through Lane.

'Are you OK?'

'Yes,' whimpered the femme.

'Carry on,' Lane told the others.

Jack raised his whip and brought it slashing down where it cut into Carol's left buttock and left a red weal. She screamed, 'No!'

Lane went to Carol's side and kissed her face. It was wet with tears. 'Do you want them to stop?'

'Do you?'

'No. But if it's too much –'

'No. Not yet.'

Again, Lane gave them the nod. Now Petra and Jack took turns to whip Carol in quick succession. Blow after blow rained down on that peachy behind, without mercy. Jack was silent and focused, like a vicious clockwork man, but Petra shouted out with each lash. First: 'Don't you like it?' Then: 'It hurts, doesn't it, Carrie?'

'I told you not to call her that,' Lane protested.

Petra wheeled around, brandishing the whip. 'You can't tell me what to do any more, Lane,' she said. 'So shut up.' And with that she lashed Carrie's arse so hard that the besieged woman broke down and let go of the mantelpiece, falling to the floor.

Lane was first to her side. She pulled her lover to her and held her.

'Too much,' sobbed Carol.

'Too much too soon, was it?' Petra asked, a cruel note in her voice.

'I'm sorry, honey,' whispered Lane. 'We shouldn't have done it.'

'Oh yes,' murmured Carol. 'We had to do it. To see. To see if I liked it.'

'But you didn't?'

'I have to feel it again. Fuck me while they do it.'

She straddled Lane and unzipped her trousers, pulling out her dildo. Everyone was ready. No sooner had Carol lowered herself on to that fat cock and bent forward than the blows rained down again. Lane held her by the shoulders and kept her close as she fucked her. Even Jack was groaning now as everyone's efforts were concentrated on Carol, who was screaming and struggling against what she had requested.

'Is it too much, baby?' asked Lane once again.

'Yes, but I need it!' cried Carol, burying her head in Lane's chest till Lane felt the tears soaking through her T-shirt.

Lane came as Carol did, from the uncontainable thrill of fucking her while she screamed and took her punishment. For that was what it was, in Lane's mind, a punishment for her infidelity and lies. Meted out by those who had already fucked her.

Carol's orgasm put an end to the whipping. As she thrashed in Lane's arms, she gradually quietened. And everyone fell silent, awed by what they had done. As she wrapped her arms tighter around her quivering lover and felt her own climax slither away, Lane wondered what they would all be capable of at the next tutorial.

'Want to make a night of it?' Jason asked Jack when everyone was ready to go home.

The white man tipped his head to one side, as if he needed to consider the request, then said, 'Yeah, OK, what the hell.'

Lane smiled in delight that the match was finally being made between her two favourite men. They left and Carol closed the door behind the last of her guests.

'Ready for bed?' asked Lane.

'I have never been so ready for bed in my life,' replied Carol, hitching the straps of her bodystocking up her shoulders in a reflex action that looked absurd as her lovely arse was still on full display, striped with red. 'But I don't think I'll be sleeping on my back for a while.'

'Does it hurt?'

'Does it hurt? What kind of question is that? Did you think it would stop hurting when they stopped whipping me?'

'No.'

'No. Well, you got what you wanted.'

'Didn't you?' asked Lane.

Carol looked down as if ashamed and dropped her bravado. 'Yes, I got what I wanted. But why did I want it? To be hurt like that? And now to be humiliated at the Special Tutorial.'

'So you will go ahead with it?' asked Lane.

'Are you listening to me, Laney? It all feels so strange. I need to talk about it.'

'So we'll talk. Come to bed and we'll talk.'

Carol shook her head. 'Not now. Now I need to sleep. Will you come up with me and keep me safe?'

Carol had never said anything like that before and Lane wondered at the changes wrought in them both by the evening's events.

'Of course I will, babes,' Lane said softly. 'Of course I will.'

TWENTY-ONE
Final Submission

It seemed like everyone knew this was to be the final tutorial. They had dressed in their sexiest kit and the fridge was full of cheap fizz. When Carol went to the toilet, she found Red, Gemma and Leila in there, snorting coke.

'How can you afford that?' she asked them, before accepting a line.

It was a party. It was just unfortunate that Carol and her coterie of experienced leaders were so late in arriving. The girls were already feeling each other up and hardly anyone was wearing more than their underwear. There were women there Carol had never seen before.

In one corner, Deville was fucking the naked Becca as if they were alone, Becca's big tits swinging back and forth. Dee greeted Carol with a long wet kiss on the mouth, oblivious to the fact that Lane was holding Carol's hand. There were skinny young men in the kitchen and more lolling on the sofas with beers in their hands.

How to get some discipline into the proceedings? Carol need not have worried because Petra and Lane were both on top form and seemed to be in competition with each other for most authoritarian orgy-mistress.

'Gather round,' bellowed Lane. 'Stop fucking in the corner, you two. Get over here . . . Hi!' She greeted Marg, and Carol remembered seeing the two of them together at the last session.

With Lane's attention distracted, Petra started up. 'This may well be our last tutorial together, girls,' she announced. Carol noticed the 'may well' and silently cursed Petra for making out there was any uncertainty.

'Tonight we have some special plans and we want you all to choose which you will take part in, then do as you are told.'

Carol didn't like watching Petra in charge. She took over, buzzing from the coke: 'Sit down for a moment, everyone, and I'll tell you what we've planned.' She looked around for Annie and located her flirting with Sheila, who was wearing scarlet bra and pants, like last time. Waving a hand in their direction, Carol continued. 'If you want to join in a wank circle, see Annie.'

There was a rush of excitement in the room. Two naked girls got up straight away and went over to Annie.

Meanwhile, Jack and Jason had rounded up the half-dozen boys and taken them away, presumably to one of the bedrooms.

Petra gave up her attempts at taking charge. She was too tempted by the wank circle. 'If you want to line up for me to fuck you with dildos or whip you, or both, come over here,' announced Carol. 'Marg, bring your bag of tricks. And anyone who's left over had better watch and wait. Later there will be a ritual flogging and I am sorry to tell you that I will be the victim.'

She had their full attention. 'And I'm sorry if I take it out on you girls who have been so loyal to me.' It was the voice of the part of Carol that could have lived forever in this one room, going through these rituals and humiliations with her troupe of young women.

Discarding her jacket, Carol prepared herself. She was wearing a deep pink bodystocking and black trousers. Saving herself for the flogging that was to come, she kept these clothes on so that no one could attempt to fuck her. Marg, her red hair freshly cropped with its tufts intact at back and front, brought the bag of goodies to Carol. The room was full of smoke from cigarettes and incense and when Leila handed Carol the bong, she refused. She wanted a clear head for what she had to do and she had already taken enough for one night.

'Do you need any help, Dr Maitland?' Marg asked Carol, who was rummaging through the sports bag, her hand closing on rubber and leather as she felt each toy, each harness. The smell that came off them was heady.

'Yes, Marg. You can hand me whichever dildo you think is best for each girl. Will you do that?'

'Yes, Dr Maitland.'

The girls lined up: Leila, wearing nothing but white Calvins that looked sharp against her brown skin, her muscles as lithe as ever; Amy, always keen to be taken; Gemma, her small breasts naked; and another white girl who was a stranger to Carol. She wore a vest and boxer shorts and looked overdressed.

'Take off your vest and pants,' Carol told her.

'Yes, Dr Maitland,' said the girl, who did as she was told. She was plump and cute but shy. As she stood there looking at the floor, her grabbable arse made Carol long to fuck her.

'I want everyone bending over,' Carol told her assistant, Marg. 'What shall we do, do you think? Make them hold their knees?'

'I could bring the chairs in from the kitchen,' Marg suggested.

'Perfect. Yes, please do that.'

Carol waited and her little group watched the wank circle. It was made up of Annie, Sheila, two naked friends, Petra, and the chunky butch called Red. One of the naked girls, lean and androgynous, had a piercing through her clit that was visible as she wanked. Others had their hands down their knickers. They were standing in a circle and Carol wondered if they would be able to stay upright. Each woman was rubbing her own clit and looking round at the others. Above the music playing on the boombox, their moans were a slow chorus. Carol managed to pick out the lyrics of the grungy song: 'Turning things around, you're the teacher, I'm the student.' Perfect.

Marg was bringing in chairs from the kitchen and Carol told her group: 'I want each of you to bend over a chair and I will fuck you or whip you, or both. Marg will choose which dildo is best for each of you. Are you ready?'

'Yes, Dr Maitland,' they replied, all compliant. Carol felt turned on by their formal obedience, so at odds with their nakedness. Her mind went back to the planning meeting when she'd said she did not want any responsibility. It was disingenuous. What she wanted was just this: to be in charge of girls who wanted to be under her.

Each girl bent over the seat of a chair, holding on tight, with her head on the seat, or leaning right down to the floor. They were beautiful.

She wondered what had happened to Lane, who would probably be astonished to see Carol take charge like this. Clearing her mind of such distractions, Carol inspected the girls. She walked up and down the short row, feeling each bum. She peeled down Leila's Calvins, breathing heavily in her excitement. She was wet with arousal and Leila's pants were equally wet.

Feeling bottoms was not something Carol had done much of in her life. But since the start of the tutorials she had found a lot of stimulation in this particular activity. Now she exercised it fully, pressing her crotch forward into each arse as she felt both cheeks with her keen hands.

'Arse or cunt?' she asked Leila, who gasped.

'Arse, please, Dr Maitland.'

'And the whip?'

'No!'

'Something for the arse here, Marg,' Carol said.

'This is a cool buttplug,' Marg said straight away. 'Stick that in her, Doctor M.'

'Good.' She took the plug from her assistant. It tapered to a rounded point. Without her having to ask, Marg lubed up the implement. Carol parted those firm brown arsecheeks and pressed the buttplug against Leila's tight hole. She had never fucked anyone's arse before. She had never offered it as an option at the tutorials. But now, because of Lane's recent obsession in that area, she was keen to try it out.

'Nice and easy now, Leila,' she soothed as she pushed the tip of the plug into that hole, which eased open and let her inside. Carol moaned as loud as Leila, watching the plug being eaten by that butthole.

'I'll leave that in you for now, Leila. You can touch your clit.'

She moved to the next girl, Gemma. 'The arse or the cunt?' she asked in between breaths.

'Please can you fuck both my holes, Dr Maitland?' asked the shapely girl.

'Certainly. Did you hear that, Marg?'

'Yes. Coming up, Doctor M.'

'What about you?' she asked the big-bummed new girl.

'Please, Dr Maitland, whip me between my legs.'

Carol felt a new fire in her own cunt. 'Good,' was all she could manage to say. She had never whipped anyone's cunt. It would take care and control.

Marg was handing over two dildos for use on Gemma. Carol started with the larger one which was the two-tone she had used on Marg, that first time. They had come a long way – and come a lot of times – since then.

'How's that?' she asked as she pushed the dildo into Gemma's welcoming cunt.

The girl moaned. 'It's good. Fill me up, please!'

When the dildo was all the way in, Carol took the smaller tool and pressed it against Gemma's arsehole. 'No!' cried the girl.

'Don't you want it?'

'Not yet.'

'OK.' Carol left her like that. 'A whip for this woman, please, Marg.' She was handed a thin strip of leather on a wooden handle. 'Won't that cut too hard into her?' she asked.

'Haven't you done this before, Doctor M?' Carol shook her head. 'You have to be real careful. Do it soft, aim at the top of her thighs and see how she takes it. It may flick across her cunt, it may not.' Then she addressed the girl. 'That's what you mean, isn't it, Lou?'

'Yes,' came the gasp.

'We've been around the scene together,' Marg explained cheerfully.

Carol told Lou to prepare herself, then she spread the girl's plump legs. Her pink cunt was wet. The lecturer took aim and swung up with the whip from below, aiming at her thigh, but the whip struck home across the girl's labia.

She screamed. 'Yes! Yes!' Her arse shuddered in the air and all the muscles between her legs were clenching and releasing.

Again Carol whipped between her legs. Again the girl screamed in pain and pleasure. After three lashes, Carol told her to rest. She returned to Gemma and, without saying another word to her, pushed the slim dildo into her arse. It opened and accepted the tool.

'Good girl.'

She went down the line, feeling each arse again and even bending down to look at where the rubber protruded from each hole. She pushed a finger into the empty, sore cunt of the girl she had just whipped, who cried out once again.

Then she reached Amy. 'What do you want?' she asked the girl. 'Cunt or arse?'

'Please can you lick me out?'

'No, I can't. It's fucking or whipping, I told you that.'

'Please, Dr Maitland!' the girl pleaded, her face pressed into the seat of the chair, her arse rising to emphasise her request.

'Give me the whip, Marg!'

'No! No, Dr Maitland, I'm sorry!' cried Amy. 'Please fuck my cunt. I'm so sorry.'

'So I should think.'

Marg handed her a studded dildo but Carol rejected it. 'Something big, please, Marg.'

'No!' cried Amy.

'Yes! Take it or leave the group.'

Now it was Carol's turn to make the same cruel threats that had been made to her so often recently. But she felt for Amy. 'What will you do, Amy?' She softened her voice. 'Do you want to go and join another group, or do you want me to fuck you with this big dildo?'

'Fuck me please, Dr Maitland.'

'Good.' Carol spread Amy's legs wider and started to push the dildo into the girl's cunt. It was thrilling to watch the way that Amy's entrance was forced wider by the thick tool.

'Very good,' she said to the young woman, who took what she was given, obedient now and moaning quietly to herself. 'Perhaps next time –' but there will never be a next time, Carol realised wistfully '– you will understand that if I give you a choice, you must choose.'

'Yes, Dr Maitland.'

That was enough for now. It was time to move back up the

line and check on the girls, to bring them all to orgasm with the pleasure and pain they had requested from the lecturer.

Nearby, the wank circle was getting hotter. As each woman reached orgasm – shouting out and keeping her eyes open wide to admire the way the other girls just kept on wanking – their knees crumpled and they fell to the floor. Eventually only Annie and Sheila were standing. They were next to each other and Carol took a moment from pleasuring those arses in order to watch the two girls giving in to temptation and starting to wank each other off. They started by just touching clits, but then Annie's hand moved to Sheila's breasts. Two of the other women got up from where they had collapsed and wrapped themselves around the two upright women, holding them up as they rubbed each other and shouted each other's names.

This was not just sex, Carol thought. It looked and sounded like the beginnings of a love affair. When they came, they fell on the floor accompanied by the other two women and all rolled there together.

'Dr Maitland!'

Carol tore herself away as the owners of a row of bottoms demanded her attention. She knew that, one by one, they would soon be screaming in release.

In the bedroom, Lane had joined the ranks of the young men who were under Jack and Jason's tutelage. The two J's seemed comfortable together and Lane gathered that they had spent more than just the one night in each other's company since she saw them last.

'Active on this side, passive over there,' said Jack, taking control.

Jason went to the passive side of the room, where he started undressing the young men. One was in his underwear but the others still wore their jeans or combats. They queued up for it, waiting to feel his hands on their waistbands, his fingers on their flies. 'Just checking you're all ready for it, boys,' he explained as he felt each packet, verifying the hardness of the goods.

This was a side to Jason that Lane had certainly never seen before. Jack, meanwhile, was briefing the active guys. There were three of them and four of the others. 'We're just going to give them what they need,' he told the men. 'You know how to do that, don't you?' They nodded. They had stripped to their underwear. In trunks and briefs, their youth seemed emphasised.

'OK,' said Jack, 'go for it!'

Lane was only going to watch but Jack encouraged her to join in. 'Get your cock out,' he said. 'We're short of fuckers.'

Lane did as she was told and advanced across the room with Jack and the others. In this bedroom full of posters of female singers, the male drive was in command.

In the mêlée, a man rolled on his back for her like a dog waiting to be stroked, and she got straight in there. Condoms and lube were being handed round and she covered and smeared her dildo and then lubed up her fingers, which she worked into this young man's hole. He was skinny and only eighteen or nineteen and he had shaved his body smooth. He took hold of his cock as she pushed her fingers in him, and said, 'This is my fantasy.'

'What is?'

'Just this. I'm not gay but I like anal sex. But my girlfriend doesn't get it. She won't talk about it because it makes her think I'm gay.'

'Shut up,' said Lane, 'I'm fucking you now.'

'Yeah! Oh yeah! A girl's fucking my arse!' He was easy to please, anyway, and she quickly entered him and stayed there while he tugged on his dick, moaning in delight.

'You like that? Tell your girlfriend all about it, when you see her. I can do the same for her if she wants.'

'Oh! Oh, yeah!' was all he could manage. He was coming, his body jerking off the floor in quick spasms as his jism spurted out.

'That's you done,' said Lane, pulling out and rolling off the condom.

She wanted to join her friends, who were in a foursome. Jack was fucking a burly guy while the guy fucked Jason – who had someone's cock in his mouth. She rolled on another condom and told Jack: 'Get yourself ready, bro, because your arse needs screwing.'

As she entered his fuck tunnel, Lane felt free. No one here was going to challenge her right to be a gay boy for half an hour and then rejoin the gorgeous women in the front room and start all over again with them.

But she was saving her first orgasm of the night for later, when she would watch her lover being flogged.

Carol caught a glimpse of her lover in the doorway just as she was relenting with Amy by pulling the dildo out of the girl's quim. The other girls had come in quick succession, the new girl shouting, 'Thank you, Dr Maitland!' and then screaming in a climax of pain from the next lash inflicted by the lecturer.

Now Carol buried her face in Amy's pussy from behind. The girl moaned loudly and immediately came. Then Lane was by their side, wanting a piece of Amy. She knelt the other side of the chair and kissed the girl as her orgasm emptied her out.

'You're cute,' she told Amy. Carol had never thought of Amy as cute and it seemed a disrespectful thing to call her, but this was not the time to quibble over terms. She did not like watching Lane kiss one of the original special students. Carol looked away. She saw Red and Billy, the two toughest girls in the room, riding a double-ended dildo with their arms wrapped tight around each other. It made Carol want to try it. Deville and Becca were fucking in the corner again. No surprises there – they were not really up to the jealousy stuff after all. But where was Dee?

On a mission, Carol went down the hall to the bedrooms. In one, men were fucking each other with much huffing and exertion. In the bathroom, once again, someone's student loan was finding its way up student noses.

But in the second bedroom, sitting on Amy's bed in her trousers, her dark breasts naked, was Dee. 'You took your time, Carrie. Shut the door.'

'I can't.' She was pinned to the spot.

'Why not? Because your girlfriend's here? She won't mind.'

'No. Because I'm saving myself for later. I'm going to be flogged.'

'So you said.' Dee was smiling.

'Well, I have to be ready for it and I have to . . . I can't explain. It's personal.'

'It's personal!' This was very funny, apparently.

Those thoughts of how erotic it would be to wait all night to come, to come only after suffering a harsh whipping, were dissipating. A new rush of desire had stopped Carol in her tracks. Dee got up and shut the door and pushed her down on the bed where she pulled off Carol's shoes and started on the waistband of her trousers, searching for the zip. She found it at the side.

'No,' murmured Carol helplessly.

'You don't want me?'

'No.'

'Why don't I believe you?' Dee kissed her and Carol moaned as those full lips met hers and Dee's tongue lunged into her mouth, stopping her from replying. She rubbed a hand through Dee's locks, enjoying the texture.

Then the young woman was on her, pulling down those trousers and ripping open the poppers at the crotch of her bodystocking. 'Going to fuck you, Carrie. Get ready.'

'No!'

'No?' Dee mocked her. 'I think you mean yes, don't you?'

Carol shook her head from side to side as Dee stopped to release her captive's tits. She rubbed her face in them and nibbled on one nipple, making Carol moan. 'Oh, yes!'

'Yes!' Dee repeated. 'You do want me, don't you?'

'Oh yes! I know you have to do it, Dee. I know you have to fuck me.'

The top pulled her dildo out of her flies and mounted Carol in one urgent but careful thrust that made her thrash on the bed. They both shouted out. Carol's fuckhole tightened around that thick cock and she let herself be screwed.

'Yes!' shouted Dee again. 'You need it, don't you? I've missed your cunt. God, you need to be fucked, you slut. I can't believe what I've seen you doing. Fucking other girls and whipping strangers between the legs.'

'You saw that?' Carol could barely get out the words.

'I saw everything and I thought: she needs it now.'

'Yes, yes, I need it!' cried Carol.

'Good.' Dee stopped speaking and shut her eyes to kiss Carol, thrusting in her in long, slow movements that made the older woman shout out each time.

'Fuck me! I need it!' She was coming now and she held Dee tight, her hands on the black woman's naked back, taking it all from her.

'You liked that, didn't you?' Dee said as she kissed Carol's face. 'You needed that, Carrie. And I needed to do it to you.' Just like last time, she fell down between Carol's legs and licked gently at her clit, making it spasm again, while working on her own clit with her hand for a few seconds before she came, kissing and sucking at the older woman's cunt and groaning with release.

Someone was outside the door. 'Get up!' Carol said reflexively.

'We're at an orgy,' Dee reminded her. 'It's good if someone walks in.'

The door opened and Lane, in bulging boxer shorts, looked down with a mixture of desire and disapproval at the sight of her girlfriend with a rival between her legs. 'We're ready for you, Carrie. I think you've finished here.'

You can only be so prepared. In the last few days, Carol had tried to imagine what it would be like to be whipped by the girls in a packed room, but now she was shaking in trepidation as Lane led her into the middle of the room where two girls took hold of her by the arms. One was Billy, who had fucked her so soundly at a previous tutorial. The other was Red. They were strong girls.

'What are you going to do to me?' asked Carol, trembling.

'What do you think?' asked Lane. 'We're going to whip you. I believe Marg and Amy have already been asked to take a special role tonight.'

Amy approached. 'I can't do it,' she said calmly. 'I never said I would, and I won't. It's disrespectful to Dr Maitland.'

'It's not!' This was Marg. 'Not if she's agreed to it.'

'Marg,' said Carol, realising that no one had banned her from speaking. 'I thought you were passive. I've never seen you whipping anyone before. I thought you would refuse.'

'No, Doctor M. I'm the best. But you told me you weren't into pain before, so I never would have thought I could get to whip you. I'm real honoured. I can return all those favours!'

Carol had nothing to say to that. But who else would whip her? Lane was casting an eye around the room.

217

'I'll do it,' said Petra from the sofa, where she had a young woman in her lap.

'No!' Lane objected, but Petra was already taking a whip from Marg.

'It's no use just holding her there,' said Petra. 'Tie her to that pillar.'

'Oh!' cried Carol. Everything was moving too fast. She had never taken any notice of the pillar before. It was square and metal, propping up the ceiling where there must have been a wall before the house was converted. It was towards the middle of the room, so Carol would be centre stage.

The girls used belts from people's discarded trousers to strap Carol to the pillar. She had given in to them by now and allowed herself to be manipulated into position. As each strap was carefully tightened she felt her autonomy slipping further away.

'Don't tie the arms,' said Petra. 'You can still hold her by the arms.' Red and Billy stood by to do just that.

Lane kissed Carol, who was trussed up now, her front pressed against the pillar. 'Be good for me,' she told her femme.

'OK,' gasped Carol.

Then Lane pulled the back of Carol's deep pink bodystocking up over her bum, invoking humiliating gasps from the women in the room. Silence descended. The two butches took her arms and held them out in a cross. Petra separated Carol's legs by placing a hand on the top of each thigh and pulling them gently apart.

'Now!' ordered Lane, as she had at the rehearsal only days ago. Then, to Carol, 'I'm right here, babes. But you stay still. No rubbing your clit against the pillar. You wait for me.'

'Coming up, Doctor M,' Marg said, as if she was about to do a favour, just as she'd promised. Her whip slashed down on Carol's naked arse. The searing pain was almost a relief. Finally the threat had become reality and the flogging had begun.

'Take this, Carol!' cried Petra as she lashed out. Then it was Marg's turn, then Petra again.

The lecturer couldn't stop herself from screaming with each stroke of that whip, although Lane whispered to her or kissed her every time. The pain was almost too much for her but it was now part of a burning sensation that had spread right across her buttocks and made her whole arse feel as if it was on fire. That feeling burnt under the surface of the skin.

She was frightened that the whip might brush her cunt, which was spread wide and was aflame in a different way, burning with desire, so that the whole of her rear was a dangerous mix of agony and lust. She remembered how she had lashed at that girl's cunt and dreaded having the same thing happen to her. But her abusers were accurate in their aim. Blow after blow rained down across Carol's buttocks. And she was able to take it because she was so firmly tied and held that no effort was required from her except to absorb the pain.

'How many?' she whispered to Lane.

'As many as they like,' replied her butch, who gave her a deep kiss and then went to inspect the state of her arse. Between blows, Carol felt Lane's warm hand on her seared arse. 'Nice,' was all that Lane said.

Her own screams were frightening to Carol. So loud, so impossible to control. But she did not want them to stop because her whole body was inflamed now. If anyone touched her clit, she would come, for sure. But with her arms held out taut by the girls, there was no chance that she could touch herself.

'Touch me!' she begged Lane when her lover returned to her side and stroked her blonde curls.

'Oh no, Carrie, not now. Now you're our whipping girl, aren't you? It's not for you, this. It's for me. I thought it all up to get my own back on you for breaking our deal and I'll tell you this – it turns me on.'

'Ohhh!' Aroused further by these words, Carol was rubbing her crotch against the pole, pressing her naked clit against the cold metal.

'Stop!' shouted Lane.

Carol stopped and so did her tormentors.

'She's rubbing herself off. I told her not to do that. She must be punished.'

'No!' begged Carol.

'Why not?' asked Lane.

'Because . . . because I want you to fuck me up the arse.' Carol's voice was quiet and humble.

'Stop the whipping!' ordered Lane. The others stood back. 'Why do you want that, Carrie?' asked Lane quietly.

'I need you now. I need you to do it to me. It's the only thing that no one has done to me tonight. It will make me come.'

'Good.' Lane asked Marg for the bag of sex toys and chose a thinner dildo than the one she was wearing. She told the girls to leave Carol strapped to the pillar and to continue to hold her by the arms.

There was a pause as Lane fitted the tool in her harness. Then Carol felt wet lube on her arsehole. It was soothing. Even the foreign feel of Lane's finger pressing into that hole was soothing. She let it in easily and revelled in the new sensation.

'How do you like that?' asked Lane.

'I like it.' The room was completely silent. Carol could see some of the girls staring at her and Lane. She buzzed with sex.

'OK,' said her butch. 'Take a bit more.' Two or three fingers pushed inside her, spreading her apart.

'It's good, Lane. It's so good. I never knew. I'm sorry, I never knew.' She was still repeating this mantra when the slim cock slipped up her arse like a couple of fingers and she pushed her sore bum back and forth to take it all the way inside her as her lover called her a good girl and, alternately, a slut.

'I'm yours,' Carol said simply. She shut her eyes as Lane's fingers finally closed on her clit. They were thrusting together into the pillar. With each thrust, Carol shouted out, packed full up her tight arse and crying out for more.

'Good girl, my good little slut,' said Lane quietly. Then: 'Finally, you understand. Finally.' And she rubbed her femme's soaking-wet clit with love as she pumped her arse.

'Yes! Yes!' They were shouting out together and Carol knew that Lane would come from the excitement of fucking her in that way, up her backside as she had wanted to do for so long.

With that thought, Carol came. She was screaming and the crowd of girls were screaming too, caught up in the moment as if it were happening to them. Lane pawed at Carol's arse with one hand as she kept that orgasm going with her other hand. And then

Lane was coming too, thrusting again and again in Carol as if she had no control over the dildo that was so far up her femme's arse.

'Untie her!' Lane was shouting before her own orgasm had even died away. She pulled slowly out of Carol. 'I can't wait any longer to kiss you, sweetheart,' she told her lover.

In seconds, Carol's body, her stiff arms, were her own once more. But she was not required to do anything with them, as her lover took her in her arms and kissed her on the floor, surrounded by the students and Petra. They had given each other everything now. They could finally rest.

'I love you,' Lane murmured in Carol's ear, her hands stroking very lightly over the painful weals on that punished backside.

'I love you too.' It seemed incongruous, but it was true.

TWENTY-TWO
New Deal

Two weekends later, Lane found Carol tending her small garden – in her bra and knickers.

'I know it's warm today, but this seems excessive!' Lane called from the back door.

Carol jumped. 'I didn't see you,' she protested. 'How long have you been here?'

'I just got here. Or would you prefer me to say that I've been watching you from the window of your flat with my hand down my trousers?'

'Whatever.' Dismissively, she bent to pull up a weed.

'Hey, what's up?'

'Just end-of-term blues, I think.'

'Well, it's been kind of a weird term, just going on what I actually know,' said Lane. 'And God knows what else you got up to that I never heard about.'

Her lover straightened up. 'Let's put it behind us for now, shall we?'

'Yeah, OK.'

'Are you going to help me?' Carol gestured at the garden.

'Er, no. I really don't want to do the gardening. If I wanted to do gardening then I'd get a flat with a garden.'

'Is that so? Then you'll just have to look after my needs while I work, won't you?'

'Such as?'

'We'll start with a cup of tea, but it may get more strenuous.'

'And then I get to watch you working in your underwear?' asked Lane.

In response, Carol removed her bra. Her full breasts, dappled with freckles, shone with sweat in the sunlight.

'Sounds all right to me. I'll put the kettle on,' said Lane. She made tea and brought it out to Carol, who sat on the back step to drink it.

'Have you seen Jack?' she asked between sips.

'What? No. I told you, I'm holding back while we work out where we're at, you and me.'

'But you do want to go with men?'

'Not right now, no,' answered Lane.

'I've just been thinking. We're going away soon, it's the summer . . . Maybe it could be just us for a bit.'

'I'd like that.' She took the mug from Carol and kissed her.

'Really, though?' asked the older woman. 'Is that what you want?'

'Yes,' said Lane. 'That is what I want. I miss you.'

'I've got something to show you.'

'What?'

'Wait and see.'

'Cool. Because I've got something to show you.'

'What?'

She shook her head. 'Uh-uh. You show me yours first, babes.'

Lane gave in to her conscience and pulled up a few weeds. By dusk, they were both hot and grubby and contented from the physical work.

'What you got for me?' Lane asked as they sat on the flagstones of the small garden, her arms round her femme.

'Oh, God, I don't think we're up to it now.'

'What?'

Carol went inside and came out with a carrier bag. She took out a double-ended dildo. 'I won it in a raffle.'

'I don't think you did. I think you've been shopping.' She

looked afresh at her lover, then back at the double tool. 'It's not that big, though, is it? Are you downsizing?'

'I thought it would do for our arses,' replied Carol, as she stood there in just her knickers, with grime on her face.

'Come here,' Lane said. Suddenly they were all over each other, grabbing a handful of tit or arse as they kissed and sucked each other's body.

'Shove it in me!' Carol begged then.

'OK. Shove it in me!' echoed Lane. They knelt up and spread lube on both ends. Breathless and grinning, they kept their eyes on each other to make it simultaneous. Lane pressed one cockhead against Carol's arsehole and felt a corresponding pressure on her own hole.

'Yes!' they both shouted as they gained entry. Then they pushed up with the dildo and down with their bodies and kissed as it slipped right inside both their tunnels.

'Fuck!' shouted Lane.

'Shh!' warned Carol. 'What will the neighbours think?'

It didn't take them long for their fingers to reach for their own clits. Face to face, Lane was trying to match Carol's timing.

'Tell me when.'

'Soon,' gasped the older woman, her hips thrusting faster. Lane dropped her head to Carol's breasts and sucked one into her mouth while she touched her own clit faster.

Then they were coming in unison, the dildo stuck tight up their arses as Lane bit at Carol's nipple. Their muted groans continued as they rolled on the ground together.

'Just you and me this summer, then?' Carol reiterated when they were cleaned up and getting ready for bed.

'Just you, me, and our memories of all the dozens of others. Oh, and this video.'

'What?'

Lane delved into her bag and pulled out a tape. She ran downstairs to put it in the VCR. 'Come and look.'

Carol came to the balcony of the mezzanine. 'Fuck!' The large TV screen in the living room was filled with arse – with four arses that Carol recognised. They were the girls she had fucked in a line at the final tutorial. Their bums in varying sizes and hues, with the ends of the dildos sticking out of their cunts and arses – it was all on television!

'Who did that?'

'Er, you did that, didn't you?' replied Lane.

'You know what I mean – who filmed it? Have the girls agreed? How did you get it?'

'That's a lot of questions, Carol. But I'll give you a clue. It seems that our friends Fee and Fennell are not quite the innocent film co-op hippies we thought.'

'What?'

'They've been involved with Marg and Amy for some time now, apparently. Fee's been getting her end away with them. Fennell can only listen through the wall till his girlie gets home with the tape. They've got a camera in there.'

'I don't believe you. Jesus, I can never look them in the eye again over one of their beansprout suppers.'

'You can't look them in the eye? They've been on a virtual journey up your jacksie, so I think it's a bit late to be embarrassed.'

'But, Lane! If the girls knew they'd been filmed –'

'Stop worrying about it. Or do you want me to call up the higher-education ethics committee and see if they'd like to view the tape and make a ruling?'

Carol had been drawn downstairs by the magnetic pull of those pictures on the screen. She ignored Lane's threat, instead asking, 'Do Marg and Amy even know?'

'Yes, they know there's a camera. But they moved out without ever asking to see this tape. Fennell dug it out when I was round there. Said he'd found me out and that a good cat-minder wouldn't be lured next door at the first sign of an orgy.'

'What, he's just joking about it? He's seen . . . Shit, he's seen everything.'

'I'm more worried about Fee seeing it. She's more analytical. She'll have drawn some damaging conclusions about us both from our sexual behaviour, I dare say.'

'Shut up,' said Carol. 'This is a good bit.'

Lane beckoned her to sit on the sofa. 'Of course, we shouldn't watch this,' she said, her eyes glued to the screen, where a whip was slashing against a vulnerable cunt. 'We should be tucked up in bed all cosy together.'

'Lane Wolfson,' replied her beautiful, naked lover, 'don't ever say that evil word under this roof.'

'What did I say?' asked Lane, all innocence.

'You know what you said. You'll be asking me to marry you next.'

'Carol Maitland,' said Lane, getting down on one knee at her femme's feet and taking her hand, 'please don't ever marry anyone else.'

She buried her head in Carol's bush and kissed her. When she looked up, Carol had pressed the SLOW button on the remote. It was going to be a long night.

SAPPHIRE NEW BOOKS

Published in June 1999

☐

RIKA'S JEWEL
Astrid Fox

Norway, 1066 AD. A group of female Viking warriors – Ingrid's Crew – have set sail to fight the Saxons in Britain, and Ingrid's young lover Rika is determined to follow them. But, urged on by dark-haired oarswoman Pia, Rika soon penetrates Ingrid's secret cult back home in Norway. The cult is spreading through the whole of Northern Europe and its devotees revel in performing erotic rites which re-enact the Nordic creation myth. In the midst of battles, sea-journeys, scarification, fire-dancing and tattooing, Rika must make a choice: will she overcome Ingrid's psychic hold, or will she succumb to the intoxicating rituals of the cult? Thrilling sword-and-sorcery in the style of Xena and Red Sonja!

ISBN 0 352 33367 7

Published in July 1999

☐

MILLENNIUM FEVER
Julia Wood

The millennium is approaching and so is Nikki's fortieth birthday. Married for twenty years, she is tired of playing the trophy wife in a small town where she can't adequately pursue her lofty career ambitions. Nikki's sapphic adventures have been conducted in secret, but her attraction to other women is getting stronger by the day. Already feisty, her sexual energies are getting the better of her, and turning this efficient marketing executive into a tyrant with a taste for road rage! In contrast, young writer Georgie has always been out and proud. But there's one thing they have in common – in the midst of millennial fever, they both want action and satisfaction. When they meet, the combination is explosive.

ISBN 0 352 33368 5

Published in August 1999

☐

ALL THAT GLITTERS
Franca Nera

Marta Broderick: beautiful, successful art dealer, London lesbian. Marta inherits an art empire from the man who managed to spirit her out of East Berlin in the 1960s, Manny Schweitz. But Marta has many secrets – for starters, she's dating a married woman, Anne. Marta is also intent on completing Manny's unfinished business: recovering pieces of art stolen by the Nazis. Meanwhile, she's met the gorgeous but mysterious Judith Compton. And as her relationship with Anne develops and blossoms, Marta's dark sexual addiction to Judith – along with her quest to return the treasures to the rightful owners – is taking her to dangerous places.

ISBN 0 352 33426 6

— — — — — — — —✂— — — — — — — — — — — — — — — — — —

Please send me the books I have ticked above.

Name ....

Address ....

....

....

.... Post Code ....

Send to: **Cash Sales, Sapphire Books, Thames Wharf Studios, Rainville Road, London W6 9HT.**

US customers: for prices and details of how to order books for delivery by mail, call 1-800-805-1083.

Please enclose a cheque or postal order, made payable to **Virgin Publishing Ltd**, to the value of the books you have ordered plus postage and packing costs as follows:

UK and BFPO – £1.00 for the first book, 50p for each subsequent book.

Overseas (including Republic of Ireland) – £2.00 for the first book, £1.00 for each subsequent book.

If you would prefer to pay by VISA or ACCESS/MASTERCARD, please write your card number and expiry date here:

....

Please allow up to 28 days for delivery.

Signature ....

— — — — — — — —✂— — — — — — — — — — — — — — — — — —

WE NEED YOUR HELP . . .

to plan the future of Sapphire books –

Yours are the only opinions that matter. Sapphire is a new and exciting venture: the first British series of books devoted to lesbian erotic fiction written by and for women.

We're going to do our best to provide the sexiest books you can buy. And we'd like you to help in these early stages. Tell us what you want to read. There's a freepost address for your filled-in questionnaires, so you won't even need to buy a stamp.

THE SAPPHIRE QUESTIONNAIRE

SECTION ONE: ABOUT YOU

1.1 Sex *(we presume you are female, but just in case)*
Are you?
Female	☐
Male	☐

1.2 Age

under 21	☐	21–30	☐
31–40	☐	41–50	☐
51–60	☐	over 60	☐

1.3 At what age did you leave full-time education?

still in education	☐	16 or younger	☐
17–19	☐	20 or older	☐

1.4 Occupation _____

1.5 Annual household income _____

1.6   We are perfectly happy for you to remain anonymous; but if you would
      like us to send you a free booklist of Sapphire books, please insert your
      name and address

      _____

      _____

      _____

      _____

SECTION TWO: ABOUT BUYING SAPPHIRE BOOKS

2.1   Where did you get this copy of *Big Deal*?
      Bought at chain book shop   ☐
      Bought at independent book shop   ☐
      Bought at supermarket   ☐
      Bought at book exchange or used book shop   ☐
      I borrowed it/found it   ☐
      My partner bought it   ☐

2.2   How did you find out about Sapphire books?
      I saw them in a shop   ☐
      I saw them advertised in a magazine   ☐
      A friend told me about them _____
      I read about them in _____
      Other _____

2.3   Please tick the following statements you agree with:
      I would be less embarrassed about buying Sapphire
      books if the cover pictures were less explicit   ☐
      I think that in general the pictures on Sapphire
      books are about right   ☐
      I think Sapphire cover pictures should be as
      explicit as possible   ☐

2.4   Would you read an Sapphire book in a public place – on a train for instance?
      Yes   ☐   No   ☐

SECTION THREE: ABOUT THIS SAPPHIRE BOOK

3.1   Do you think the sex content in this book is:
      Too much   ☐   About right   ☐
      Not enough   ☐

3.2 Do you think the writing style in this book is:
        Too unreal/escapist ☐   About right ☐
        Too down to earth ☐

3.3 Do you think the story in this book is:
        Too complicated ☐   About right ☐
        Too boring/simple ☐

3.4 Do you think the cover of this book is:
        Too explicit ☐   About right ☐
        Not explicit enough ☐

Here's a space for any other comments:

SECTION FOUR: ABOUT OTHER SAPPHIRE BOOKS

4.1 How many Sapphire books have you read?

4.2 If more than one, which one did you prefer?
    _____

4.3 Why?

SECTION FIVE: ABOUT YOUR IDEAL EROTIC NOVEL

We want to publish the books you want to read – so this is your chance to tell us exactly what your ideal erotic novel would be like.

5.1 Using a scale of 1 to 5 (1 = no interest at all, 5 = your ideal), please rate the following possible settings for an erotic novel:
        Roman / Ancient World ☐
        Medieval / barbarian / sword 'n' sorcery ☐
        Renaissance / Elizabethan / Restoration ☐
        Victorian / Edwardian ☐
        1920s & 1930s ☐
        Present day ☐
        Future / Science Fiction ☐

5.2 Using the same scale of 1 to 5, please rate the following themes you may find in an erotic novel:

Bondage / fetishism	☐
Romantic love	☐
SM / corporal punishment	☐
Bisexuality	☐
Gay male sex	☐
Group sex	☐
Watersports	☐
Rent / sex for money	☐

5.3 Using the same scale of 1 to 5, please rate the following styles in which an erotic novel could be written:

Gritty realism, down to earth	☐
Set in real life but ignoring its more unpleasant aspects	☐
Escapist fantasy, but just about believable	☐
Complete escapism, totally unrealistic	☐

5.4 In a book that features power differentials or sexual initiation, would you prefer the writing to be from the viewpoint of the dominant / experienced or submissive / inexperienced characters:

Dominant / Experienced	☐
Submissive / Inexperienced	☐
Both	☐

5.5 We'd like to include characters close to your ideal lover. What characteristics would your ideal lover have? Tick as many as you want:

Dominant	☐	Cruel	☐
Slim	☐	Young	☐
Big	☐	Naïve	☐
Voluptuous	☐	Caring	☐
Extroverted	☐	Rugged	☐
Bisexual	☐	Romantic	☐
Working Class	☐	Old	☐
Introverted	☐	Intellectual	☐
Butch	☐	Professional	☐
Femme	☐	Pervy	☐
Androgynous	☐	Ordinary	☐
Submissive	☐	Muscular	☐

Anything else? _____

5.6 Is there one particular setting or subject matter that your ideal erotic novel would contain:

_____

_____

SECTION SIX: LAST WORDS

6.1 What do you like best about Sapphire books?

_____

6.2 What do you most dislike about Sapphire books?

_____

6.3 In what way, if any, would you like to change Sapphire covers?

_____

6.4 Here's a space for any other comments:

_____

_____

_____

_____

Thanks for completing this questionnaire. Now either tear it out, or photocopy it, then put it in an envelope and send it to:

Sapphire/Virgin Publishing
FREEPOST LON3566
London
W6 9BR

You don't need a stamp if you're in the UK, but you'll need one if you're posting from overseas.